EDGE OF STEELE: A CHRISTIAN ROMANTIC SUSPENSE

STEELE GUARDIANS SERIES - BOOK 6

SUSAN SLEEMAN

Published by Edge of Your Seat Books, Inc.

Contact the publisher at contact@edgeofyourseatbooks.com

Copyright © 2023 by Susan Sleeman

Cover design by Kelly A. Martin of KAM Design

This book is a work of fiction. Characters, names, places, and incidents in this novel are either products of the imagination or are used fictitiously. Any resemblance to real people, either living or dead, to events, businesses, or locales is entirely coincidental.

1

Ryleigh's future was going up in smoke. Literally. Right before her eyes.

She cupped a mask over her mouth and plunged into the smoke and blowing sparks. Roaring, intense flames consumed the sawmill down the hill. Building by building. Sparks jumping. Walls burning. Flames higher than the nearby tree canopy eagerly waiting to catch fire. One building nothing but sticks of charred wood.

Smoke. Dark. Swirling like fire-filled dust devils. The sky yellowy-orange. Ominous.

Armageddon.

What on earth had caused this?

She'd never expected this sight. Not ever. She'd simply driven to Shadow Lake this morning to perform a surprise evaluation on the Steele Guardians' guard working at Shadow Lake Logging.

Ward. Their guard.

Ward Byler, a veteran deputy and now one of their finest workers, was on duty. Had he been caught in the flames? And the millworkers? What happened to them?

Her vantage point didn't allow a clear enough view to

assess. She had to move closer. To see. To help. To find Ward.

She adjusted the N-95 mask she kept in her SUV and hurried ahead. The heat grew in intensity on the already warm July day. Neither deputies nor fire department had arrived on scene.

She scanned ahead. Couldn't see anyone. Early after-noon on a Friday and the workers should still be milling lumber. Flatbed trucks lined the side of the road, their beds empty and waiting for freshly sawn Oregon logs. Cars filled the large parking lot, all signs pointing at a crew working this location.

Her throat tightened. Had all the workers perished?

Maybe Tobias Hogan, the owner of Shadow Lake Logging, knew. Or was he here? Inside? He was usually at the company office or explosives' depot located only minutes down the road. Surely he knew about the fire and would be here checking on his employees.

She reached the mouth of the driveway, sparks jumping on the heated air down a slight incline, the nearby trees charred black. The fire raged through the front buildings, the rear structure already consumed. Took everything in its path and burned out. Mostly smoke in the back of the complex now. Some flames sizzled at the top of trees. Other trees stood like blackened sentries guarding the mill.

A door on a truck parked ahead opened, grabbing her attention. Ward, dressed in a Steele Guardians' uniform, dived out as if in a race for his life and bolted her way. He settled a mask over his soot-splotched face and square jaw.

"I'm glad you're here. It was a bomb." His words tumbled out like a gymnast at the Olympics. "No threat this time. Just an explosion."

No threat? Odd.

The company had received several bomb threats. The

reason they'd hired Steele Guardians to stand watch over the people who worked at the sawmill and the loggers clearing land nearby. But the threats stopped after they'd put a guard on duty twenty-four/seven and added security cameras around the main office area.

Now this. An actual bomb. *Unbelievable!*

What should she do? As a former FBI agent, she was the closest thing to a first responder and had to do something. But what?

She stared at the fire devouring the stacks of wood in the distance. The rear building looked like a pile of burned toothpicks dumped in every direction—the explosion.

She looked at Ward. "I assume you called 911 and the fire crew is on the way."

"Called right after the bomb went off, but they're a volunteer department so it takes time."

"Anyone hurt?"

"Don't think so. Today is a maintenance day and all the workers are on a trip with the boss."

"Say what?"

"Mr. Hogan takes one day a month to maintain his equipment. While that's happening, he rents one of those fancy Greyhound-type buses and takes all the workers out for lunch, and then they do something fun. They're going bowling today. Says the perk helps retain workers."

Explained why Tobias wasn't on site yet. "What about the maintenance crew?"

"They meet up with the others for a long lunch, then come back to work while the others go out for some fun. The night shift joins them too. So only one guy was on site when the bomb exploded."

He took a long breath and pointed at the white Chevy pickup he'd tumbled from. The driver sat behind the wheel. "The day supervisor, Virgil Eckles. I was on my way to ask

3

him a question when kaboom. If I hadn't gone, I..." He shuddered and looked over his shoulder. "I'd have been right there by the buildings. As it was, the blast threw me a good distance. Nothing broken, thank God. Anyway, Virg got a call from his wife. She's pregnant. Due any day. So he stayed back and was just about to go home when the bomb went off."

Ryleigh kept her attention on the site, searching for what she didn't know. She did know she felt like a failure. Shadow Lake Logging was her first client since she joined Steele Guardians and everything had been going fine.

Until today. Until this. A bomb. A fire. All under her watch.

Now what? How did she not only ensure the safety of anyone here, but save the reputation of the family business? Of course, safety was first and the only thing she should be concerned with, but she'd be lying if she didn't admit the other issue would remain in the back of her mind.

Please don't let it impact my decisions.

"I need to talk to Eckles." She hurried toward the man sitting behind the wheel. From this distance, all she could see was his bald head and blue shirt.

Could he be their bomber and was he in his truck because he'd set the bomb? Or was that simply a coincidence?

She stopped next to his truck and signaled for him to lower his window. He opened the door instead as Ward stepped up to them.

Eckles put on a mask, pushed out of the truck and slammed the door, the sound echoing in the eerie air. "Don't want my truck to take on more smoke than it already has."

She introduced herself. "Are you sure this was a bomb?"

"Positive. I've used my share of explosives on the job enough to know an explosion when I hear it. The blast occurred in Building A. Then a fire broke out. Jumped to the next building and soon everything else went up. Didn't take long, what with all the lumber and sawdust around."

Okay, sounded like his explosives background gave him the know-how to construct a bomb. "Are explosives stored on this site that might've been set off by mistake?"

He shook his head. "Closest ones are at the main office under lock and key in the explosives' depot."

Thank goodness for that, at least. "Who has a key?"

"Tobias, of course. Me and Uri. He's the night supervisor. That's it." Eckles tugged on his mask to shift it higher. "You aren't thinking one of us done it, are you? It's them tree huggers, I tell you. Probably the ones who have been sending the threats too. They've protested all over the state but haven't shown up here. At least not until today."

She agreed. The ecoterrorist group Sovereign Earth seemed to be the likely culprits behind the threats, but her research hadn't uncovered any proof yet.

A vehicle slowed and parked down the road. She glanced that direction. A large pickup. Not the sheriff.

"I'm going to check the area that's burned itself out," Eckles said. "See what I can see."

"Not looking for victims, are you?" she asked. "Because Ward said all of the crew went to lunch except you."

Eckles's eyes creased. "Right. But I'm in charge of the day shift, and I have to be sure. See with my own eyes. You know?"

She did know. Being an FBI agent was all about team-work and making sure you never did anything to put another agent in harm's way. She still carried that commit-ment with her.

"Could be another bomb in the area," she said.

"Lady, if there was, the heat and flames would've made it blow." The burly man started ahead.

She stepped in front of him. He pushed past her.

"You're going at your own risk," she called after him. "Watch for an explosive device. If you see anything, hightail it back here."

She or Ward could tackle Eckles to stop him, but the man knew the risk, and he had a point. If the bomber had planted another device, it would have to be between them and the original explosion, and the whole area had burned now. That left the possibility near zero. But not zero, and she wouldn't let Ward follow if he even wanted to.

She faced him. "Is Eckles a solid guy or do you like him as a suspect for the bomb?"

"Solid. Couldn't see him behind the bomb, but then, if my years as a deputy told me anything, it told me you can't trust a superficial opinion."

"Yeah.

Ward lifted his shoulders, his gaze tightening. "Here comes the company's new security manager. Been here for a couple of weeks but only met him once. Seems like a stand-up guy."

"A security manager? No one mentioned him." She spun to look down the road at a tall, broad-shouldered man. His face was turned toward the fire, and he marched toward them, purpose in his step.

"Sorry, I figured Tobias told you he'd hired the guy."

The owner hadn't said a word to her. Now why was that? Did this new guy plan to fire Steele Guardians? "What's his name?"

"Oh, man, sorry." Ward rubbed his forehead with a sooty hand. "I don't remember. An unusual name though."

She changed her focus to the manager as he strode her way. Sure steps. Confident. Authoritative. Would he become a problem for her and their company account?

"What do you want me to do now?" Ward asked.

Ryleigh faced him. "We need to set up a perimeter and make sure anyone who arrives stays behind it until the property is deemed safe. That includes us and this manager."

"But what if someone needs our help down there?"

She glanced at the devastation. Could anyone survive that blast and inferno? Doubtful. "They'd likely be calling out. With the possibility of another bomb, I can't risk anyone else's life. Emerson County Sheriff's Office isn't big enough to have a bomb squad, but hopefully, when they get here, they'll have someone with explosive experience who can clear the area."

Ward made a grumbling sound. "It's hard to stand down. I'm sure you get it since you just left law enforcement too."

He got that right. If only she were still an agent. This bombing could well be domestic terrorism, and the FBI would offer their services to the local sheriff. As an agent, she'd be in the thick of finding whoever committed this crime instead of standing on the fringes and watching her family's company lose a much-needed account. Maybe lose their reputation.

That was if the ATF allowed the FBI to get involved when they usually had priority on bombings. The sheriff would have to notify them as soon as possible.

"I have to ask you both to move back for your safety," the deep male voice came from behind, familiar to her as it had often filled her dreams.

She spun. Stared at the man who'd walked up the driveway. The man who'd walked out of her life a few years ago.

"Finn," his name whispered out on the last breath she could manage.

She blinked. Blinked again.

"What are you doing here, Ryleigh?" he asked through a mask, sounding none too pleased.

She drew in a breath and let it out. Tried to draw in

another one, her brain acting sluggish as if every bit of oxygen had burned in the fire. She knew why she was there. She just couldn't find the words.

Ward looked at Finn then at her, his forehead creasing.

Ryleigh couldn't think about her guard right now. She couldn't think at all.

"Excuse me. I...I gotta make a call." Ward bolted toward Eckles's truck.

"As far as I know, no one has called in the FBI," Finn said, ignoring Ward's movements. "Means you can't be here in an official capacity. So what gives?"

She took a step back and lifted her shoulders, a reply finally forming in her brain. "I came to check in with Tobias on how my guards were performing and happened upon the fire. Why are you here?" she asked. She knew the reason but needed to buy time to digest the fact that he was standing there. In front of her. All six-foot-two of him, solid as a rock.

He cocked his head, drawing her attention to his red hair that fit his Irish heritage on his mother's side. "I'm the new head of security. Didn't Tobias tell you?"

Best to stick to short replies before she said something she would regret. "No."

"That's odd. He said he was going to send an email to the Steele Guardians rep to introduce me. You sure you didn't get it?"

Trust me. If I saw an email containing your name, I would remember.

"No email." She needed to move on. "Took you long enough to get here."

"Had to evacuate the office and depot, then checked the area to be sure a bomb hadn't been planted there as well."

Of course he'd done the right thing. And likely without hesitating—unlike her. SEALs were trained to assess and act. Not that she hadn't been trained for emergencies too, but he had far more experience in facing life-threatening situations. She ought to know. She'd worried for his safety long after he'd bailed on her.

Car doors slammed from the area where Finn had parked. Two men in turnout gear pounded toward them, moving at a high speed in the afternoon heat. Both guys were tall. Both took sure steps. But only one of them was a childhood friend.

"Ryan?" Ryleigh asked. "You're a firefighter?"

"Hey, Ryleigh." Ryan Maddox flashed her a smile, and she remembered the years as a kid following the lanky, blond boy around the Maddox family resort every summer. "We'll catch up later. Who's in charge here?"

Finn held out his hand before she could speak. "Finn Durham. Security manager."

"Ryan Maddox." Ryan gripped Finn's hand. "What do we have?"

"A bomb detonated in the back building about twenty minutes ago now." Finn jerked a thumb over his shoulder, pointing at the buildings that had been decimated.

"Anyone injured or trapped in the blaze?"

"Not that we know of," Finn said before Ryleigh could. "All the workers are offsite all day. The supervisor was in his truck at the road, and the guard was on his way to talk to him."

"That's good news." Ryan looked at the other firefighter. "Go ahead and radio this in and update others. We could need a wildland crew if this spreads to the surrounding trees."

The guy nodded and stepped away.

Ryan turned his attention back to Ryleigh. "We're a volunteer group. Troy and I live the closest, and the others should be here with the equipment soon. For now, you all need to—"

"Ms. Steele," Eckles shouted from behind what was left of the front wall of the back building. He stepped out. "You'll want to see this."

"What is it?" Finn demanded in his Navy SEAL domineering tone before Ryleigh could respond.

"A body," Eckles said. "I found a body."

Ryan bolted toward the supervisor before Finn could even turn. Finn should wait for Ryleigh to head to the scene, but she stood frozen in the swirling heat, and he didn't really want her to see the body anyway, so he jogged down the drive.

Please let her stay behind.

Her footfalls sounded, and she caught up to him.

Drat.

She grabbed his arm, slowing him down. "Hold up. We do this together."

He jerked back and rubbed the area she'd touched. Earned him a raise of her eyebrows, but he wasn't about to tell her it impacted him. A lot. Or make some stupid comment. Seeing her again had turned his brain to mush, and he wasn't functioning at full capacity.

"You should stay here," he said. "A person's been killed. It's dangerous."

"Um, hello." She rolled her eyes. "I was an FBI agent. I'm trained—"

"*Was* an agent?" He eyed her. With her cute short haircut that he learned was called a pixie cut after he'd taken seven-year-old Avery into his life, Ryleigh reminded him of a young girl instead of an FBI agent. "You left the agency?"

"Two months ago to work for the family."

Wow! Just wow. "You used to bleed blue. You and your whole family. I never thought you'd leave the bureau."

She fisted her hands on her curvy hips, a perfect place to rest his hand in the past when they'd walked side-by-side.

She held his gaze. "And *I* never thought you'd leave the SEALs. At least that was the excuse you used when you ended things between us." She paused, her gaze intensifying. "And yet, here you are."

So she was still mad at him. Not surprising, but he couldn't get into a personal discussion now. "Long story."

"Yeah, for me too, and not one to get into now. We need to find out this victim's identity and determine if they're responsible for the bomb." She lifted her chin as if she expected him to argue. "And you won't stop me."

"We'll see how it goes." A noncommittal response, but he didn't want her wrapped up in a bombing. Didn't want her in danger. Actually, now that he thought about it, he was thankful she'd left the FBI. He didn't like thinking she went into potential danger every day, much like he'd done for years.

She took off, and he lengthened his strides to catch up.

They neared the blaze that still roared in the first building like a flickering monster hungry for the wood, and the heat knocked him back. They skirted the flames dancing and licking as sparks jumped from place to place, desperately trying to catch onto fuel before burning out. The smoke thickened and darkened the area decimated by the bomb. It had not only flattened the building and felled several trees but also charred the ground.

"Looks like a burnover," Ryan said from behind the last standing wall. "The area burned hot and fast, leaving only embers."

Ryleigh surged ahead and rounded the wall. The roar of

the nearby flames filled the air, but Ryleigh's gasp sounded above the hum of destruction.

He turned the corner. She stood over the victim charred beyond recognition, her eyes wide, her hand clamped over her mask. The victim was lying on his side, his limbs pulled tight against his torso.

Horrific. Like many of the tragedies Finn had seen as a SEAL. He'd learned the victim's position was called the pugilistic stance—pugilistic meaning boxing. When a body burned, the elbows and knees constricted and fists clenched in the heat due to the shrinkage of body tissues and muscle dehydration—resembling a boxer's stance. Charred, black debris surrounded him, and glowing embers were the only hints of fire trying to stay alive.

Question was, who had succumbed to the fire?

The burly day supervisor, Virgil Eckles, stood over the victim. His eyes were tight, his body rigid.

Finn stepped over to him. "Can you ID this guy?"

"Smokey." The name came out on a choking sound, and Eckles looked away.

"Smokey, really?" Finn shot another look at the body to see if he could recognize the night supervisor. The man oversaw the last half of a fifteen-hour work day in the summer when there was an abundance of light outside to move logs and materials.

But this guy? The body, if you could even call it that, was Smokey?

No way Finn could ID the victim by sight. "You're sure?"

Eckles glanced back at the victim. "I mean, I can't be one hundred percent sure, but what's left of those boots are Smokey's."

"I'm not familiar with Smokey," Ryleigh said, her tone tight.

"The night supervisor, Uri Gates. Got the nickname on

his first logging job when he started a fire with a chainsaw. The name stuck with him. Anyway, that hunk of boot that's left is his. His right leg is shorter than the other, and his right boot has a custom lift."

Finn gave a side glance at Ryan. "How on earth did that piece of boot survive the blaze?"

Ryan pointed at a steel spade lying near the body. "It must've fallen onto the tip of his foot and blocked the fire. I moved it to see if there was a lead on his ID."

"Why didn't the shovel melt?" Ryleigh asked.

"Steel melts at two thousand degrees," Ryan said. "Must not have gotten that hot in this area."

Ryleigh squatted, her focus pinned on the remaining piece. "If his boots are custom, not likely that someone else would be wearing them. Or perhaps that's not a lift, and the sole is that thick. Could someone else have a similar pair without a lift?"

"Not likely anyone on our crews." Eckles shoved his hands into his pockets. "That brand's price is out of reach for most of us. You could buy a couple pairs of sturdy work boots for one pair of those."

"So why can Gates afford them?" Finn asked.

Eckles cocked his head. "He's too new. Don't know a lot about him, so I can't say."

Maybe he was paid to plant a bomb. "What was he doing here at this time of day?"

Eckles shrugged. "Could've come in a few hours early for his shift, but I doubt it. He didn't seem like the go-getter type to me. Didn't even know he was here."

"That's odd, right?" Ryleigh asked.

"Yeah," Eckles said. "He had to know Tobias wouldn't be here, and there would only be a skeleton crew doing maintenance. He'd pretty much have the place to himself."

"You think he had something to do with the bomb?" Ryan asked, sirens sounding from the road.

Eckles narrowed his eyes. "Just don't know him well enough to speculate, but him being here instead of at lunch with the others *is* suspicious."

Ryleigh stood. "We can speculate all we want, but it might not even be Smokey. Top priority is to get a positive ID."

Finn looked at Eckles. "You know what type of vehicle Smokey drives, and is it parked in the lot?"

Eckles nodded. "He's got one of them new Jeep Gladiators. Lime green. Can't miss it, but I didn't see it in the lot or on the road."

Ryleigh frowned. "Had to have hiked in then. If you were out front, he could've come in on the logging road back here. If so, he couldn't have parked close to here or his Jeep would be toast."

Finn squinted through the smoke to peer down the road leading away from them. "Don't see any vehicles."

"Say he's our bomber," Ryan said. "Wouldn't he want his truck nearby for a fast getaway?"

"I would," Finn said. "We'll look for the vehicle. I'll call him too. See if he answers. If so, we're not looking at Gates. I'll also check with Tobias to see if Gates is with the guys. If I don't get ahold of him, odds are better that we're right."

"He's single." Eckles's slumped shoulders rose for a flash of a second, then fell as if he was holding heavy logs. "No girlfriend and never married. Lives alone. So no one at home will report him missing."

"Then let me make that call," Finn said. "If he doesn't answer or isn't with Tobias, I'll send someone over to his place to check on him."

Ryleigh met Finn's gaze. "Even if we don't find Gates,

we'll still need a positive ID. A chunk of boot isn't enough by a long shot. We'll need dental records and/or DNA."

Finn nodded and held his hand out to Eckles. "For now, I'll take your key to the explosives' depot."

Eckles batted his eyelashes. "My key? But why?"

"It's for your own protection," Finn said. "The sheriff will want to search the depot and check the inventory. I'd like to be able to tell them you didn't have assess from this point and could alter things."

Eckles eyed Finn for a moment then jerked his key off a ring and slapped it on Finn's palm.

"Thanks, man." Finn pocketed it.

Vehicle tires crunched over gravel and air brakes sounded from the road.

Ryan jerked his head in that direction. "That'll be the rest of the crew. Maybe the sheriff or deputies too. They'll cordon off this area, and you all need to move back to the road for safety."

Finn clamped his mouth closed to keep from saying anything. He was used to being in charge, not taking orders. He knew how to handle himself in more dangerous situations than most men. Likely more than Maddox here, except when it came to fires. Finn knew the basics though. They were unpredictable. Could turn on you in minutes. Took this guy out, after all. They all needed to take care, and he would listen to Maddox.

Sort of.

Finn eyed the firefighter. "You have the explosives training needed to clear the area for any additional bombs?"

Ryan snapped his shoulders back. "Our crew is trained in the basics. Nothing advanced."

Okay, fine, Finn's question had annoyed the guy. "Just asking because I've had advance explosive training while serving in the Navy, and I'm glad to clear the area."

"Explosives, really? As a sailor?" Ryan's eyes crinkled with amusement.

"He was a SEAL," Ryleigh said, sounding unimpressed.

Ryan scrubbed a hand over his short blond hair. "Oh, right. Then yeah. You've probably got the goods to do it. But this is a crime scene, and I still need approval from the officer in charge before you can search."

Finn opened his mouth to argue. Stopped. Wouldn't hurt to wait a few minutes to follow protocol. This body was going nowhere, and if everyone moved back for safety, then another bomb wouldn't threaten them.

Besides, if he remained at the scene, so would Ryleigh. Sure, he'd broken up with her after a whirlwind relationship. Had thought of her and played the what if game on a regular basis. He was the one who ended things and shouldn't have such intense feelings over seeing her again, but he did.

And when he cared about someone? The protective instinct he'd developed to protect his sister, Hadley after losing his parents rose up.

So no matter what Ryleigh wanted, he'd do anything— everything—to be sure she didn't get hurt. Even if he died trying.

2

Finn slid between the barriers erected by the firefighters to keep people back at the road and jogged down the hill, turning to make sure Ryleigh hadn't tried to follow. She stood with Ryan, chatting. Looking all too comfortable. Had she dated him or just been friends? The ease she had with him was enviable. An ease Finn had once had with her too, and he missed that.

A log fell in front of him, snapping his head around.

Focus man. Can't help anyone if you're dead.

He began his search, swinging the light as he moved, the heavy smoke swirling around his feet. The brighter-than-usual beam of Ryan's flashlight cut through the haze, clouding the daylight as Finn's grid took him back and forth. Through still-standing trees. Under fallen ones. Over brush. Through scrub. Until he reached the detonation zone.

He flashed the light over the body and the area surrounding him. Bits and pieces of the bomb lay scattered in the wreckage. Looked like slivers of plastic and metal. Tiny. Fragments really. One larger chunk held some kind of electronics. Surprising that anything survived the high heat, but hopefully the debris would lead to the bomber. Thankfully the firefighters wouldn't have to hose this area down if it didn't spark up again, and the evidence would be spared.

He looked around the smoldering ruins for any sign of another device but found nothing of concern. He searched outside. High. Low. Nothing there either. On the way back, he avoided the flames still licking greedily over the first building. They'd jumped to nearby trees during his short trip and were ramping up into a wildland fire.

Hurry now!

Every second he took delayed the firefighters from moving in and preventing a full-fledged wildfire.

Still, be careful.

Trees could be replaced. People couldn't. He knew that too well with the loss of his parents and recently, his best friend Felicia, who'd died, leaving her daughter Avery in Finn's care.

He slipped through flames spreading on the grass. Felt the heat licking at his feet. His legs. Fighting to ignite his clothing. Him.

As a SEAL, this would've just been another day on a mission, but he was out of place here. Adrenaline-packed and thrilling for sure. Something he missed. How he missed it.

Too bad.

He picked up speed and raced toward the road.

"We're clear," he called out and handed the high-intensity flashlight back to Ryan.

The crew sprang into action. Barriers moved. Pump trucks rumbled ahead. Firefighters went silent and marched forward. A crew at war. The enemy, flames.

He was jonesing to join them. To battle the foe. But he hung back. He was retired from danger. Any danger. Now more of a desk jockey than anything.

Tough for him if he still craved excitement. He would sit

this out. He was now Avery's father, and she needed him. She was all that mattered.

If only he could really internalize that and stop these cravings for the thrills.

A uniformed guy jerked a thumb over his shoulder. "Thanks for your help, but you need to keep moving back."

Finn complied, slipping between the wooden barriers, but he wasn't eager to join Ryleigh again. Sure, he was attracted to her. What man wouldn't be? But now their obstacle to being together was gone. He'd left the team. It no longer stood between them. He could finally consider a future with her.

Didn't matter, though. They were still living worlds apart, and he wasn't about to move Avery when the hurt from losing her mother was still so fresh.

More importantly, Ryleigh was angry with him. Big time.

So what did he say to her? Was now the time to have that talk?

Man, he just didn't know. He'd never been so uncertain about a woman in his life.

He looked ahead and found her watching him with that familiar spark of interest in her eyes. She didn't look away at being caught admiring him. Of course not. She was completely confident and sure in herself.

She stood by his truck, and when he reached her, the first thing that came to mind slipped out. "I'm still shocked that you left the bureau."

She shrugged as if it was no big deal, but he knew it was a huge life-changing decision. Just like his had been.

"The family needed an IT person," she said, her tone devoid of any emotion, but her eyes held a certain unease. "And I'm the only one with those skills."

Could she be regretting her decision? "They could've hired someone."

"As they would tell you, why do that when there's a family member who can step in?"

He couldn't see her mouth, but he suspected she was smiling fondly over her family. Even if she regretted retiring from the bureau, she would make the best of it for her family. They were everything to her—everything—and she would never knowingly let them down. Nor would they let her down. Ever. They were a unit. Tightly knit, just like his SEAL team. Sure, the SEALs weren't his blood relatives, but they were his family all the same.

"One of the things I remember most about your family is how tight they are," he said.

She arched a brow and watched him for a long moment. He wished he could remove the mask and see her expression, but the particles clinging to the air were better breathed through filtration.

"You should also remember that once we make up our minds we don't back down," she said. "As the security manager you need to know that I fully intend to investigate the bombing."

She eyed him, and pixie haircut or not, he had no problem seeing the retired FBI agent now. "Did you know I was the rep on this account for Shadow Lake Logging?"

No matter how he answered her question, it wouldn't bode well for him so he simply shook his head.

She fingered her gold necklace but didn't look away. "Still, you had to recognize the name Steele and remember our family was in the security guard business."

"I did, but I didn't know you'd started working with the company. And if you managed the account, Tobias would deal with you, not me." Even to him, his answer sounded lame.

"Too bad or you could've contacted me." The words flew out like fired bullets. "Warned me."

Wow, warned! Stronger reaction than he expected. "I didn't realize you would need a warning."

She let out a long breath behind her mask. "I can't get into this now. Not here with an uncontrolled fire and remains waiting to be recovered. I need to make an investigative plan and implement it."

He would do the same thing, but he didn't need to share that now as it would likely just make her madder at him. Still, they both had the same obstacle to overcome if they were to begin an investigation. "The local sheriff will try to muscle you out when he gets here."

"Let him try." Her shoulders went up. "This bomb occurred on my watch. *Our* guard was on duty. I'm involved, and I won't go anywhere until I find the person who planted that bomb."

He opened his mouth to continue arguing, but a patrol car raced down the road and careened to a stop, taking her attention. A tall, built guy with blond hair jumped out. He wore black tactical pants and a khaki uniform shirt, had a gun at his hip, a badge on his belt, and a black face mask dangling from it. A patrol officer would be wearing a full uniform. Had to be the sheriff.

"Russ," Ryleigh said.

The sheriff stared at her and blinked a few times, a blank look on his face.

"Ryleigh Steele," she said.

"Ryleigh." He cracked a hint of a smile. "I heard that Tobias took my recommendation and hired your company for security. Just didn't know which Steele serviced the account."

"That would be me." She clenched her hands. "Now we have a bomb, and I need to find out who's behind it to save our company's reputation."

Russ's hands drifted to his waist. "You need to leave that to me."

"Or me," Finn said, as he wasn't going to step back for anyone, not even the law, and the good sheriff needed to know that.

Russ's eyebrows rose. "And you are?"

"Finn Durham. Shadow Lake Logging security manager."

"Oh, right," Russ shifted his belt. "The former SEAL Tobias is bragging all over town about snagging for the job. I'm Russ Maddox. Emerson County Sheriff."

"Maddox?" Finn asked, as when Ryleigh mentioned her summers up here when he was dating her, she'd said there was more than one Maddox boy that she'd hung out with. "Any relation to Ryan?"

"Brother."

"Small world."

"Even smaller than you think," Ryleigh said. "I also worked with their oldest brother at the FBI. Reid was an agent too, but now he runs their family business."

Russ gave Finn a quick once over. "You must've drawn the short straw if you went from a SEAL to this gig."

"It's complicated," Finn said, giving him as vague of an answer as he'd given Ryleigh.

All they needed to know right now was that he was here, had his sights set on finding the bomber, and he wasn't going anywhere until he had eyes on his target.

Thankful Russ trained his attention on Finn, Ryleigh took a long breath. She needed to get her act together and appear more in charge for Russ. Finn too. She especially had to stop letting Finn take over.

He probably wasn't doing it to get at her. Or at least she didn't think he was. But taking control came naturally to him, the reason he'd risen to commander of his SEAL team. Hard to compete with those innate skills.

She lifted her shoulders and crossed her arms. *No. Stop.* That just emphasized her short nails that she'd polished a soft pink, making her even more girly looking.

She shoved her hands into her pockets instead. "I know you want me to leave this alone, Russ, but I can't. Won't. So you'll just have to accept that."

Russ shook his head. "This's just like the time you thought you could swim well enough to go into the river. I'd warned you about the current and ended up rescuing you from it."

Grrr. Why bring that up now? "You can't judge me for something that happened when I was a kid. I'm older and wiser and have law enforcement training now."

Russ smiled politely, a practiced smile he probably used to pacify people on the job. "I was surprised you became a law enforcement officer like the rest of the family. Thought there were too many rules for a free spirit like you."

Fine. Try to pigeonhole her. She'd faced that her whole career and knew how to handle it. She lifted her chin. "I served a little over five years with the FBI. Left two months ago to join the family firm."

He continued to eye her skeptically. "I still can't let you two impede my investigation."

His bossy tone grated on her, and Finn's rigid posture said he agreed.

Russ took a wide stance, his boots planting on the ground and kicking up dust. "And I won't take kindly to you siccing the feds on me either."

"I don't plan to." She held his gaze even when it felt uncomfortable to do so. "But you have to call the ATF."

"Do I?"

Now he was just being ornery.

"Come on, Russ. You can't avoid the feds. You're an excellent sheriff, but we both know the ATF handles bombings. Plus, my research into the prior threats says this could well be the work of ecoterrorists, so the FBI will likely be pulled in too."

Russ took a few steps closer. "Are you forgetting the victim in the ruins? Because I'm not. Murder falls under my jurisdiction, and I'm not passing that off to anyone. And I'm sure not calling anyone in—feds or otherwise—until I do further discovery."

Risky decision for sure. "You're willing to face the fallout from that move?"

"I've been at this job long enough to know what I'm doing. Leave things to me. You too, Durham." His last words were fired at Finn like Russ had lifted his gun and discharged a bullet.

No way she would give up. But…"I'll back off while you assess the scene. Give you at least that much, but I'd like to offer a suggestion."

"Go ahead." He crossed his arms.

Grudging agreement. More than she expected. "You can gather the information you need faster with professionals at your fingertips."

"That's a given, so explain."

"The body is too badly burned for an ME to handle, and you'll need a forensic anthropologist to recover the remains. The Veritas Center in Portland has an expert forensic anthropologist who I would recommend using."

He snorted and lifted his hands. "You know my budget would never stretch to that and their pro bono funds might not cover such a large investigation."

He didn't outright say no, so… "Doesn't hurt to ask. They

could also process this scene for forensics. And they just hired a guy with extensive experience with explosives. He could analyze the blast and bomb fragments. Plus, you won't find anyone better at collecting evidence than Sierra Rice. I could ask for their help pro bono."

Ryleigh expected Russ to scoff at the offer, but he gave a sharp nod. "I'll keep that in mind."

Great. Now she had to close the deal. "Let me give you my cell number, and I can work on that for you."

"I said I'll keep it in mind." He took his mask from his belt. "I'll get your contact info when I take your statement. Stay here until I come back." He strapped on his mask and marched off.

She glanced at Finn. He didn't move, but his gaze tracked Russ. "Nice guy."

"Do I detect a hint of sarcasm in your tone?"

"Just a hint?" He chuckled.

She might be battling Russ, but she didn't like Finn dissing her old friend. "He actually *is* a great guy. Or at least when I knew him he was, but he was always the serious one of the family, and a lot of people take him the wrong way. Right now, he's just doing his job as sheriff to keep us in line and protect his investigation."

Finn changed his focus to her and leaned against his dusty truck. "Which you plan to ignore."

Busted. "As do you."

"Yeah. As do I." He searched her face. "What if we stopped arguing and agreed to work together? Pool our resources."

Seriously? How would that be a good idea? It wouldn't be. Not at all. "With our past? I don't think so."

"I'm sure we can put that aside to locate a bomber. At least I can."

"Of course you can. You were the one who walked away

without a backward glance." The words came out harsher than she'd planned.

He recoiled. "I had to go."

"Because you couldn't leave your SEAL team." She paused, letting her comment linger on the smoke while she tamped down the feelings threatening to steal her ability to think clearly. "Like I said before. Here you are. No SEAL team in sight."

"Trust me," he said, but she didn't. "It wasn't my choice. I had to leave."

Nearly overwhelmed with emotion, she couldn't form the right words, so she eyed him, challenging him to explain,

He let out a sigh. "You remember my friend Felicia? She died a couple of months ago and left her daughter in my care. When Avery was born, Felicia asked me to take care of her if something happened to Felicia. Man, I..."

He shook his head, his eyes darkening. "I never thought it would happen. So I said yes and didn't give it another thought. Then Felicia *did* die, and I had a decision to make. Come take care of Avery or let her go to foster care."

He swallowed, his Adam's apple bobbing as if he was fighting to get his emotions under control. "I can't be a single parent to Avery and still be deployed all the time."

"Oh, Finn." Ryleigh clutched his arm.

He jerked back, sliding along his truck and resembling a captured animal trying to escape.

Oh, man. Wow. The second time she'd touched him, and the second time he retreated.

What was up with that? Now was not the time to ask. Now was the time to offer her sympathy at the loss of his friend who'd been by his side since his parents died when he was ten.

She shoved her hands in her pockets so she didn't try to

touch him again. "I'm so sorry, Finn. I know how close you were to Felicia."

His eyes were vacant and panicked at the same time. Gone was the invincible man she'd known. He moved even further toward his truck's tailgate and lifted his shoulders. "I'm just trying to trust that God has a plan for this and do my best to move on and help Avery deal."

His tone lacked conviction. Like he was repeating words he knew he should believe but didn't. She wanted to know more, but she wouldn't press him. They didn't have that kind of relationship anymore. Any relationship. The hours they'd once spent under the stars, talking and getting to know each other were over.

Way over.

Better to stick to facts. "How old is Avery now?"

"Seven." He lifted his mask to scratch his face, but she noted he was chewing the inside of his cheek, a habit she remembered well, proving his uncertainty. "But losing her mom has made her grow up pretty fast."

Ryleigh would struggle mightily to survive if she lost her mother. "I can't even imagine."

"Sadly, I can."

She raised a hand to clap it over her mouth, then felt her mask and let it fall. "How insensitive of me."

"No worries." He looked away as if he was trying not to remember that day on the slopes when the avalanche had spared him and Hadley, but took both of their parents. "Anyway, it helps me understand Avery when she lashes out or even when she cries inconsolably. So there's that."

How was he even dealing with this? Coping? His life had been upended in so many ways, and he was obviously struggling big time.

She had to cut him some slack. A lot of slack, actually. "Was Felicia sick or was her death unexpected?"

"Unexpected. Sudden." He rested his arm on the truck bed as if trying to keep that rigid SEAL persona in place. "She had an undiagnosed brain aneurism and collapsed during one of her shifts at the ER. You'd think if a rupture happened in a hospital, they could save her. But no way."

"Oh, man. How rough for everyone. I'll keep you and Avery in my prayers," Ryleigh said sincerely. They both needed prayer right now like they needed to breathe. "And we can work together on this."

His eyes flashed wide open and he stared at her.

She would be staring too, if she were him. Did this mean she forgave him for choosing his career over her? Not hardly. Or was she letting his loss color her decisions, and she felt sorry for him so she agreed to join him in this investigation? She honestly didn't know how she felt and sure shouldn't make hasty decisions. Especially one she was already regretting.

Maybe it could work. He *did* have strong investigative skills from his SEAL days. Carefully scrutinizing situations that arose on a mission was a must-have ability for a SEAL. That, combined with her law enforcement experience, could make them a power couple in the investigation.

They'd been a real power couple in life too, but that ended far too soon.

He bent forward, grabbing her attention. "Are you planning on calling your friends at the FBI?"

She shook her head. "Russ should be able to handle the investigation his way. Besides, friends or not, my former associates are even less likely than Russ to share findings with us."

"Then what do you propose?"

"No agency will provide us with official forensics results. That's a given. But if I get Veritas onboard, maybe Russ will let them share the info with us."

"You think he will?"

Did she? "He's by the book and our odds aren't good. Not unless it serves his purpose."

"Not having access to forensics results would be a real blow. The bomber will likely be identified by the forensics."

"Or it could just confirm any suspect we discover."

His eyebrow went up. "And how do you propose we go about finding legit suspects?"

Yeah, how? She glanced around until an idea came to mind. "While we wait to give our statements, we move as close to the action as we can to listen in. Maybe we'll overhear something of value. Then if Ryan is still battling the fire, we wait until we can talk to him."

"And if he has nothing to offer?"

"We call in our own expert. I've investigated the recent bomb threats Tobias has received. I believe this is the work of Sovereign Earth, a nationwide ecoterrorist group. Problem is, I've struck out on actually pinning the threats to them." She planted her hands on her hips, a habit she picked up in the FBI to try to make herself seem more forceful. "So instead of wasting time on going through my research again, we get help."

"I take it you have someone in mind."

"Yeah, someone who can run circles around me on the computer."

"Whoa!" Finn pushed off the truck. "Ryleigh Steele modest about her IT skills? Never thought I'd see the day. This person must be something else."

She laughed. He was right. She did tout her skills—not an unusual thing in the IT world. "I have two people in mind, actually. Nick Thorn at Veritas is the top IT expert in the area. He doesn't have a background in terrorism, but he has top-of-the-line equipment and mad skills to run deep searches. Then there's Colin Graham, who I worked with at the FBI. He ran the IT aspect for their domestic terrorism team but recently left the agency too."

"Where is he now?"

"Oddly enough, he works at Shadow Lake Survival. The Maddox family business."

"You think he'll help us?"

"I hope he will, but he left the FBI because he was burned out on all the bad out there. Especially the terrorism aspect. He might run the other way, but it might help convince him to join in the search if I ask in person."

"Then that sounds like our first stop." He held her gaze. "*After* we interrogate Ryan."

She flashed up a hand. "Hold up there. You might have interrogated people while serving as a SEAL, but in the civilian world, we just question."

Hopefully, he would keep her warning in mind, but would he?

Any hint that Ryan was holding back on them, and Finn would likely revert to his SEAL training and find a way to make Ryan talk. Something she would have to stop if they had any hope of succeeding in this investigation.

3

Ryleigh tore her gaze from the fire that smoldered and smoked in the charred tree line where firefighters seemed to be winning the war right now. She focused on Tobias Hogan, stepping their way. He wore jeans and a plaid shirt and resembled a skinny Santa Claus. Or at least Ryleigh had always thought of him that way.

He usually had the jolly personality too, but today the wrinkles around his eyes were even deeper, and his mouth was pursed behind his flowing white beard. He stopped short of her and Finn, where they'd been waiting on a truck tailgate for Ryan.

Tobias plunged his hand into his silvery hair. "Any news on Uri?"

Finn stood and shook his head. "I called him, and it went to voicemail. Then I sent one of the men over to check on him, and he didn't answer his door. And we didn't find his vehicle either."

"Sheriff Maddox will do a welfare check," Ryleigh added. "This gives him probable cause for a forced entry, so he can go inside Gates's house."

Tobias frowned.

"Any idea why he might've been here at this time of day?" Finn asked.

Tobias fired a heated look at Finn. "Not setting off a bomb, if that's what you're getting at. He's an upstanding guy as far as I know."

"I meant no offense, sir." Finn's apprehension surprised Ryleigh. "It's just that he hasn't been working with us all that long. There might be something he's hiding, and we've yet to find out."

"Find out what? You know I ran background checks on all my employees after we got the first threat. None of the guys have a criminal record or hint of radicalism."

Ryleigh stood too. "I mean no offense either, but that only tells us that he was never apprehended, not that he didn't commit crimes. He could easily be affiliated with an extremist group, and the check you did wouldn't have that information."

Tobias pressed his full lips together. "You know a lot about all that cyber gibberish. Can't you check into him that way?"

She wished that the earlier work she'd done had paid off, and she had a lead to share right now. Maybe then Tobias would be more apt to keep her family's company on. But she didn't, so she worked extra hard not to let the disappointment in her failure show. "I can look into him, and we'll also ask a former FBI agent and the IT expert at the Veritas Center to research him too. A three-pronged attack could result in finding the key piece of information we need."

He gave a sharp nod, and his beard whispered over his chest. "What about working with the sheriff?"

"Ryleigh offered her services to Maddox," Finn said. "He refused and was closemouthed about his findings before he took off."

Tobias's eyes pinched tight. "That won't help any of us. Let me give him a call. Our families go way back, and he owes me a few favors."

"Family friends or not, Russ does have to follow proper procedures," she said, though she really didn't want to defend him right now.

Tobias frowned. "Still, I'll work on him."

She appreciated Tobias's help, but it was better for her to work on Russ directly. He wasn't easily influenced, and he would do what he would do despite Tobias's pressure. "I know we've been through all of this before when the threats started coming in, but have you thought of anyone other than ecoterrorists who might want to do something like this?"

Tobias shook his head. "And I've been thinking about it. A lot. But no one else comes to mind. Gotta be those Sovereign Earth people. That's the only thing that makes any sense."

She agreed but... "Problem is, there aren't any local members of the group, so someone from out of the area has to be doing it. I can check local motels and hotels for possible suspects but a warrant will likely be required to get any info."

"Russ can get one." Tobias nodded at a vintage red pickup parking down the road and two men stepped out. "There's Reid. Maybe I can ask him to put some pressure on Russ too."

She should've recognized the driver as Reid Maddox, but she hadn't caught a good look at his face. The two men quickly marched toward the back of their truck.

"Perfect timing. I wanted to talk to him anyway." She faced Tobias. "The former FBI agent I mentioned is Colin Graham, and he's a part of Reid's team."

She didn't wait for Tobias to ask any questions, but

headed down the road, skirting the large log trucks still hugging the side. Finn had said drivers would be coming back to return the vehicles to the office location.

She got closer to Reid's pickup and two sets of footfalls trailed behind her. Finn and Tobias of course. Thankfully the awkward silence between her and Finn had ended. They'd earlier given their official statements to Russ, and as predicted, he didn't share a bit of information. Then she and Finn had made phone calls, checked email, and otherwise sat staring as water trucks came and went while the fire-fighters battled on and the flames diminished.

The other guy with Reid looked up.

Colin! It was Colin.

She sped up to where they'd set up a pair of tables and were now unloading other items from the truck bed.

"Steele," Colin said, a smile she couldn't see behind his mask lighting his eyes. "Long time no see."

"Hey, Colin," she said so Finn and Tobias would know who she was talking to. "Nice to see you."

Colin set down a box of individual packages of potato chips. "Russ said you were here when they found the body, but I didn't expect you'd still be on scene."

She stopped by the tailgate loaded with food and drinks likely for the firefighters. "We're waiting to talk to Ryan, but then we planned to come see you."

"Me?" His large brown eyes widened.

"I have a favor to ask," she said. "But why don't we help you get this set up as we talk? I assume it's for the firefighters."

"It is." Colin cast a quizzical glance at Tobias and Finn, who stopped next to Ryleigh.

Reid stepped closer. "Ryan called to say the blaze was contained, and the guys could use a meal." His piercing blue eyes fixed on Finn. His look could cut right through a person if he wanted, but he was a kind, Christian man underneath. The contrast had always made him most interesting to watch. "Ryleigh and Tobias are old family friends, but I don't know you."

Finn didn't balk under Reid's intensity but held out his hand and introduced himself to Reid and Colin. "Ryleigh mentioned you both."

Reid relaxed, but only a fraction. "I was sorry to hear about Felicia's passing."

Finn flashed a wide-eyed look at Reid. "You knew her?"

Reid nodded. "My daughter Jessie attends elementary school with Avery."

"Right," Finn said. "I need to remember how small Shadow Lake is and that everyone knows everyone."

"Not everyone." Colin's sarcasm wasn't even mildly hidden. "But as an outsider, I can say it sure feels like it. Not that people haven't been friendly. Maybe *too* friendly if you get my meaning."

On the summers Ryleigh had gone into town with the Maddox boys, she'd witnessed the local gossips in full force. "Have you been fixed up on blind dates yet?"

Colin snorted. "Man, have I, but I've managed to put them off. So far, anyway. You too, Durham?"

"I've met my share." Finn's voice was strained.

"I wouldn't be surprised if you're introduced to all the single women with kids in school by the end of the month." Colin's eyes crinkled above his mask.

Finn shoved his hand into his hair. "Avery and I have enough casseroles in the freezer for a month of dinners. I appreciate the food. Just not sure I'll appreciate the offers that will come when I give the dishes back."

Ah yes, he was reluctant. Not a surprise. He'd always made a point of ignoring women who threw themselves at him. One of the reasons he'd been so interested in her. Sure, she was impressed that he'd survived the sheer torture to become a SEAL, and she liked that he was a hero, but she worked with heroes every day and came from a family of them too. So why put SEALs, in particular, on a pedestal?

Reid shifted and toed the dirt. His wife died a little over a year ago, and the single women were likely starting to approach him too. He waved a hand over the bed of his cherry red Ford truck and looked at Colin. "If you'll get things unloaded and the tables set up, I'll go tell my brother we're here."

"We can help." Finn grabbed a bin of disposable dishes and silverware and took them to the table.

"You're in charge." Reid nodded at Colin as he passed.

Colin gave a mock salute and looked back at the others. "Let's get to it. These guys are bound to devour this stuff." He picked up a cooler and carried it toward the table.

Tobias followed Reid, and they stopped to talk. Ah yes. He was putting that pressure on Russ that Tobias said he would exert.

Finn picked up a large platter of sub sandwiches in an open cardboard box and headed for the table by Colin. "So you work in the Maddox resort that Ryleigh used to come to in the summers."

Colin set down the cooler. "Not hardly a resort anymore.
"

"It's now Shadow Lake Survival." Ryleigh grabbed the nearest item, a trashcan, and stepped over to Colin. "A few years ago, they started the business to teach survival skills to people who want to live off-grid. It's an immersion kind of course and really intense."

Finn looked at Colin. "There're enough customers for that line of work?"

Colin nodded. "With more people working from home and moving from cities, the business is booming. That's why they hired me. Hired my brother Devon too. He's a former Clackamas County deputy. Also recently brought Micha Nichols on board. He served with Russ in the military."

"From what I've heard, you guys are always booked." She unfurled a bag in the trashcan.

Colin turned to study her. "What's this favor you mentioned?"

"Before I ask, I want you to know I respect your decision to walk away from domestic terrorism."

"Okay. Butter me up first. I get it." His eyebrows rose. "But..."

"But we believe this bomb could be a result of ecoterrorism."

He stopped moving. "And..."

She settled the can by the table. "And I've done all I can think of to find a solid suspect, but I've come up empty-handed. You have such a deep understanding of this kind of crime, I hoped you could find something I missed."

He simply stared at her. She got it. He didn't want to do this.

As much as she respected him and didn't want to inflict any further distress on him, she couldn't give up. "I know this is a big ask, but a man has died. With so many threats sent to Tobias, I'm worried this might not be over."

He scrunched his forehead. She hadn't convinced him. Far from it.

"Tobias reported the threats to Russ, right?" he asked.

Good. At least he hadn't given her an outright no. "He did, but from what Tobias told me, Russ struck out too. Of course, this bomb changes everything. Russ now has a murder to investigate. He's bound to throw additional resources at it, but they don't have a budget for hiring someone with your skills."

Colin reached into the cooler and shifted chunks of ice

to expose bottled water. "I'm sure we could get Nick Thorn at Veritas to help. They do pro bono work all the time. I know him and would be glad to ask."

"Already in my plan, but he doesn't have a terrorism background like you." She moved closer, hoping he would look up again as she planned to plead with more than her words. "And remember, not long ago you would've done exactly what I'm doing if you had an expert who could help."

"Yeah. I would've." He ran a hand over deep brown hair styled in a buzz cut then let out a long breath. "I've finally let that all go, and I really don't want to drag it up. Especially not so soon. I've just started sleeping well at night again."

Ouch. That cut her to the core. But if she could bring in a killer and at the same time save her company's reputation, she would pull out all stops. "Trust me. If I thought we could do this without you, I wouldn't ask."

"I don't know."

She hated taking advantage of their friendship, but she had no choice. Yet to be fair to him, he needed to know her motivations. "You know I want to bring in the bomber at all costs, right?"

"That goes without saying."

"But once the news media finds out Steele Guardians knew about the threats and failed to stop this bomber, it could be disastrous for our family business."

"Why didn't you say that in the first place?" He lifted his mask to his forehead and scratched his chin. "Your family took me in on Thanksgiving that year I couldn't go home. They made me feel like one of the family. I'll do it for them. You too, of course, because you're one of them."

"Thank you, Colin." She threw her arms around his neck and gave him a quick hug, something she would never have done while they were fellow agents, but it felt right at the moment.

"If I'd known I'd get a hug out of it, I would've said yes right away." Colin grinned, his face blooming in attractiveness.

Why couldn't she fall for a wonderful guy like Colin?

But not her. She always liked men who bordered on a bad boy. Men like Finn. Guys who weren't available. A challenge. Even now. He'd hurt her big time, and he still got to her. Truth be told, she'd never forgotten him and had imagined what might've been off and on since they split over two years ago.

Totally odd for her. She was a free spirit as Russ had said and rarely lived in the past. She moved on. Tried new things.

And yet, here she was caring about what he was thinking. That had to stop and it had to stop right now.

4

Finn unloaded and set up chairs near several tables for the men, his gut churning as he watched Ryleigh and Colin reminisce about their past at the FBI. That after a shared hug. Finn wanted to march over to Ryleigh, stamp his claim on her, and warn this Colin fella off.

Seriously, where had that come from? Finn had never been a jealous guy. No need to be when he usually had no trouble convincing the woman he was interested in to go out with him. Not bragging. Just stating a fact. SEALs were chick magnets and women flocked to them. He didn't play that up like some of the guys did. In fact, he never put it out there until after a first date. But Ryleigh had been different. She hadn't succumbed to his charms on that date. Far from it.

He'd met her at church when he was on medical leave and visiting his cousin in Portland. One look at her, and he'd fallen hard. He'd tried to get her attention, but she didn't pick up on his most obvious signals. He'd had to get the pastor to introduce him. Seriously. She unsettled him so badly that he'd had to ask a pastor to be his wingman. Didn't matter. Finn was hooked and would do whatever it took to meet her.

Did she care? Nope. She was more interested in what her family was up to than talking with him. Took her sister, Mackenzie, to act as a go-between to procure that first date. Even then, Ryleigh seemed more interested in everything around them than him.

So he broke his hard, fast rule and told her he was a SEAL on that first date. Waited for a positive reaction. Got little to nothing other than respect. What he wanted, right? No. He'd wanted her to be the one to ask for a second date. Or at least hint that she wanted it instead of a reluctant agreement.

He'd learned on the first date that she was an eternal optimist and a real free spirit. Fine. He had to play into that. Plan an adventure together. He did some recon with her sister and found out Ryleigh had never been on a hot air balloon ride. That would be an adventure a free spirit could get behind, so he arranged a flight over the Willamette Valley.

What an afternoon. She finally opened her eyes and really saw him. Well not until they were back on the ground. In the air, she was bursting with joy and wonder at her surroundings. Her big eyes blazing with enthusiasm. Her face filled with astonishment. So beautiful he could barely remember to breathe, and he'd hardly seen the landscape.

He would never forget that day. Her smile. Her passion. Her pure joy.

In fact, he never had forgotten it or her, and after he'd gotten Avery settled, he'd planned to look her up again. He had to apologize for the way he'd left things after the amazing month they'd had together before his leave ended, and he had to deploy again.

Everything came crashing down on him that day. All the rules. The problems. The reasons they didn't work. Why relationships with a SEAL often failed.

He lived in California when not deployed. She might be a free spirit but family was everything to her, and she was entrenched in Portland. He wouldn't mind living in Portland again. He liked the city just fine, but he couldn't leave the team. They were his extended family.

So he'd ended things. Bam. Just like that. Cold turkey. The way he did everything. Decide. Act. Move.

But man, oh, man. He wasn't proud of how he'd left her, but he'd thought he had no choice at the time. If they'd tried a long-distance relationship, he would just have dragged out the inevitable breakup. Better to rip the Band-Aid off instead of taking a gentle approach and getting more invested in a future they couldn't have.

Besides, as a free spirit, he hadn't thought she would be upset. Certainly not hold it against him two years later. But there she was cozying up to this Colin guy and forgetting Finn was even there.

Leave it alone. Move on.

He settled the last chair in place and spotted Reid and Ryan stepping down the driveway, ten other firefighters trailing behind.

Finally.

Soot covered Ryan. His face. Turnout gear. Gloves. All of it. And his facial muscles were tight, his eyes droopy.

The man had just given his all, and he deserved a major thank you. Along with this spread of food and drinks.

But what did Finn plan to do?

Pounce on the guy and pump him for information. Not something Finn wanted to admit, but finding the bomber had to come first. The only thing more important to Finn was not to let it become all-consuming, take over his life, and let little Avery down. Nothing could be more important than the motherless little girl.

Not even following these unwanted feelings and trying

to rekindle a relationship with the captivating Ryleigh Steele.

~

While worn and exhausted firefighters fueled up, Ryleigh shoved her phone into her pocket from calling her family to update the situation and leaned against a logging truck next to Finn. She'd also had a long discussion with Colin about how he could help, and he was fully on board.

He grabbed another platter of chocolate chip cookies from the truck. "Email me all the details for the searches, and I'll get on it the minute I get back to the compound."

"I'll do it right after we talk to Ryan." She smiled her thanks.

He returned her smile, and she could actually see it as the air had cleared, and they'd ditched their masks. Problem was, she also had a clear look at Finn's unbearably handsome face, and she kept sneaking glances.

"You're both former feds," Finn said, seeming totally ignorant of her struggle. "Does this bombing fit the FBI's definition of ecoterrorism?"

"It appears to." Colin uncovered the cookies. "But this situation is odd."

Finn pushed off the truck, his gaze interested. "How so?"

Colin tossed the plastic wrap in the trashcan. "I've never seen an ecoterrorist group engage in an action like this where there was a potential loss of life."

"These groups usually want to protect life," Ryleigh added. "Means they direct their attacks on property, hoping to cause economic harm to industries that destroy the environment. Sovereign Earth believes logging in any form is bad."

Colin strode back to the truck. "Then if we go with their

philosophy, they'd need to be sure no one would be on site. Means they could have someone on the inside who knew the place would be deserted at lunchtime today."

Finn frowned. "Or they're just good at recon. This place runs on a routine schedule. If I watched the site long enough, I could predict what would happen at any given time of day."

Ryleigh agreed. "Besides, wouldn't it be easier to set the bomb to detonate on a regular day after the second shift ended, and our guards would be the only people in the area?"

Colin cocked his head. "Good point, but maybe they thought the bomb would start a fire like it did, and a volunteer response could be slower at night."

"Sounds possible," Finn said. "If not quickly contained, a fire could wipe out the trees the group was trying to protect."

A grave expression tightened Colin's face. "I really need to get a look at those threats."

Ryleigh opened her phone to her photo app and held it out to Colin. "I scanned them. You can take a quick look now, and I'll email them to you too."

He swiped the images and studied the files one at a time. "They're certainly framing the threats as protecting the environment, and no doubt the message is consistent with an ecoterrorist group."

"Looking deeper into ecoterrorism seems like the way to start for sure," Finn said.

Colin's lips turned down in a deep frown. "Yeah, but we don't want to count Virgil Eckles out. He was onsite and could be involved. I'll start with him before digging into Sovereign Earth and then widen the search to include all ecoterrorism."

"Wouldn't it be faster to limit our focus to groups with their sights set just on logging?" Finn asked.

"You'd think so, but these groups can be very erratic and unpredictable," Colin said. "A group protesting one environmental issue could be enraged over something they see or read in the news and jump on the anti-logging bandwagon in support of another group."

Finn nodded, but his attention drifted to Ryan, who had come to his feet and was stretching.

"Excuse me," Finn said and made a beeline for Ryan.

"Me too." Ryleigh gave Colin an apologetic look. "We want to ask if Ryan saw anything related to the bomb."

"Then I'll join you. The device used could tell us who's behind it."

She hurried to follow Finn. By the time she reached Ryan, he'd planted his hands on his hips.

Had Finn gone in guns blazing?

Ryan looked at her, at Colin, then back at Finn. "Okay, what gives? You're not ganging up on me to see how I'm doing."

"We're hoping if you saw any bomb fragments that you could tell us about them," Ryleigh said.

His eyes widened. "Guess my tight-lipped brother is being his usual self, and you want to pick my brain."

"He is," she said, as there was no point in denying it.

Ryan eyed Ryleigh. "And you're going to try to find the bomber on your own?"

"Not alone," she said. "I'll work with Finn and Colin. Nick at Veritas too."

"But you won't be working with Russ?" Ryan pointed at a patrol car pulling up on the road behind them.

Drat. Why did Russ have to pick this moment to show up?

45

"Right," she said to hurry Ryan along before Russ joined them. "So if you saw something…"

"I did actually," he said, as Russ's car door opened.

"Out with it," Finn snapped. "Before your brother gets over here."

She wasn't surprised at Finn's outburst, but she was surprised he'd made it this long without exploding.

"Please," she said to Ryan making sure her tone was soft and conciliatory to make up for Finn. "Finn's just a bit impatient, and he means nothing by it. Right, Finn?"

"Right, but let's get to the point." His tone continued to hold a sense of urgency. "What did you see?"

"One unusual thing. A piece that looks like a photoelectric cell."

Now he had Ryleigh's full attention. "They used it to detonate the bomb?"

"Looks like it," Ryan said. "We spotted computer fragments too, which I suspect are out of place in the mill."

"Only computers are in the machinery," Finn said. "So if you saw parts of a typical computer casing, they're not from the machine."

"That's what I saw," Ryan said.

Colin cocked his head. "In all my ecoterrorism research, I've never seen a photoelectric cell being used."

"If the cell was the detonator," Finn said. "The computer fragments could suggest the bomb was controlled by a computer. That would allow them to time the explosion somewhat."

"Explain," Russ demanded from behind them. "And make sure you mention how and why you possess such knowledge."

Finn turned slowly. "SEALs are trained in explosives. All types and all methods of detonation. You never know what you might encounter on an op."

"Okay that covers why you know about it." Russ kept his gaze pinned to Finn. "Now give me the what."

Finn stood tall and strong under the intense observation. "When you think of photoelectricity think of electricity produced by a light beam. So photoelectric cells work when light hits them. The brighter the light, the greater the electricity produced. These cells are used in everyday life. Automatic faucets in public restrooms for example."

"You wave your hand," Colin said. "And the cell sends a signal to a solenoid, which pulls the valve open and the water comes out."

Finn nodded. "Bombs controlled by these cells are often called "when dawn breaks" bombs as they go off when the rising sun hits them."

Russ frowned. "Then why didn't this one detonate at sunrise today?"

"Based on Ryan's mention of computer parts, seems possible that the cell was controlled by a computer programmed to only detonate when a certain level of light was reached."

"Doesn't sound precise though," Ryleigh said. "If the bomber knew when the workers would be out of the building, why not just set a timer? Or even detonate with a cell phone?"

"That I can't answer," Finn said. "But I do know bombers tend to stick to the same script—use the same switches, explosives, and wiring—so maybe the photoelectric cell is what he knows."

Russ faced Ryleigh. "I've thought about your earlier offer. I'd like your assistance on this investigation and have you call in the Veritas team if they'll do the work pro bono."

Ryleigh tried to keep her mouth from falling open, but this was the last thing she expected from Russ.

"Good way to catch flies," Russ said.

"But I...you...are you sure?"

"Positive. I need to gain as much information as I can over the weekend before I call in the feds—who aren't known for sharing."

"You know I'm not a law enforcement officer anymore." She didn't really want to throw out things to change his mind, but she didn't want him to agree only to backtrack either.

"You can serve as an official expert," Russ said. "But I can deputize you if that makes you feel better."

Clearly, he'd given it some thought. "No need as far as I'm concerned."

He gave a sharp clap of his hands that echoed through the stillness. "Get on the horn to Veritas, and let's get this moving."

She nodded, but her mind raced with items she would need to do. First off, call Veritas, second, find a place to stay in town. She couldn't make the four-hour drive back and forth to Portland each day.

"Give me an hour," Russ added. "And we can meet at my office to form a plan of attack."

"I'll be joining you." Finn thrust his chest out as if he expected a fight.

"We could use an explosive expert on the team, so why not?" Russ said.

Finn blinked. "Well, good, then."

Russ looked at Colin. "Can Reid free you up to help us in the IT area?"

"I already asked for Colin's help," Ryleigh said. "But he hasn't had a chance to ask Reid for the time off."

"I'll take care of that," Russ said.

Reid managed the day-to-day aspects of the business, but Russ was a full partner as was Ryan, so Ryleigh supposed any of them could make such a decision. Hopefully, Reid would be okay with this one.

Russ fixed his sights on his brother. "Anything else you want to tell me about the fire or bomb?"

Ryan tilted his head. "Burned hot and fast, but not unexpected with all the wood. Could be solvents or other chemicals that you might want to check out with Tobias, but I don't think he'd have done this for insurance or anything."

"A possibility we still need to consider," Ryleigh said.

"And we will." Russ looked at Ryleigh and Finn and gave them directions to his office. "Okay, people, let's move. We have a bomber to find in less than two days."

5

Ryleigh wasn't the least bit surprised by Russ's rapid end to their discussion, but Finn gaped after the sheriff, who rushed up the hill with sure and solid steps. Russ knew his mind and didn't like to be challenged. Finn knew his mind too. Ryleigh had seen him in action enough to know. And as leader of his SEAL team, he was used to men following his lead no matter what and ensuring the chain of command wouldn't be broken. But he wasn't in charge in his current job. Tobias was. The Finn she'd known would be experiencing extreme frustration.

He shifted his attention to the group. "Is Russ always this abrupt?"

"Abrupt? That was calm Russ." Ryan chuckled.

Colin dug his phone from a cargo pocket. "I'll still check in with Reid and meet you all at Russ's office."

Finn held out his hand and gave Ryleigh a tight smile. "After you."

They climbed the incline, and she took out her phone. She scrolled through her contact list until she came upon Blake Jenkins's name and hit dial. As Veritas Center's criminal investigator, he coordinated their team's efforts in all major investigations. A bombing and murder required a big response. *And* a big ask in terms of pro bono costs.

The phone rang, and she offered a prayer for success with Blake.

"Blake, hi," she said when he answered. "Ryleigh Steele here."

"Ryleigh." His deep tone rumbled through her phone. "How are things at the FBI?"

"Actually, I retired and now work for the family business."

"Big change, I imagine."

"I figured life would be more boring, but today has proved otherwise." She explained the situation and their needs. "You know Emerson County doesn't have the funds to pay for such an investigation, so our request also includes your team subsidizing the investigation."

"Isn't the sheriff calling in the ATF and FBI?" As a former sheriff, Blake would know the proper procedure. "If they pool their resources, they'll have everything they need."

"He is, but he has the murder aspect to work and wants to gain as much information as he can before he calls them to take control of the narrative."

"We wouldn't want to step on the fed's toes." Blake went silent then let out a breath.

Oh no! He was going to say no. She was counting on a yes, but she knew this was a big request and shouldn't have had her hopes so high.

Please!

Blake cleared his throat.

Here it comes. A big fat no.

"But as a former sheriff," he said, "I totally understand this guy's wishes."

She should've thought to play up the sheriff card right up front. "Does that mean you'll do it?"

"Depends. I can usually commit our resources but not with this. Way too big of a pro bono request to act on my own. I'll have to get the partners buy-in."

"I hate to ask this but—"

"You want an answer like yesterday and us on scene within an hour."

"You read my mind." She laughed.

"Not hard to do when you think like every law enforcement officer out there." He chuckled. "We already have a partners' meeting scheduled in half an hour, and I can get back to you after that."

"Thanks, Blake. The sheriff and I really appreciate it." She ended the call and shared the information with Finn.

He raised an eyebrow. "You think they'll go for it?"

Did she? "It'll take a lot of resources, but all the partners have a heart to help, so yeah, I do. Or at least I'm hopeful."

He narrowed his gaze. "What else do we need to do before the meeting?"

"I don't know about your tasks, but I need to make lodging arrangements and call one of my sisters to see if one of them can pack a bag and bring it down here for me."

He stared at her for a long moment. "Avery and I still live in Felicia's big house. It's really more house than we need, but I don't want to move Avery. Anyway. My point is, we have several spare bedrooms, and you can stay with us."

Another surprise, but this time she managed to keep her mouth closed. "I don't think that's a good idea."

He gritted his teeth. "It's just a place to sleep, Ryleigh. Nothing else. No big deal."

"But we'll be together so much of the time already. Adding even more time isn't wise."

"Afraid you'll fall for all of this again?" He ran his hands over his body and laughed.

"Easy for you to joke like that. You weren't the one who was hurt."

He sucked in a sharp breath.

Right. She'd nailed him, and it hurt him. She should feel bad for that. And she did. Somewhere deep down, but the other part of her—the part she would later have to repent for—was glad he was hurting too. Even if he'd been the one to walk away, maybe he didn't want to and had been heartbroken back then as well. She had to at least admit it was a possibility.

"I want to talk about that." His tone had grown husky. "Ask for your forgiveness and make it right, but not here in public."

"I understand." Or at least she was trying to.

"Then just agree to stay with us and after dinner tonight we can talk."

She still couldn't commit. "I'll think about it."

He didn't look away. No surprise. He didn't like to lose at anything. Even something as simple as her decision of where to stay.

"At this time of year," he said. "Tourists are flocking to the lake, and you'll be hard-pressed to find another place on such short notice."

He had a point, though she didn't want to admit it. Maybe the Maddox family had room for her at their compound instead. "Like I said. I'll think about it."

She nodded at Colin. "We should help clean up here and get going."

She marched away from Finn and up to the table. She covered the sandwich platter while Colin consolidated several boxes of chips into one.

Maybe he could help with her lodging needs. She looked at him. "Do you live on the Maddox compound?"

He nodded. "All the staff does. Reid and his daughter Jessie have the main house. Russ and Ryan live in the two big cabins near the lake, and the rest of us are in smaller cabins. They recently built more cabins for paying guests too. Even with the added ones, they're almost always full."

"Are they occupied right now?"

"Yeah. Busy time of year, and the weekends are big for us."

So if she wanted to hunker down on the Maddox property, she would have to ask one of the brothers to bunk with them. No way she would stay with Russ and his intensity. She wouldn't mind asking Ryan but wouldn't want to intrude on Reid and his daughter. Maybe it was just easier to take Finn up on his offer and hide out in her bedroom. She would have to decide soon.

She put her attention to her chores, and they finished the clean-up.

"See you at the meeting," she said to Colin and Finn and headed for her SUV.

Inside, she sat for a moment and inhaled the coconut air freshener. Enjoyed being on her own and the lack of need to be on guard every second. Away from Finn. Away from her thoughts. Just sitting in the quiet. Alone.

Colin drove past and waved.

If she wanted to arrive at the meeting on time she had to get going. She took a cleansing breath and cranked her engine.

Click.

No response.

She turned the key again. Another click.

No. No. No. Not again.

She slammed a fist against the wheel. She'd had the

54

same dead engine one morning last week, and her vehicle had been towed. The mechanic said he'd replaced the alternator, and the car was good to go.

Obviously not.

Argh! Today was a gift that just kept on giving. She couldn't handle another stressor, could she?

She gripped the wheel and rested her head on her hands.

What did she do next? Pray for sure. Mostly for her attitude as it raced down a steep incline toward the pits.

A knock sounded on her window.

She startled and sat up.

Finn stood there. Of course he did. He would've waited until she got on the road to follow her and be sure she was safe. He'd done that often enough when they'd been together for that short month.

He was a protector. Something she was used to from her family of current and former law enforcement officers, and it had never bothered her in the past. Not so at the moment. Now she didn't want to need him for anything. But it seemed like she might need him not only for lodging but transportation as well.

She lowered the window.

He leaned forward. "Car trouble?"

She explained about the repair.

He pointed at the front end of her vehicle. "Want me to look under the hood?"

"Not sure you can do anything. It just clicks like it did before."

"Still, it could be something different. Like the battery. "

"But Russ is expecting us, and we don't have time to troubleshoot. Can I grab a ride from you now, and I'll call for a tow on the way?"

"Your tow options around here are limited, but I know a

good local mechanic. We could stop by his garage to give him the keys. He can bring it in to work on while we're in the meeting." He pulled her door open as if he expected her agreement.

She didn't want to give in so readily, but that was childish, and besides, she didn't have much of a choice. She got out and followed him to his truck. He opened the door, grabbed a worn pair of combat boots sitting on the floor, and tossed them in the back where he'd strapped in a child's booster seat.

The contrast struck her hard. So many military families struggled to balance family and service to keep the country free for people like her, and she never really appreciated it enough. Sure, on the one day a year when the country remembered them, she did too, but since she'd split up with Finn, she'd tried hard not to think about the danger he raced into most of the year.

She prayed for the service members as she climbed into the truck that smelled of vanilla. The big vehicle had buttery soft leather seats, and he kept the interior immaculately clean. His military days had taught him organization, and he continued to apply it in his life. She remembered how neatly he could fold laundry when she shoved things into drawers.

He got behind the wheel and put his hand on the key. He sat for a long moment, not moving. He looked at her. "I have to be right up front with you about something."

Please don't let him say he's in love with another woman.

"Okay," she said.

"I have to stop work at five-thirty to pick Avery up at daycare before it closes at six. On the weekends, I head home to relieve her sitter at the same time."

"Oh, okay." She let out a silent breath. Why in the world was she so thankful that he didn't tell her about another woman in his life? She might be attracted to him, but she wouldn't give him another chance. *If* he even wanted one.

"When we get home, we'll have dinner and free time for Avery since there's no homework with school out. Lights out for her is at eight, and we can work from the house after that if you want to."

"Sounds fine," she said and didn't dispute that she would be staying with him again. If she secured other arrangements, she could tell him then.

He arched a brow and kept looking at her.

"What?"

"The Ryleigh I knew lived for her work."

"Yeah, well, the Ryleigh you knew has changed." *A major hurt like you inflicted can do that.*

He opened his mouth as if he planned to reply but turned the key instead. The big engine rumbled to life, and he pulled onto the road.

She sat back, but she wanted to continue the conversation. Obviously, he didn't. Too bad. She was a big girl and had moved on from him.

Right?

Ryleigh ignored Finn and got out her phone. She stared at the black screen for a moment. Which sister did she call to bring her clothing? Mackenzie or Teagan? Only Mac knew about Finn, and they'd kept it between them, sparing Ryleigh an inevitable review of the breakup by her family.

The question was, which one would be the least nosy about him?

Likely Mackenzie. If Teagan got a hint of Ryleigh's attraction for Finn, she would press and press until she got the info she wanted, where Mac would be more patient.

She punched Mac's contact number, and her sister answered right away.

Ryleigh quickly explained her need and asked her sister to help.

"Glad to do it, but if I leave now," Mac said. "I won't get there for hours, and I'll have to spend the night. I can hit Ryan up for a room. Where are you staying?"

"Not sure yet." If Ryleigh did stay with Finn and had a working vehicle, she could meet Mackenzie at Ryan's cabin, and her sister wouldn't even have to know about Finn. "Text me once you get to Ryan's place, and I'll come get my things."

Ryleigh thanked her sister and ended the call before Mac could ask additional questions. She looked at Finn. "Are there any car rental places nearby?"

"You can use my truck if you need it after work hours. Otherwise, during the day, I can drive you."

"I have to meet Mackenzie at Ryan's tonight."

He cast her a suspicious glance. "It's none of my business but why can't she drop your things at my place?"

"Because," she said and left it at that to look out the window.

"Because you don't want her to know we're working together after the way I bailed on you," he said, his tone deep and emotionless.

"Yeah."

"She'd give me a piece of her mind, I'm sure."

"And then some."

"I can handle it, if it's easier for you."

"It's easier for her not to know."

"Then take my truck if your vehicle isn't fixed."

"Okay," she said, more to silence him than anything. She would ask Russ about rental cars. If she decided to stay with Finn, she didn't want her every move controlled by him. By any man. By anyone. She liked to be free to do her own thing when the mood struck.

He drove them to a well-maintained garage painted a bright green and white on the edge of town. He parked and held out his hand. "If you give me your keys I can arrange for the tow and repair."

"I can take care of my own car."

He let out a long breath. "Is this the way it's going to be between us? Everything a fight?"

"No, I..." No point in arguing. She got out her keys and dropped them on his palm.

"Be right back." He exited his truck at top speed, likely thinking she might change her mind and snatch her keys back.

What was the big deal for him to arrange for her tow and repair? He knew the mechanic, and it would be faster and easier for him to handle it. So why be disagreeable?

Because Finn had hurt her, that's why! Big time hurt her. And she didn't want his help with anything. Not now anyway. Maybe after they hashed out their differences she would change her mind, but she just couldn't see that happening.

Petty of her when he was simply being kind. But feelings had a way of taking over. Especially hurt feelings. And they colored everything in sight. Everything, until she let them go and reason returned.

Right now the only way to do that was give this whole situation to God. She should've done that the minute she clapped eyes on the infuriating man.

She closed her eyes. Prayed. Sincerely. Earnestly. Asking God for the ability to trust His reason for putting Finn in her life again. To let down her carefully erected wall and be accepting.

The door clicked, and her eyes startled open.

"You okay?" Finn asked, sliding behind the wheel.

"Just praying."

"Sorry to disturb. Go ahead and resume, and I'll get us to the sheriff's office." He glanced at his watch. "We should arrive right on time."

She looked out the window but didn't go back to prayer. Instead, she watched as they drove into the small town with narrow streets lined with small older houses at first and then turned into a commercial area. An ice cream shop, café, and stores with bright banners lined both sides of the streets. The sidewalks were filled with tourists buying souvenirs and antiques, laughing and enjoying themselves, oblivious to the recent bombing and murder not far away.

Hopefully, when they heard the shocking news, it wouldn't ruin their vacation. Days spent in town with her sisters and the Maddox brothers had always been a high-light of her summers. The lazy, idyllic sun-kissed days were different from life in the big city.

Ah, simpler times. She longed for them. She sighed.

Finn glanced at her.

"Sorry. Just going down memory lane. Maybe I told you how I used to hang out in town a couple of days every summer with the Maddox brothers. Or we just came in to grab an ice cream cone."

"Did we pass their property on the way in?" he asked.

She shook her head. "Other side of town. About ten miles out. We rode bikes to get cones. We ate the ice cream and then rode back, but by the time we reached the resort, we had to jump in the lake to cool off." She laughed.

"Sounds like fun."

"It was. I had the best childhood."

"I wish I could say the same thing."

Her heart constricted. "I'm sorry, Finn. That's the second time I was insensitive about the loss of your parents."

"No. Not at all." He waved a hand. "You can't downplay your life just because I had some hard times. I had ten great years and memories before my parents died. And the rest was okay too. Mostly thanks to Felicia's friendship."

"That's very mature of you."

"Not hardly." He shook his head. "I figured God gave me a raw deal and had a chip on my shoulder for a long time. Wasn't until I became a SEAL that I figured out life is better if you learn to live *with* your hurt instead of living *in* it."

He glanced at her. "I don't know if that makes sense, but it's what got me through BUDS to get my trident. I discovered if I focused on the pain, it won. If I put my focus on the prize, I won. Same in life now. Focus on God. I win. Focus on all the painful things. I lose."

"Makes perfect sense." She let his comments settle in and looked out the window at the town receding and the highway ahead that led to the sheriff's office and jail. She'd been living in the hurt of their breakup. Totally. She really hadn't seen it until now. Running into him again told her that. She'd let it color so many parts of her life. Especially dating. Or more specifically—not dating for fear of being hurt again.

Would a change of perspective help with that?

Couldn't hurt.

She looked back at him. "That's a great way to look at life."

"You're way too quick with the compliments today," he said. "I wish I could say I was living with things right now, but I'm not. Sometimes, maybe, but not all the time. This latest curveball has thrown me. Some days I succeed. A lot of them I don't."

"I get that," she said to reassure him. "Not long after we broke up, my cousin Thomas was murdered. That took a lot out of our family. In some respects, we're all just coming out of the terrible loss."

"I'm real sorry that happened." He cast her a sympathetic look. "Did they catch the person responsible?"

"Yes, and he's been convicted and is serving a life sentence."

"That's something at least."

"Yeah, sure. It is." She swallowed the pain down to continue without tearing up. "But honestly, we all thought the conviction would bring more peace. It didn't. Just a sense of finality." Tears won out and pricked her eyes. She had to change the subject. No way she would cry in front of Finn today.

She pointed out the window. "There's Russ's office."

Finn turned into the parking lot for the single-story building that covered a city block and had been built since she'd last vacationed here, so sometime in the past ten years.

He parked in a visitor's space, and they got out. The sun had dipped below a thick stand of trees, and a chill in the air sent a shiver over her arms. Or maybe the chill was from their mission.

They were hunting down a bomber. A killer. And getting distracted for any reason and failing was not an option.

6

—————

Finn held the door for Ryleigh to the wide lobby that served as a waiting area for the sheriff's office. Large signs pointing to the right directed visitors to the jail. A hint of lemon cleaner lingered in the air, and the tile floors were spotless. Of course they were. The Russ that Finn was coming to know would insist his facility be tidy and clean.

Ryleigh headed for the front desk. Finn wanted to brush past her and take charge, but he had to do a better job of letting her do her thing and resist taking over.

The woman with silvery gray hair cut short and straight to her narrow chin looked up from behind the desk and flashed a smile. "Help you?"

Ryleigh stepped forward. "Ryleigh Steele and Finn Durham to see Sheriff Maddox."

"Oh, you!" She stared past Ryleigh to Finn, and he didn't like her over-the-top exclamation. "The SEAL who has every unmarried woman in town's heart aflutter."

"Retired SEAL," he said, but did so between clenched teeth.

"Right. Well. Just the same to them." She tsked. "Now I

know you're here to see Russ, but I can't let you go without mentioning my niece. She's just darling."

Finn flashed up a hand, hoping his expression would warn off even a charging bear, which was the way a lot of these women had attacked him. "Best not to keep the sheriff waiting."

"Oh, right. Right." She picked up the handset. "I'll let him know you're here, and then we can continue our conversation."

"Sorry. I need to speak to Ms. Steele before we meet with Maddox." He took Ryleigh's elbow and nearly dragged her away from the window. "Now you see what I face."

She fought a grin but didn't contain it.

"It's not funny."

"It is. Kind of. If you'd relax and go with it."

Easy for her to say. She didn't have to deal with it. "If I'd been thinking, I'd have told Tobias to keep the fact that I was a SEAL private, but I never thought he'd blab it all over town."

"It's a big deal to some people."

"But not to you."

She took a long moment before answering. "I'd never want to downplay what you achieved. Not many men can do it. Or downplay the danger you put yourself in for others, but a lot of men and women go into danger every day. That puts them on the same playing field for me."

He'd always admired her logical take on life. Or at least on this, even if it did make him work harder to have to meet her. "And well it should be."

"I always liked that about you," she said, seeming happy to be remembering one of his good points. "You're humble and never bragged or used your SEAL status to get anything."

Busted. "I did. Once. On the first date with you. Broke

one of my rules. I was hooked and you were like, yawn, who *is* this guy—if you noticed me at all."

She wrinkled her nose. "Was I that bad?"

"My ego took a beating for sure."

"Sorry. We met at a time when I didn't want a relationship to interfere with my job."

"And now? Are you in a relationship?" he asked, hating that he wanted to. No, needed to.

"No."

"Looking to get involved?"

"Hmm." She tapped her chin. "I have to work longer hours to prove myself in the family business right now. But as long as the guy can accept that the job is a priority for me, then I'm okay with starting something up."

But not with him were the read-between-the-lines words she didn't say.

The door near the main desk opened, and Russ poked his head out. "Follow me."

Finn held the door again and trailed Ryleigh and Russ down the long hall painted a light beige. The sheriff passed his office, but Finn paused to take a look inside. The space fit the guy. Big desk to match the ego. Neat, organized, and dust free to match his orderliness. Shelves filled with legal books to match his by-the-book stance.

Or none of Finn's observations could relate to the guy's personality. Hard to tell at this point.

Sure, Finn had been taught to make snap impressions in his job as SEAL, but in the civilian world he usually had more time and needed to keep more of an open mind. After all, Ryleigh said the sheriff was a good guy and not as full of himself as he'd appeared.

He led them into a brightly lit conference room smelling of fresh coffee and holding whiteboards on two walls. One of those long walls also contained a large window overlooking the rear of the property and a forest of tall ever-greens. A large map of Emerson County was centered on the third wall, and a huge flat-screen TV on the fourth.

"Grab some coffee if you want." Russ waited by the door and closed it behind them.

Finn nodded at the pot for Ryleigh, but she shook her head. He was still amped up from a soda at lunch and didn't need any caffeine, so he scouted a place to land.

Colin already sat in a chair facing the door, Ryan across the table. No way Finn would put his back to the door even in a secured sheriff's office, so he rounded the table to claim the seat next to Colin. Ryleigh evened out the numbers and pulled out a chair next to Ryan. A young woman with an iPad and keyboard sat at the far end of the table.

Ryan smiled at Ryleigh as she took a seat next to him.

Would she look at Finn that way again after he explained tonight? He didn't expect her to fall for him again. No matter how much he was still into her. Nah, that was a pipe dream. But they could be friends. *Friends, ugh.* So not where he wanted to go. No guy liked being put in the friend zone, but that would be better than her gut-wrenching dislike.

Russ stood at the head of the table where a stack of stapled papers sat in a neat pile. "My assistant, Allison, will be recording details." He gestured at the woman. "Allison, meet the team." He went around the table and gave names and basic info. "Get your contact info to her before you leave. I'll start a group for email and texts so we're all in the loop. Don't leave anyone out on important details."

He took a long breath. "Goes without saying that every-thing we discuss is confidential." He ran his gaze over them, locking in place with each person to gain their agreement. Seeming satisfied, he picked up the stack of pages. "Copies of the official report. Likely nothing you don't know other than the victim's details, but read it over carefully right now and give me any corrections or feedback you have."

He slid the pages down the table. "You should know. My deputy who checked on Gates found the place ransacked, and you'll see that reflected in the report too."

"Interesting," Ryleigh said. "Could point more to Gates being a player in the bombing."

Finn studied the information and paused at the suspected victim section. Uri Francis Gates. Nickname Smokey. Single. Age thirty-six. Last known address before Oregon was Birmingham, Alabama. Oregon driver's license and his truck was registered in the state.

That was basically it, and Finn had items he wanted clarified. "I remember that Gates's work application at Shadow Lake Logging doesn't mention any jobs in Alabama. He listed his last employment here in Oregon. As far as I know, Tobias checked references, so was Gates a logger in Alabama too?"

Russ went to the largest whiteboard and divided it into columns with the headings of *Assignment and Responsible Person*. "Ryleigh, follow up with Tobias. See if he confirmed Gates's employment and if he was employed as a logger in Alabama. If so, why he omitted it on the application."

"Are odds good that he logged in Alabama?" Ryleigh asked. "I've never thought of them as a logging state."

"Alabama, Oregon, and Washington are the top three logging states in the country," Finn said.

"I knew Alabama was on that list from previous ecoterrorism activities. I'll get the deep dive running on the day supervisor, Eckles, and Sovereign Earth, then I can do one on Gates. That might bring up details for Alabama."

"That's your first task." Russ wrote the assignment and Colin's name on the board.

Finn slid a business card to Colin. "Would you email a

copy of your report to me as soon as it's done, so we don't repeat the work?"

Russ frowned at Finn. "He'll send it to everyone at once."

"Right." Finn knew how to work as part of a team and could deal. He just didn't remember how to work on a team where he wasn't in charge. It had been far too long. Time to get with the program though, as his days of being the top dog were over. Long over.

"Any other comments on the report?" Russ asked.

He received a shake of heads in reply.

Ryleigh's phone rang from where she'd placed it on the table. "It's my contact at the Veritas Center calling back. I should take his call."

"Go ahead," Russ said. "Put him on speaker. Our future actions depend on them, so let's find out if they want to play ball."

∾

Ryleigh punched the speaker button on her phone and shared the names of everyone in the room with Blake before setting the phone on the table.

"Blake Jenkins here." His deep voice rumbled through the room, grabbing everyone's attention. "We've decided to partner with you, pro bono of course, but I have a few logistics to work out before we can get started."

Ryleigh pumped her fist, but resisted shouting out her joy. "Thank you, Blake."

"Pretty hard to say no to helping stop a bomber."

"This is Sheriff Maddox." Russ planted his hands on the table and leaned toward the phone. "I can't thank you enough for helping. If I can ever repay, let me know."

"Will do, Sheriff," Blake said. "Our team is packing up, and we'll leave in time to arrive by eight a.m. tomorrow. We assume it will take more than a day to thoroughly process this scene, and we'll need overnight accommodations. I'll email a roster of staff who will be making the trip."

Russ scowled. "Lodging might be tough. This time of year, motels and cabins are booked up, but we can accommodate quite a few people at our family compound."

"We're not opposed to roughing it in tents if that's the only option."

"We can take the tents if needed." Russ looked at Ryan, who nodded.

"Okay, then next," Blake said. "When I hang up, Sheriff, I'll email a contract to you. If you want the other task force members to be privy to our findings, you'll need to spell that out on the last page. What's your email address?"

Russ shared his email. "What else can we do?"

"Lunch, snacks, and drinks provided at the jobsite are always appreciated. If we don't have to leave the site, we can work faster."

"Of course." Russ went to the board and noted the food needs but put Reid in charge of things.

Ryleigh hadn't wondered until now why Russ hadn't included Reid on the team instead of her. As a former agent, Reid would have the same resources as she did. Maybe more, as he'd been an agent longer than her before he retired. But then her family connection made her hungry for a resolution to the investigation, and Reid might not have the same drive.

"One last thing," Blake said. "I'll need a representative at the crime scene at all times in case we need to make snap decisions. We'll work from sunup to sundown, so please make those assignments."

"Roger that," Russ said.

"That's it for me," Blake said. "If you don't have any questions, I'll see you tomorrow."

No one spoke up.

"We're good to go. Thanks, Jenkins." Russ looked at Ryleigh and sliced a hand in front of his neck to tell her to end the call, which she did.

"I'll give up my cabin to bunk in my brother's cabin," Colin said. "Gives you two extra bedrooms."

Ryleigh remembered Colin saying his brother, Devon, worked for Shadow Lake Survival too.

Finn leaned forward. "Ryleigh will be staying at my place, but I have an extra room."

He would say that. She opened her mouth to correct him, but stopped. What was the point? If the Veritas team needed all the rooms at the Maddox compound, there wouldn't be any space for her. She had no choice but to stay with Finn. Time to start accepting that.

Russ turned to a different whiteboard. "Let's note our potential suspects."

He wrote Uri Gates—Smokey—on the board. "The most obvious one to me. His place was tossed. Someone was looking for something. It's possible he set the bomb, and it detonated before he could get away. But we have no motive at this time."

Ryleigh agreed completely with his assessment. "Did anyone find his phone?"

Russ shook his head. "My deputy dialed the number while at Gates's place. It didn't ring or vibrate there. Maybe the anthropologist who recovers the body will find it on him, or it could be in his vehicle."

"Though I doubt Tobias is behind the bombing," Ryleigh said. "We can't rule him out. Could be an insurance scam, and we should search the business."

Russ nodded and jotted down Tobias's name. "I've already declared his office a crime scene. Sent everyone home. Posted a deputy on site twenty-four/seven. Warrant for the search should come in at any time. We'll need to get forensics over there too."

"Since you've posted a deputy at the mill office, I should call Tobias," Ryleigh said. "He might not want to spend money on posting one of our guards there too. But I'd be glad to double our guys up at the bomb site to protect the Veritas staff when they arrive."

"Ask if he stored solvents or other chemicals at the mill," Ryan said.

"Yeah, go ahead and ask," Russ said. "But forensics will give us a definitive answer. If you ask now and he lies to us about it, that'll tell us something. If the warrant comes in by the time we wrap up, we can talk about completing our search first."

Finn looked at Russ. "Virgil Eckles should be on the suspect list. Not that we have a motive for him, but he had access to the company's explosives and he was the only one on site—other than Gates and Ward—when the bomb detonated. I collected his key to the explosives' depot. Means the only people who can access it now are Tobias and me."

Russ held out his hand. "I'll take both of those keys. It'll protect you from any suspicion of manipulating the inventory after the bombing."

Ryleigh thought Finn might hesitate, but he handed over two shiny brass keys. "I implemented a restricted key system when I started. Only one locksmith can duplicate keys, and Tobias and I are the only signers on the account. They won't make keys for anyone else. I also inventoried all explosives at that time, and the inventory jived with deliveries and usage. So if anything is missing, it happened since then."

Ryleigh might not be happy with Finn, but she was impressed with his actions. "I had security cameras installed on the exterior at the office and depot. Maybe we'll catch our suspect stealing the explosives."

"And I added a sign-in requirement for all visitors to the office," Finn said. "So we can review that footage and compare them to the logs."

Ryan snapped his chair forward. "This isn't an individual suspect, but Colin mentioned ecoterrorist groups protesting logging."

Russ added it to the board and turned. "Who else might gain from setting the bomb?"

Yeah, who? That was the big question Ryleigh had asked since she'd taken on the account. "A competitor maybe who's trying to put Shadow Lake Logging out of business or at least severely cripple them. I checked into that but didn't find anyone who wanted to harm Tobias or his business. Or any competitors who'd received threats either."

"Still, it's a possibility, and we'd be remiss if we didn't consider it." Russ made a quick note and then pointed his marker at the item. "What's the fastest way to get a list of these competitors?"

Colin tapped his laptop sitting in front of him. "I'm sure Ryleigh has one, but I can compile a thorough list online in a few minutes. I'll have it to you before I leave today."

"Would be good to compare the two lists," Ryleigh said.

"Good." Russ added Colin's name as the point person.

"This isn't a suspect," Ryleigh said. "But we should also have Colin look for bombers who specifically use photoelectric cells. That could point us to a prime suspect. At least for construction of the bomb."

Russ looked at Colin. "Is that something you can do?"

"Absolutely. I can write a search algorithm that will find anything you want on the internet." Colin leaned back. "But ViCAP might be a good resource too, and I don't have access for that search."

The FBI's Violent Crime Apprehension Program database held information about violent crimes, but was restricted to law enforcement officers.

"I'll take that." Russ put his own name into the responsible person column then turned. "We're speculating on the photoelectric cell, but it's better than sitting around and waiting for forensics. Gates's house needs to be searched too. See if we can find any bomb schematics or ties to an ecoterrorist group. Maybe information about Alabama. I already have a warrant for that search."

Ryleigh checked her watch. "Finn and I have time to do that right after this meeting."

"My deputy forced open the patio door for his welfare check, and you can get in that way, but make sure to secure it as a crime scene." Russ added it to the board along with a note to search Eckles's property too. "I'll get a warrant for this, and then we can proceed."

"What about Gates's truck?" Finn asked. "Has it been located?"

"My deputies are looking for it." Russ recorded the item on the To Do list. "Let's take five so I can check my email from Veritas. Go ahead and give Allison your contact info while we break and review this info to see if there's anything we missed."

He left the room, and they each shared their information. Colin opened his laptop, his fingers flying over the keyboard.

Finn looked at Ryleigh. "You think we can do a thorough search before I have to pick Avery up?"

"If Russ doesn't keep us here much longer."

"We've covered all the basics," Ryan said. "At this point, we'll need Colin's reports or forensics to give us further direction."

The room went quiet, save Colin's fingers clicking on the

keys, until Russ returned holding a stack of papers. "Contract signed and I asked that all reports be emailed to everyone." He looked down the table. "Allison, please email a list of the team's contact information to Jenkins ASAP."

He slid the stack of papers down the table. "Our guests are coming tomorrow."

Ryleigh took a page and read down the eleven experts' names while Russ noted the rooms available by location on the third whiteboard. Impressed by the extent of the Veritas response, Ryleigh looked up to see Russ had completed housing assignments, filling every open space except for Finn's spare room.

Well then. It was official. She was stuck staying with him. Finn glanced at her. He had to know the implications, and she tried hard to hide her frustration.

"Looks like we're getting ousted." Russ looked at his brother. "We can either pitch a tent or stay with Mom and Dad."

"Mom and Dad, for sure." Ryan grinned. "Would give Mom an excuse to spoil us like she always wants to do."

"I'll give her a call. Reid too, so he knows to expect guests and get meals ready for the Veritas team." Russ didn't add that to the board but glanced down the table. "Any conflicts with taking a turn babysitting the crime scene for the Veritas team?"

"I'll have to relieve my sitter or pick Avery up from daycare by six each day." As if expecting a challenge from Russ, Finn lifted his chin.

"Got it," Russ said, no question at all.

"And my car is in the shop so I'm dependent on Finn for a ride," Ryleigh said. "But I hope it's fixed tomorrow sometime. Or I could rent a car if there's a local place."

"Nada around here," Ryan said. "You'd have to go to Medford."

"I can keep you and Finn grouped together," Russ said. "Won't change the schedule much." He faced the board and wrote out the four-and-a-half-hour time slots.

"I need to get to the office at a reasonable time, so I'll take the early shift." Russ put his name next to the five a.m. slot. "Ryleigh and Finn after me, then Ryan, and finally Colin, our resident night owl, ends the day."

Ryleigh didn't mind her midday shift, but she had a request and leaned forward. "Since I'm the one who called Veritas in, I'd like to be there to greet them when they arrive in the morning, if that's okay?"

"Sure thing," Russ said.

She looked at Finn. "Could we be there by eight?"

"Can do," he said.

"Anything else we need to cover?" Russ asked.

"I'm ready with that list of competitors," Colin said.

Russ grabbed a marker and crossed the assignment off the board then added a new item to investigate the list. He looked at Ryan. "You take this. Your experience with wild-land fires makes you most familiar with logs and the best one to speak their language."

"You got it," Ryan said. "We don't have a group at Wilderness Ways, so I have time."

"Wilderness Ways?" Finn asked.

Ryan's eyes sparked. "An organization for troubled teens. I'm the director."

Finn scratched his cheek. "I thought you worked with Shadow Lake Survival."

"I work part-time for both. But if the family business keeps booming, I'll soon need to go full-time there and find a director to replace me at Wilderness Ways."

Finn shifted to look at Russ. "You going to retire to work for the family too?"

"Never."

"That's what I said and look at me." Ryleigh chuckled.

"I won't give in to pressure. I help out when I can, and that's the best I can do right now." He clapped his hands. "That's it, people. I'll assign a deputy to babysit the crime scene so we can meet again tomorrow. Time to be determined."

7

Ryleigh studied Uri Gates's two-story townhouse from the quiet treelined road, Finn by her side. Gates's place was located in one of the few newer developments in town. Newer according to Shadow Lake standards, built in the past twenty years. The building's crisp white paint with black trim stood out next to the neighboring unit covered in dingy yellow paint.

She and Finn walked up to the side of the building and into a strong wind that buffeted her face. "No doorbell or security cameras on the property."

"Not a surprise since he basically just moved in," Finn said. "Or maybe he's not into that."

They entered the postage stamp-sized backyard through a squeaky gate to the sliding patio door in back. Both of them slipped into disposable gloves and booties, and Finn slid the door open. It grated along the track sending a horrific rasping sound into the air.

"Hope the neighbors don't think we're breaking in and report us." Finn gestured for her to go first.

"Guess it's good that Russ insisted on deputizing me

before we left so I can flash my new shield at anyone who bothers to question us." She grinned.

He returned her smile with the one that got her heartbeat racing.

Do not fall for that again.

She stepped over the threshold and forced her attention to the dark family room, coming up short at its trashed state. Sure, Russ had said the townhouse had been tossed, but the extent exceeded her expectations. The intruder had sliced open the cushions on a small sofa and spilled the innards across the room. The coffee table was upended. The debris brushed against a glass-enclosed gas fireplace with sparkling crystals in the base.

She picked her way through the mess to a modest-sized kitchen that butted up to the family room with two stools perched at the black granite counter. Stainless appliances gleamed as if recently polished. Maybe because his lease had been signed only a month prior. The contents from oak cupboards were swept onto black tile floors. A jug of vinegar had spilled, leaving the caustic odor radiating through the air.

Finn came up beside her. "Wonder if they found what they were looking for."

"Who knows," she said. "Let's go upstairs and see if the mess continues. Remember this is a crime scene so watch where you walk."

She led the way down a short hallway that took them to the front door and a steep stairwell leading upstairs. On the second floor, she found two bedrooms and headed for the closest one.

The mattress had succumbed to the same fate as the sofa, and the drawers had been yanked out of the nightstands, odds and ends salted across the faded beige carpet.

She pointed at the far wall with two doors. "I'll check the closet. You do the bathroom."

They separated, and she could barely get in the doorway with all the clothing scattered on the floor. Mostly heavy-duty work clothes but jeans and T-shirts too, and several pairs of work boots and sneakers, all with a built-in lift in the right shoe. A wooden organization system lined the closet walls, but stood empty. She squatted and dug through the items, carefully feeling clothing pockets for any hint of a lead. She came up empty.

Finn returned.

She stood. "Anything?"

"I found antidepressants in the medicine cabinet, but that's it."

"Interesting, but I don't know how that helps. Unless he was suicidal and decided to take the company out with him."

"He seemed well-adjusted to me, and I don't think he formed any grudges against the company in the short time he was there."

"Yeah, doesn't make sense. But then do we really know the people we work with?"

"I did. At least my SEAL team, but this guy was pretty new and likely on his best behavior at work, so if he was feeling down, he was hiding it well."

She nodded. "Let's search the other bedroom."

They went down the hallway, but the second bedroom was devoid of any furnishings. Still, she ran her fingers over the walls and floor of the closet looking for any hidden doors before giving in. "Nothing."

"We still have his truck. If the deputies' search turns it up."

Trying not to let her disappointment ruin her mood, she headed down the stairs and gave the family room another quick search. "Nothing, but I still want to get Sierra Rice over here. She could locate fingerprints from whoever broke in and trashed the place, giving us a solid lead to pursue."

"We should talk to the neighbors too," he suggested. "Or at least I always found neighbors to be great sources of intel."

She nodded. She'd thought he would be helpful, and he was proving his worth.

She pulled the door closed behind them and affixed the seal Russ had provided. "Wish I could lock it, but this will at least let us know if anyone tries to enter."

They put their heads down against the wind until they reached the sidewalk and headed toward the dingy yellow place next door. The townhomes had immaculate landscaping, probably taken care of by the homeowners' association. With the buildings blocking the wind, the late afternoon sun warmed her back as she approached the front door of the yellow house. Up close, she noted the color now faded to match the sky, looked like it had once been royal blue.

Ryleigh knocked and got out her shiny new badge in a small portfolio.

"What do you want?" A gruff female voice came from the other side of the door.

Ryleigh held up her credentials to the peephole, giving the woman a clear look at it.

She opened the door and stood, hand on a cane with five prongs and looking up at Ryleigh. Stooped over her cane, Ryleigh had a hard time telling her height, but her wrinkled face and frail posture made Ryleigh think nineties or older.

"I'm Bertha Samuels." She clicked her teeth. "Suppose you want to know about the new neighbor too."

"Mr. Gates, yes," Ryleigh said.

"Knew he was trouble from the first time I laid eyes on him."

"Is that so?" Ryleigh let her comment hang in the warm summer air, hoping that the woman would elaborate.

"He was moving in, and I came out to greet him with a plate of my famous peanut butter cookies. Now with my arthritis, it's no small feat to bake these days, but the guy is one of those gluten-free people." She rolled her eyes. "Rejected my cookies, and right off the bat he made sure I knew that he worked from two until ten and expected me to be quiet in the mornings when he slept late."

"I'm sorry," Ryleigh said as she didn't know what else to say.

"I never." Bertha shook her head. "Telling me to be quiet. I'm the most respectful neighbor he could hope to have. I knew he was from out of state by his southern drawl. I almost told him to go back to Alabama."

"How did you know it was Alabama?"

"Plates on his truck. He got them changed though, so I guess he was planning to stick around. But you know those loggers. They're a flighty bunch."

Ryleigh didn't know any such thing. Most of Tobias's workers had been with him a long time.

"When was the last time you saw Mr. Gates?" Finn asked.

Bertha craned her neck to see him. "Now, aren't you a tall one?"

"Yes, ma'am." He gave her a charming smile.

"Good looking too." She chuckled. "I saw Uri yesterday morning, which was odd. He left in his truck around nine. Haven't seen him since."

"Thank you, ma'am." Finn smiled again, really working Bertha in a manner that was getting the information they needed.

No way would Ryleigh interrupt.

"Have you noticed anyone else at his place today?" Finn asked. "Or anything else out of the ordinary."

"I'm assuming you know about the deputy who came to check on him this afternoon. He stopped by to ask me the same questions." Bertha eyed Ryleigh with watery blue eyes. "Maybe you should try talking to each other."

"We should at that." Ryleigh smiled.

Bertha turned her focus back to Finn. "Then there was another person. A guy. Some might call him fat, but in my day, he would've been called heavy. He had on a baseball cap. A black one. And he kept looking down so I didn't see his face. But he seemed to know where he was going, like he'd been here before. Still, I took a look out front for his car, but nothing was parked on the street that didn't belong to a neighbor. So I don't know how he got here."

"How long did he stay?" Finn asked.

"About thirty minutes, I guess. I thought about calling the cops, then figured he could be coming by to pick up some clothes or something for Uri."

Finn nodded. "Was he carrying anything?"

"Not when he arrived, but when he left, he had a plastic grocery bag with something in it."

Finn glanced around. "Doesn't look like you have any security cameras that might have caught him."

She shook her head and shifted her other hand to the cane. "Wouldn't know what to do with it if I did have one."

"Anything else suspicious going on?" Ryleigh asked, hoping to bring an end to the questioning.

"Nothing related to Uri, but I could tell you all about who's sneaking around behind their spouses' backs." She shook her head. "May the good Lord call me soon so I don't have to keep seeing the downward spiral of people's morals."

"Thank you for your time, ma'am," Finn said.

"See how polite you are." She smiled. "You wouldn't cheat on a spouse, would you?"

"No, ma'am. I sure wouldn't."

But he would bail on the woman he was dating. Namely me.

"Thank you for your time, Ms. Samuels," Ryleigh said.

"No Ms. for me like you younger girls." She tried to straighten up but failed. "I was a Mrs. for seventy-eight years and proud of it."

"And well you should be, ma'am." Finn smiled. "Again, thanks for your time."

Ryleigh walked away. The door closed and the lock snicked into place behind them.

Finn caught up. "I know what you're thinking."

She glanced up at him. "You do, do you?"

"That I might not cheat like Bertha said, but I'd walk away."

"You got me."

"Will I ever live that down?"

She shrugged. "Guess it depends on our talk tonight."

She caught the disappointment in his gaze, but she kept going. She couldn't commit to forgiveness until she knew his full reason for treating her so badly. She knew as a Christian, she needed to forgive him no matter what, and she honestly thought she had. But today God had made it clear. She was still holding the breakup against Finn and had to do better.

Ryleigh leaned back in the passenger seat of Finn's truck and read the group text from Russ. She quickly replied with an affirmative to Russ's text then swiveled to face Finn, who was driving them to the daycare center to pick Avery up.

"Russ's text says the warrant for Shadow Lake Logging's

office came in." She dropped her phone into her pocket. "As an employee, you'll have to sit this one out, but Russ wants me to join him. He'll pick me up at your place."

Finn didn't even try to argue but gave a quick nod. "Even if he did include me, I'll be watching Avery."

She turned her attention to the late afternoon sun beaming over the daycare building just down the road. They'd finished their search by four-thirty, giving them plenty of time to pick Avery up before the center's six p.m. closing time.

Finn turned the corner. "I wonder if Tobias is going to can me."

So that's what he'd been preoccupied with on the drive.

"Why would he do that?" she asked.

He flexed his fingers on the wheel, maybe relieving stress. "I'm in charge of security, and his whole operation was blown to bits. I couldn't do a much worse job than that. I'd can me if I were in his place."

Yeah, she might too. And what about Steele Guardians? "Same goes for our security services. He might dump us as well."

Finn gripped the wheel. "I can't help but feel like we deserve to be fired, but even in hindsight, I don't know what we could've done differently."

Should she have done a better job? "I probably should've called Nick or Colin to review the threats earlier on."

"Maybe," he said, as if he didn't want her to think she'd failed.

She wished he would've totally disagreed with her, but even if he had, she knew she was right. She should've kept digging into the threats until she had at least one strong suspect to go after. But after the bomber didn't follow through on the first threats and then they stopped coming, she'd foolishly believed they'd been idle threats. She'd let other things take her focus. And now a man had lost his life in a very gruesome way.

She resisted sighing as Finn pulled into the daycare parking lot and stopped his truck out front.

The bright primary colors of the building made the place look cheerful and inviting, and brightly colored playground equipment peaked above a sturdy wooden fence on both sides of the lot. Children's giggles and joyful screams rang out.

"Avery has always gone here after school and in the summers." He shifted into park. "I don't really know how to evaluate the place, but she seems to like it. At least she doesn't complain about coming, and it's what she was used to, so no point in changing it."

He took out the keys and opened his door. "Be right back."

Well, that answered the question of if he expected Ryleigh to come inside with him. If she joined him, it would likely start tongues wagging. Probably why he was avoiding it.

Still, she was anxious about everything that was going on, so she slid out to pace. Ryleigh hoped staying at Finn's house didn't disrupt this child's life any more than it had been. The poor thing. Losing her mom—her only parent—so suddenly.

The door opened, and Finn came out with a thin little girl wearing a tie-dyed T-shirt and blue jean shorts. She had frizzy blond hair down to the middle of her back and no bangs. The sides were clipped back with bright blue barrettes. An excess of freckles dotted her high cheekbones, and she was missing two upper teeth, and the ones that had come in were spaced wide apart.

Now what did a seven-year-old respond to? Ryleigh had

babysat when she was a teen, but that was ages ago, and her memory was vague.

Finn and Avery marched up to her. Finn introduced Ryleigh. A guarded look tightened the little girl's face. Man, how rough to be seven and so uneasy. If the child smiled, she would be adorable.

"We're working on an investigation together," he told Avery.

She looked up at him, her cautious look changing to full-fledged worry. "What kind of investigation?"

"Just one at my workplace," he said off-handedly.

Avery scrunched her eyes. "You mean the bomb that went off today. The one at your work."

Finn grimaced. "How did you hear about that?"

"I heard a couple of teachers talking about it when I was coming back from the bathroom. They didn't know I was there. I was worried that..." She shrugged.

"That I was there and might've been hurt?" Finn squatted next to her.

She nodded.

Finn rested a hand on her shoulder. "I'm sorry you had to hear that, Peanut. I wasn't anywhere near the bomb. If I'd known you heard about it, I would've made sure you knew that."

She lifted her pointed little chin. "But otherwise, you weren't going to tell me, were you?"

"No. No point in you worrying for nothing."

Wow, that was honest. Ryleigh would probably have tried to sidestep the question.

Avery's chin wobbled. "Will this investigation be dangerous?"

"Not likely."

"Will *she* help you stay safe?" She jerked a thumb at Ryleigh.

He nodded. "She used to be an FBI agent."

Avery's eyes widened, and she looked up at Ryleigh. "Really?"

"Really."

"Do you have a gun and everything?"

"Yes." Ryleigh stopped short of telling her that she was carrying right now.

"Did you shoot anyone?"

"No."

"How come?"

A question Ryleigh had gotten all the time as an agent. "I never found myself in a situation where I needed to."

"I would've shot someone." Avery turned and climbed into the truck then slid between the seats and shed her backpack to scramble into her booster seat.

"Spoken like a seven-year-old." Finn grinned.

Ryleigh laughed and got into the truck as did Finn. Avery's seatbelt clicked, reminding Ryleigh to put on her own, something she never failed to do. Ryleigh didn't know why she was so frazzled over meeting Avery, but maybe it made her think about what it might be like to have a child with Finn.

Not a place she wanted to go.

She turned to look at Avery. "What was the best part of your day today?"

"I dunno."

"You always like the art projects," Finn said as he backed out of the space.

"It was okay."

"What did you make?" Ryleigh asked, trying to keep the child engaged.

"Paper hot air balloons that we hung in our classroom. They're decorations for a party we're gonna have soon."

"What color was yours?" Ryleigh asked.

"Pink and purple."

Finn looked in the mirror. "Your favorite colors."

"I guess." She looked out the window.

Man, she was a tough act. Finn really *did* have his hands full.

Ryleigh turned around in her seat and faced the dash. She would wait for Avery to talk to her next time and not try to start a conversation. Who knows, Avery might not say a word. Which was sad, because Ryleigh really wanted to help the child relax and find some joy in her day. She hoped Avery had fun when she was in her known environments like school and daycare and especially at home. But maybe her grief still usurped her joy at this point.

Finn navigated through the small town with people walking dogs and riding bikes. An idyllic area, and here sat a traumatized child who couldn't enjoy any of it right now.

They arrived at the large box of a house with two stories and a wall of windows in the front. After pictures Finn had shared of Felicia, who'd been a quirky dresser, the plain traditional style was just as unexpected. Finn pulled into the garage, and they all got out. Avery ran ahead and inside without a word.

Finn looked at Ryleigh. "I'm sorry for Avery's rudeness but not surprised. She's really hurting. I'd call her on it, but I don't know if that's a good idea or if it'll harm her more."

Ryleigh couldn't even imagine having to make such a decision. "Have you considered counseling for her?"

"Way ahead of you there. She's going but just sits and looks at the counselor. Not a word out of her, so no progress yet, but I'm not giving up."

Ryleigh was about to comment when Russ pulled into the driveway. "That's my ride. I'll be back as soon as I can."

"Let me know if you'll be later than six-thirty. I like to make sure Avery eats by then."

"You don't have to hold dinner for me. Just go ahead as you usually do, and I'll find something."

"I'm glad to have you join us. Just call if it's going to be late."

"Will do." Feeling like an old married couple and not hating it, she fled to Russ's patrol car and got into the passenger seat. He was on the phone and held up a finger.

She buckled her seatbelt and then sat back, looking at his computer set up. A laptop was fixed in a holder with a navigation screen mounted next to it. The radio played dispatch calls that came over loud and clear. No calls nearly as urgent as the bombing, unless you consider a bull getting out of his pasture urgent.

"Get back to me if it turns up anything helpful." He ended the call and placed his phone in his pocket before backing out of the drive. "That was my deputy who's running the ViCAP search. He struck out with the use of a photoelectric cell in the state. He's expanding his search nationwide."

"I really think that's the kind of detail that would make it into ViCAP."

"Agreed." He set off at a clipped speed. "Give me details on your search of Gates's house."

She gave him a report, including the talk with the neighbor. "I'll get Sierra over to Gate's place first thing in the morning."

"About that. I gave Jenkins a call and asked if they could bring additional staff so they could process the logging office too, after we lock it down tonight. He said he would try, but it was up to Sierra as she runs the trace evidence department."

"Would be great if you had more forensic staff to keep from stretching her group too thin." She looked at him. "No offense to you, of course."

"Hey, none taken. I'd love to have the budget for that."
He cocked a half smile. "We could call in the state, but then
I'd have to call ATF, and I'm not ready."

"You're seriously not worried about blowback on that?"

"Why? All it could do is end my career as sheriff." He
chuckled.

He made light of it, but she didn't get that vibe from him.
"Seems like the job is kind of important to you, though."

"Yeah. I'd like to think I'm good at it and I still make a
difference, so I'm not ready to leave. But if my decision
costs me the job, so be it. In this business you have to do
what you think is right no matter public opinion. I think
this is the right move that the local voters would appreciate.
Especially if they knew my motive is to find and stop a
killer."

"But you haven't told the public that a bomber is at
large," she said.

"No need. The grapevine already has." He turned onto
the road leading to the mill and Shadow Lake Logging's
office. "There's no indication anyone outside of the mill and
logging business is in danger, and my staff is warning the
other local companies to be alert."

He glanced at her. "You miss the law enforcement gig?"

"At times. I have to admit to enjoying this investigation.
Not that a man has died though or even convincing Colin to
come out of retirement."

"Yeah, he was pretty broken when he came here. But he's
really lightened up the last few weeks." Russ turned his
blinker on for the office sitting down in a lush valley on the
right side of the road. "He's a real asset to the family business, just like I know you are to your family."

She sat back. "Who'd have thought when we played
together as kids that we'd be working on solving a murder
together."

"Well, we *did* play cops and robbers." He grinned. "Remember the cap guns and holsters your grandad got us."

The smile sent a wave of love for her grandad through her heart. "Gran was so mad at him. Said we had plenty of time to play cops when we grew up if we wanted to."

"But she didn't make us give them back. That was the important thing." He turned into the driveway and cast her a mischievous grin. "Don't tell anyone, but I still have mine."

"Me too." She looked at him and laughed. "I wonder if anyone else kept theirs."

"We should ask." His smile faded. He lowered his window and stopped next to his deputy guarding the mouth of the driveway along with one of Ryleigh's company guards. Tobias's truck was parked on the side of the driveway. "Let Mr. Hogan through too."

The uniformed deputy gave a crisp nod and stepped back to let Russ pass. Russ rolled the car slowly down the driveway to the two-story cinderblock building that looked more like a bunker than an office.

They got out and waited for Tobias to park and cross the lot. Russ handed her a pair of booties and disposable gloves and held onto an additional set.

He took a step forward as if he couldn't wait for Tobias to arrive. "Thanks for meeting us, Tobias. We have a warrant to search the premises." Russ held it out. "That includes your explosives' depot."

He frowned at them. "You didn't need a warrant. You just had to ask, and I'd let you look at anything you wanted to see."

A perfect answer to point to his innocence. Or was he lying and playing them? She believed it was innocence.

"First up," Russ said. "I'd like to get all of the keys for the depot."

"In my office." Tobias spun and marched up to the

building where he unlocked the door and disarmed the alarm.

"Hold up," Russ called out. "We'll check for explosive devices."

"You think they've put one here too?"

"Can't be too careful." Russ slipped on his booties and gave a pair to Tobias. "Put these on when I call you back to your office."

Russ held out his hand for Ryleigh to come in.

She encased her shoes in the blue fabric, and they stepped side-by-side into the waiting area, their feet whisking over the checkerboard tile floor. They split, each taking a different side of the long hall that led to a bathroom, break room, and offices, including Tobias's at the end of the hall. Logging photos filled the walls, covering decades of this business's existence.

She went into Tobias's small office with a desk, credenza, and a round table with four chairs. Every surface was covered with paperwork. The first time Ryleigh had seen the disorganization, she'd almost pivoted and walked out. She figured if he worked in such clutter maybe his business was a mess too, but she'd stayed and learned that he ran a tight ship.

She searched high and low, moving things when she was uncertain, but just found more of Tobias's junk and released musty odors into the air. Or at least it looked like junk to her.

She went back into the hall. "It's clear."

"You can come back now, Tobias," Russ yelled.

He hurried down the hall, his feet sloshing in the booties, and brushed past them. "Might look like I don't know what I'm doing in here, but I have a system."

Not one, Ryleigh had ever heard of. She was a messy person at heart but this office fell on the hoarder spectrum.

He squatted down by an ancient black safe and spun the dial. He took out a small wooden box and gave it to Russ. "The master's in here and here's mine." He removed the key from his ring and gave it to Russ.

Russ put on gloves and withdrew a plastic evidence bag from his back pocket, then put everything in the bag. "I need to confirm that your two supervisors, Finn Durham and you, had the only four keys."

"That's right."

"And you haven't had any new ones cut." Russ stowed the bag in one of his cargo pockets.

"I haven't."

"Then next I'd like to see the explosive inventory."

Tobias took a ledger book out of his safe. "I'm old school and make the guys record everything in front of me or Finn now that I hired him, in the same log I been using since I started this business. No point in changing things that work just fine."

Ryleigh thought it would be a whole lot easier to keep an inventory on a computer, but if this worked and was accurate, she couldn't fault him just because he was old-school.

"Let's all head out to the depot and take a look at what you have there," Russ said.

"Sure." Without argument or fuss, Tobias closed and locked the safe, then stepped down the hall and out the door.

No one could say the man didn't cooperate. Either he was being helpful because he was innocent or because he was guilty and confident he wouldn't get caught.

Only time would tell which answer they would find.

8

With sunset around nine o'clock at this time of year, Ryleigh wasn't surprised when they stepped outside to see the sun bright in the sky or hear birds chirping in nearby trees that surrounded the clearing. The crew had parked large logging equipment in lots on the far side of the property. Next to them sat a shed with red and white signs warning of explosives plastered on its log exterior.

Tobias looked at Ryleigh. "I was hoping you'd come to tell me you have this investigation figured out already."

"Sorry, we're just getting started, and it'll take time," she replied. "But while we're walking, I can ask you a few questions to speed things along. First, do you still want one of our guards stationed here? Or since there'll now be a deputy here all the time, should we focus on the bomb site? I think the forensic workers could use the protection if that helps make your decision."

He didn't reply, and she hoped the answer wasn't that he just wanted to cancel their contract.

"I'm sure my deputies will have things covered here," Russ said.

Tobias nodded. "We have a first-rate sheriff's department, thanks to Russ. Might as well keep your guards at the mill property."

"Okay, so next I want to ask you about Uri Gates."

He pursed his lips. "What about him?"

"I know you did a background check when you hired him, but did you call his references too?"

"Of course I did." His offense at her question flowed through his tone and rigid posture. "Called his last employer here in Oregon. Tom Watson. A good friend. Said Uri only worked for them for a month when my supervisor opening came up. Tom said Uri was a good worker, and they were sorry to lose him, but he'd been a supervisor before and that was really the job he'd been looking for."

"What about prior jobs?" she asked. "Did you follow up on any of those?"

He shook his head, and his long white beard flowed back and forth. "Tom and I go way back. I figured his word was good enough for me." Tobias stopped walking to stare at her. "Why? Something bad in Uri's prior work history?"

"I don't know, but he came here from Alabama, and we think that might be a red flag."

"Oh, that." Tobias waved a hand and started walking again. "He told me he got divorced and wanted to leave the past as far behind as he could. Oregon fit that bill for him."

"So you knew he'd previously logged in Alabama?"

"Yep."

"But it's not on his application. Why was he trying to hide it?"

"Not hiding it at all. His former wife is the admin assistant at the logging office in Alabama. He doesn't want her to know where he is. If I called, she would find out."

Sounded plausible but still something they needed to follow up on, and Russ's pointed look aimed at her said he expected her to take care of it. "Can you give me the contact info for this logging office and his former wife's name?"

Tobias stopped by the depot's solid door and glanced between her and Russ. "You thinking Uri set the bomb?"

"We're just covering all the bases."

Tobias stood back. "Remind me before we go, and I'll look up the info on his personnel record."

Still wearing his gloves, Russ dug the key from the bag. "If Dr. Dunbar confirms Gates perished in the fire, we'll have to contact her for the death notification call."

Ryleigh had forgotten all about that fact. Russ might've tasked her with confirming Gates worked in Alabama. Russ would have to call the local police to send someone to notify the wife in person that Gates had died in the fire, and then Russ would follow up by calling to ask questions.

Ryleigh didn't want to dwell on this and moved on. She looked at Tobias. "I don't really understand why you even need explosives in logging."

"To protect my workers."

"Explain," Russ demanded.

"Most everyone knows logging is a dangerous occupation, but some trees make it even more so. Sometimes when we start felling a tree with a chainsaw, it'll get hung up on its way to the ground. Those trees can get so twisted or bent that their tension makes it almost suicidal to touch them with a chainsaw. We call them widow-makers. So it's safer to blast from a distance than trigger a natural booby trap."

"I never knew," Ryleigh said.

"And insect-killed trees are also big hazards. They often rot from the inside. So you go to take them down and they can shatter or fall in unpredictable directions. Again, the explosives keep the logger out of danger."

"As long as they know how to handle the explosives," Russ said.

"Yes, there is that, and tons of regulations. Which is why we limit the people who can handle them."

Ryleigh nodded. "We're also wondering if you stored solvents or other chemicals at the mill."

Tobias rolled his eyes. "No way. Only a fool would do that. With all the wood and sawdust around, it would be a tinder box if any of it caught fire." He let out a long breath. "Exactly what happened. Could've been just from a single spark from the bomb."

Russ inserted the key in the heavy-duty lock on a solidly built door and frame.

"How long before I can clean up the mill and get the men back to work?" Tobias asked.

Not something Ryleigh could answer. She left it to Russ.

"It'll be quite some time." Russ pulled the door open and put on a fresh pair of booties.

"What are we talking? A week? More?" Tobias's tone had skated high.

"It's not something we can predict." Russ eyed him. "Your mill is a crime scene, and no one will be allowed on site until I tell you. Same thing goes for this place. I expect you and everyone who works for you to comply."

"Here? You're locking this down too."

"I have to, Tobias. Surely, you can see that."

"But my loggers. Office staff. They need their paychecks."

Russ's gaze softened. "I wish we didn't have to do it."

Tobias glared at Russ. "You're gonna lose a lot of votes from this."

"I'm not in the job to be popular." Russ held Tobias's gaze for a long moment. "I'm sheriff to uphold the law and make sure every resident remains safe under my watch."

Wow. Russ had a huge responsibility. Sure, she'd known he ran a county sheriff's office and that alone would bring a lot of pressure. But to feel personally responsible for every citizen of the county had to weigh heavy on him. No wonder he was such a serious guy. The best thing she could do for him—besides supporting him while a sworn deputy—was to lift him up in prayer and put him in God's hands. Only God was up to the huge task Russ had taken on his shoulders.

He switched on the interior light and turned to look at Tobias. "You wait out here while we clear the place and do a quick inventory."

Tobias's shoulders drooped but he didn't speak. She figured it must be hard to own a business for so many years and then see other people go through it without a care. She squeezed his arm. "It'll be okay."

He blew out a breath. "Just don't know if I'm too old to rebuild. I'd be happy to retire but so many people around here depend on these jobs."

"God will give you the answer." She released his arm, and after donning her new pair of booties, she followed Russ inside the small shed-like building.

The walls were lined with tubes of explosives that resembled giant sausages encased in different colors of plastic—big white ones and smaller red ones. The space had a distinct odor, but she couldn't place it. Likely from the explosives. Each package had a date marked in black marker, perhaps the date the item was checked into inventory so they used the oldest product first.

Russ set the inventory record book on a nearby shelf. "You count the red ones, and I've got the white."

She used her finger to tap the red tubes as she went up and down three rows in open cardboard boxes facing forward. She found a total of seventy tubes and went to the inventory book, which said she should find seventy-six. She counted again. Still only seventy.

"I'm short six tubes," she said.

"There's seventy-two of the white," Russ called out.

She looked at the inventory. "Should be seventy-eight tubes."

"No way I miscounted, but you try it."

She moved to the white ones and used her finger again, going up and down the vertical towers. "Same as you. Seventy-two."

"So six tubes are missing of each color." Russ scowled. "Who all accessed the inventory since Finn took it?"

She glanced at the form. "All three key holders, but Gates was the last one, taking three tubes of each last night."

"Maybe he took the missing ones on this visit and used the extra ones in the bomb."

"I'm really starting to like the guy for this bombing," she said.

"Me too," Russ said. "But we can't rule out the other key holders, including Finn."

She ran her finger down the ledger columns. "According to the form, he hasn't ever taken anything, and he had the inventory confirmed and signed off by the assistant."

"Just because the paper doesn't say he took anything, doesn't mean he hasn't."

"True," she admitted, but felt like a traitor to him.

"We need to get that security footage from the outdoor cameras ASAP." Russ met and held her gaze. "For now, this shortage stays with task force members only until I can figure out a way to use it to our advantage."

He was a shrewd sheriff, and her respect for him kept growing. "What if Tobias asks?"

"Then we play dumb and move on." He picked up the inventory sheet. "Let's get to counting the blasting caps and other supplies."

She nodded and followed him out of the building,

praying that when they reviewed the video files, Finn wasn't caught anywhere near that building. And if he was, his hands weren't filled with explosives.

~

Nearing six, Ryleigh went through Finn's still open garage and knocked on the interior door. She tapped her foot as she waited for him to answer, her mind still overflowing with thoughts on the missing explosives. She really didn't think Finn was involved, but even if he didn't show up on video, he could still be guilty. After all, he knew about the cameras and would know how to avoid them, maybe disable them.

The door whooshed open, and he flashed a quick smile. "How did it go?"

"Tobias wasn't happy we shut down his total operation. He's concerned about paychecks for his workers."

"I guess that would include me."

"You going to be okay?"

He nodded. "I never had enough time to spend my money as a SEAL, so socked a lot of it away." He pulled the door all the way open and stood back.

Ryleigh entered a combo mudroom/laundry room painted a deep purple with white cabinets. Laundry was stacked in baskets on the washer and dryer and the room held a slight odor of bleach.

"With getting up to speed in the new job, I'm a little behind on my chores," Finn said. "Head to your left for the kitchen."

She made the turn down a short hallway that opened into a throwback kitchen from the fifties. Pale yellow metal cabinets ringed the room, combined with a retro powder blue refrigerator, and black and white checkerboard floors.

Frilly white curtains hung across the window over a white porcelain sink and were flanked by white laminate countertops. A blue Formica table with chrome edging and chairs sat in the middle of the room.

"Wow, is this all original?"

"It is and was the reason Felicia bought the place. She loved it. Me? Not so much. Dishwasher is ancient. Fridge barely holds anything, and the freezer? Forget about it. I have to go to the store all the time and that's just for two people. How did families live with such a kitchen back in the day?"

"With the mom typically staying home, she had more time to shop and do dishes, I guess."

He stilled and watched her. "Would you ever do that? Be a stay-at-home mom, I mean."

She'd never really given it a thought. "I don't honestly know."

"Not that I would expect it."

"Um, Finn. I'm only staying for a few nights, not marrying you." She grinned up at him.

"I wasn't...I mean..." His face flushed fire engine red. "I'll need to get dinner started. We planned to have burgers on the grill, and last night I made a packet of veggies to cook alongside it."

Ah, a change of subject. For some reason she wanted to continue to tease him, but gave in to the dinner talk. "What can I do to help?"

"I'd like to eat outside. Avery seems to like that best. Sometimes I can even get her to kick a soccer ball around with me after dinner."

"We're cooped up inside so much during the rainy season and the weather is gorgeous today so that sounds perfect. And I'm not sure if I told you, but I played a lot of soccer when I was younger."

He smiled, broad and potent. Ooh, this might be a dangerous decision. Thank goodness they had Avery to keep things platonic between her and Finn.

"I'll light the grill then gather the things I need," he said, all business now. "But if you want to grab cleaning supplies to wipe the outside table, that would be great. You can find stuff in the laundry room."

They split off, and he stepped out the french doors to the back. She set her purse on the kitchen table then went back to the laundry room. Music played somewhere in the house. Likely Avery's room, but Ryleigh wouldn't go see. She found some disinfecting wipes and headed out the same door Finn had gone through.

The fenced backyard was wide and flat and had a concrete patio with a dining set and grill. A wooden play structure had been placed near the fence with mulch underneath, and a manicured green lawn filled the rest of the space.

Finn stood at the gas grill looking very domestic. A sight she never thought she would see, but it was far more attractive than any of the dreams she'd had of this man.

She doubted she would ever start anything with him again, but she didn't trust her heart not to betray her and give him a second chance. Especially when they could so easily fall into the personal realm like this.

Something she had to guard against and focus on what she needed to do. Finding and stopping the bomber before he struck again.

~

Finn couldn't decipher Ryleigh's mood as she stared at the kitchen cabinet, an odd expression on her face. Looked almost like longing for this lifestyle, but that would be odd.

She hadn't been the settle-down kind of woman when they dated. Made her the perfect woman for him. But seemed as if that might've changed. If her anger at the breakup told him anything, anyway.

She shook her head, then charged outside with a stack of plates and silverware as if needing to get away from him. She set the table with a fury. Almost like she was mad at the dishes. He was tempted to ask what was going on in that pretty head, but no reason to go there until after Avery was fast asleep and couldn't overhear their discussion.

He left to grab the burgers and the veggie pack from the refrigerator and to tell Avery he'd started cooking. He found her in her room, sitting at her desk, drumming the beat with her finger on the wood and reading a book.

"Burgers on the grill for dinner." He crossed the room to her. "And we'll eat outside. It'll all be ready in less than thirty minutes."

She peered intently at him. "I like burgers. Mom didn't know how to grill. I like that you grill."

What? A compliment. That was a first. "I'm making them just for you."

"Doesn't *she* like burgers?"

Ouch. And a slam. "Ryleigh does too. At least she used to when I knew her before."

She scrunched up her face. "Before when?"

Oops. Maybe shouldn't have brought that up, but now that he had... "We dated a couple of years ago."

Avery's eyes narrowed. "You gonna go out with her again?"

"We're just working together," he said, doing his best not to reveal that he wanted to date Ryleigh.

She curled her legs up in her purple swivel chair. "Why did you stop going out?"

"I had to deploy all the time, and it wasn't fair to her for me to be gone so much."

"I remember that. You would go away, and me and Mom would pray for you all the time." She remained focused on him. "But you quit that for me."

"I did."

Avery tilted her head. "How come you didn't do it for her?"

Yeah, why didn't I? His desire to stay with the team. The only explanation, but it sounded so selfish that he couldn't say it. "Ryleigh's a grown-up and didn't need me like you do."

Avery blinked up at him. "Don't grown-ups need other people?"

"Yes, but not usually for all the basic things like a place to live and food."

"And love." Her vulnerable tone touched him deeply. "We all need love."

"Yes, we do."

She clutched her book tightly. "I love you, Finn. Please don't marry her and leave me alone."

He squatted by her chair and took her hand. "I'll never leave you, Peanut. Never."

"You pinkie promise?" She held out her little finger.

He quirked his finger with hers and gave her a reassuring smile. "Pinkie promise."

She threw her arms around his neck and held tight. "I hated it when I had to live at that foster home until you got here. I never want to do that again. I don't want to be alone again."

"You never will be." He only hoped he could keep that promise. He would never let this child down, but he couldn't do anything to prevent a freak accident. Or a health issue like her mother succumbed to.

He leaned back and brushed her hair from her face. "Want to help me cook the burgers?"

"Okay, but the grill is hot. I could get hurt."

The little girl he'd known before her mother died had never been this fearful. He hoped he could bring her security back. "I'll show you how to stay safe."

"Okay."

He turned to leave and saw Ryleigh at the door. She stepped forward. "Sorry to interrupt. I just came to tell you a timer is going off in the kitchen."

"Means the grill's ready." He held out his hand to Avery. "Let's get those burgers cooking."

She gave Ryleigh a triumphant look, then grabbed Finn's hand and dragged him from the room and past Ryleigh.

Curious. Avery still saw Ryleigh as competition for his affection. No need. No need at all. He had plenty for both of them, something he was just coming to learn, thanks to Avery. Made his upcoming talk with Ryleigh even more important.

9

After dinner when they were relaxing around the table, Ryleigh couldn't look at Finn without seeing him in Avery's room. His tender look for the vulnerable child. His gentle explanations. Ryleigh's heart had melted in so many ways. Seeing the big, tough guy being so loving and soft. The child's obvious pain at losing her mother. Finn's hope in making a good life for the broken child.

Ryleigh wanted to swoop in and hug both of them. To hold them until the big bad world disappeared. Until Avery got over her loss. But Ryleigh couldn't do a thing to help. In fact, she was a problem. Avery seemed worried Ryleigh was going to steal Finn.

She wasn't of course. Was she? Not steal him, but if she was with him for long, she would probably cave and let him back into her life if he asked. Did he even want that?

"What do you say, Ryleigh?" Finn asked.

She blinked as she had no idea what they'd been talking about. "What?"

"Would you like to kick the soccer ball with Avery?" Finn asked.

"Oh, soccer. Yeah. Sure."

"I'll get the ball." Avery trudged toward the storage shed as if being forced to participate.

Ryleigh looked at Finn. "No secret that she doesn't want to do this."

"No, which is odd because she loves soccer. For some reason, she sees you as competition for my affection."

Ryleigh needed some clarification. "I'm not putting out that vibe, am I?"

"Quite the opposite."

"Then why?"

He shrugged. "Who can know the mind of a seven-year-old, especially one who's living with such a major hurt."

Avery came running back, black and white ball in hand. "Got it."

Ryleigh took off her boots and socks. She didn't like the idea of playing barefoot, but she liked it better than wearing boots.

"You start." Avery tossed the ball to Ryleigh.

A goal was set up at the far side of the yard so Ryleigh dropped the ball and moved it down the field and into the goal. She turned to look at Avery. "I thought maybe you would try to block me."

She nibbled on her lip. "Is that what you want me to do?"

"Yeah." Ryleigh dribbled the ball back to Avery. "It's more fun to have a challenge."

"Okay. Go for it."

Ryleigh considered going easy on the child, but that wasn't fair to either of them. She positioned the ball, and Avery took a defensive stance in front of her. Since Ryleigh had no one to pass it to, she would use a banana kick to curve the ball around Avery and then take control of it again. A banana kick was usually used to make a goal, but she thought it would work well here too.

She kicked the ball. It did exactly what she hoped, spun, and curved around Avery. The child expected the ball to go straight, so she moved in that direction, but Ryleigh was ready to take control at the true location and drive the ball downfield. As she raced across the yard the blades of grass tickling her bare feet, she heard Avery struggling to catch up. Ryleigh didn't slack off and fired the ball into the net.

She turned to gauge the child's reaction. Ryleigh really hoped Avery understood competition and wouldn't be crying.

She wasn't. She looked up at Ryleigh in awe. "That was amazing. How did you make the ball go that way?"

"Would you like me to show you how to do a banana kick?"

"Yes, please!"

Ryleigh placed the ball on the grass. "Your plant foot is next to the ball. Kicking foot. Toe up. Ankle locked. Hit the outside of the ball."

Ryleigh demonstrated slowly without actually kicking the ball hard.

"I want to try." Avery's excitement bubbled from inside.

Ryleigh stepped back and enjoyed seeing the child's enthusiasm as she attacked the ball and gave it a pretty good go for her first attempt.

"That's a great start," Ryleigh said. "Just remember to keep your ankle locked."

She ran after the ball and tried again.

"That one was much better," Ryleigh called out.

Avery looked up, a big grin on her face. "Wait till they see this at practice. They're gonna think I'm a pro."

"You might want to practice more before unveiling it for your friends. It's usually used to score a goal, so especially practice it with the net."

"I will. Right now." She stood at the ball and kicked, then looked up. "That was better. Now another one."

"Five minutes until bedtime," Finn called out.

Avery scowled. "Aw, do I have to? I want Ryleigh to teach me more."

"Maybe tomorrow," Finn said, but he put little confidence behind his words.

"Okay," Avery said. "I can get some good practice in five minutes."

She turned her attention back to the ball, and Ryleigh jogged over to Finn.

He leaned back in his chair and smiled. "Looks like the jealousy is gone."

"For now, anyway," Ryleigh said, knowing how fickle a girl can be because she'd once been one herself. She remembered changing with every whim, so yeah, she'd broken through with Avery, but what would happen once the ball went back into the shed?

For now, Ryleigh enjoyed sitting in the soft night air with Finn and watching the little girl do her best to make that soccer ball curve. She planted her foot, followed through, and the ball flew, then curved into the net.

Ryleigh came to her feet. "Great job, Avery!"

"You saw it." She bolted across the lawn toward them. "Did you see it too, Finn?"

"I did. It was awesome." A broad smile crossed his face.

"I'm gonna do it again."

"Sorry, Peanut. Time's up."

"Aw." She stabbed her toe into the grass, then lifted her shoulders, her joy gone. "I'll put the ball away."

She ran off, and Ryleigh's heart creased for the little girl. "She was transported beyond losing her mother for a while there and now her loss is back."

"Breaks my heart."

"Mine too."

Avery jogged back and looked at Ryleigh. "Can you tuck me in tonight?"

Ryleigh worked hard to hide her surprise. "Sure."

"Go ahead and get your teeth brushed and your PJs on," Finn said.

She skipped into the house.

"This is so very domestic," she said to Finn. "I never imagined I'd see you in this role."

"Honestly, me either. But God put me here, so I know it's the right place."

Ever practical, but did he really believe it? "And how do you feel about it?"

He didn't answer at first just stared at his hands. "I miss the team. Especially when I'm at work. The security job puts food on the table and lets me be home every night for Avery, but it doesn't challenge me." He looked into the distance again. "But I'm doing my best to live up to that motto—live with my pain not in it."

He was trying for sure, but if she was right, he was failing more often than not. She got that as she really hadn't wanted to leave the FBI, but her family was more important.

"Still, you're in pain just like Avery," she said. "You have the loss of your friend plus the loss of your life as you knew it. I kinda get that with having left the FBI. I would like a bit more excitement too, but figure I can find that in other areas of my life."

"Not me." He let out a long breath and looked at her. "At least not with dangerous things. I promised Avery I would never do anything to risk my life, so no skydiving or base-jumping or anything like that."

"I admire the sacrifice you're making." Without a thought, she reached across the table to squeeze his hand, an action that just seemed right and natural between them.

Heat flared in his eyes as he locked gazes with her. A shot of adrenaline rushed through her. *Oh, man.* She really did still have feelings for this man. Big time.

"Ready." Avery burst out the door, her cute pink pajamas covered with puppy dogs.

Ryleigh jerked her hand away, the mood evaporating.

Avery eyed them suspiciously. "Are you two holding hands?"

"I just rested my hand on Finn's for support." Ryleigh stood. "You know like when someone hugs you or rests a hand on your shoulder when you've had a tough time."

"Like friends or moms do." Avery's tone held her usual cautious note.

"Exactly." Ryleigh started for the house. "How about that tucking in?"

"Ready!" Avery's suspicions vanished, and she cast a sweet smile at Finn, then ran over to him. She kissed him on the cheek. "Night, Finn."

His wide-eyed surprise said this hadn't happened before or if it had, not often.

Avery grabbed Ryleigh's hand and dragged her to the bedroom. "Finn is reading me a story. We're reading Nancy Drew mysteries. They're my mom's from when she was a kid. She got them from her mom. They loved 'em."

"And do you?"

"They're a little bit old, but yeah, because Mom loved them, I do too." She grabbed a book from her bookshelf and flopped on her bed. "Have you read them?"

"Yes. Every single one and I liked them too."

Avery chewed on her lip. "Do you have a mom?"

"I do."

She dropped the book, *The Secret at Shadow Ranch*, on her rainbow bedspread. "Mine died. Just like that. One day she was here. Then she was gone. I miss her."

"I would miss my mom too." Ryleigh sat next to Avery. "My cousin recently died, and I miss him a lot."

"It hurts."

"Yes."

"Real bad. Sometimes I just want to go under my covers and never come out." She picked up her pillow and rested it on her knees.

Ryleigh sought the right words as the child was opening up, and Ryleigh didn't want to discourage her by saying the wrong thing. "Have you talked to Finn about it?"

"Nah." She pressed her face into her pillow.

Ryleigh had to swallow down tears that were threatening to spill. "Did you know his mom and dad died when he was ten?"

Avery's head popped up. "They did?"

Ryleigh nodded. "And he totally understands how you feel, and talking to him might help."

She squished her eyebrows together. "He didn't tell me."

Maybe Ryleigh shouldn't have said anything. "He might not want you to feel bad for him while you were already feeling so bad. Plus, he's not a real big talker. Kind of a silent type of guy."

"He's been trying though. Real hard." She frowned. "But I've been mean to him."

"I'm sure he understands." Ryleigh picked up the book. "A lot of people in our family talked to a counselor when my cousin Thomas died. That helped too."

"I've been going to see one, but I don't know what to say to her."

"Maybe pretend she's a friend who wants to help. Like me."

"You're my friend?"

"Sure thing."

She threw her arms around Ryleigh's neck and held tight. Ryleigh hugged the skinny little girl back.

"This is a mom hug," Avery whispered. "Soft and squishy. Not hard and solid like Finn."

Ryleigh could see why this child would crave a soft mom hug, and Ryleigh was glad to provide it, but Ryleigh's craving? One of those hard, solid hugs that Avery took a pass on. Ryleigh had to get a grip or being alone with him tonight could very well be dangerous to her heart.

10

Everything was riding on this talk with Ryleigh, and as the sun slowly dipped in the sky, Finn didn't want to screw it up. But how should he handle it? He'd always struggled to convey the deep-seated attachment to his SEAL team. They were brothers. Even more than brothers. Men he trusted with his life. No questions asked. They had his back and would be there for him. Blood brothers wouldn't always heed that call. SEAL brothers would never turn away.

Never.

Even now that he'd left the team, if he called, they would come running as soon as they could. But the only help he needed was with Avery accepting him. And what could the guys do with her that he hadn't been able to do?

They were like him. Used to attacking a problem head on. Find the solution and implement it. Sometimes in seconds. But Avery? She was a take your time and go slow situation. Feel your way as you go. No set plan. No instructions. Nothing a guy could train for. Run ops practices for. All he could do was be patient and take cues from her and pray he wasn't screwing things up. Screwing her up.

So far, he was failing. Or at least her response to him had said as much. But the kiss earlier?

He rested his fingers on his cheek, feeling for the emotion again.

Never had a kiss touched him so deeply or profoundly. He'd wanted to race after her and ask if they were good now. Solid. More like father and daughter than almost stranger and child.

"She's off to sleep." Ryleigh's voice came from behind. "I think she's going to open up to you now."

"You think?" He made sure to extinguish the hope her comment brought.

Ryleigh sat next to him. "I told her you lost your parents. She said you hadn't told her. I'm sorry if you didn't want her to know."

Oh, wow. "It's not that I didn't want her to know. I just never thought it was the right time to tell her."

"I think it'll help, but if not, again I'm sorry. I would never want to interfere in the great job you're doing here."

He snorted. "Like I'm succeeding."

"You are. By letting her take her time in opening up and gaining her trust. I think you're doing an amazing job." She smiled at him.

A smile he didn't deserve. Not yet. "I wish I could say the same about when I left you. I really botched that, didn't I?"

Her smile fell. "You did."

"I meant it when I said I would never leave the teams. I didn't plan this, and I almost didn't do it. Leave, I mean."

"What made you change your mind?" She twisted to face him as if his answer was crucial.

He took a moment to organize his thoughts as explaining himself was likely one of the most important things he ever had to do. Failure was not an option. "I wanted to say no, but then I remembered the time I spent in foster care before social services found my estranged grandparents. My dad's parents had died, but my mom's were alive. Mom had a drug problem when she was young, and they eventually disowned her. She got clean and her act together, but didn't want to see them. She understood on one level that they'd had to cut ties when she was using as she was toxic, but she still wished they'd given her more chances. So she had no desire to see them, and we never did. They didn't even know my sister or I existed."

Ryleigh arched a brow. "But you loved living with them and are still close to them."

"Yeah. They were good to us." He smiled at the memories. "I was a lot like Avery, but I had an extra chip on my shoulder. I resented them at first for what they did to my mom. But then we talked about it, and I eventually understood. They'd prayed every day that she would come back to them. The estrangement was two-sided, and I couldn't blame them alone." He shook his head. "And now, here I am in a similar situation. I'm at a loss for what to do."

"Channel your little child and you'll know." She grinned.

"Easier said than done." He rubbed his face, trying to erase his ongoing frustrations. "But back to your question. I didn't have a good experience in foster care, and it was only for two months until they located my grandparents. I know there are great homes out there, but the one we were in was awful. I kept imagining little Avery in a place where the adults were just in it for the monthly checks, and I couldn't let it happen to her. So I took emergency leave that day and ended my military career soon after."

"Did she have a bad experience?"

"Actually, no. She was placed with a great family. So I wondered if I should be taking her away from that, but foster care placements are often temporary. Just because she was placed with this family now didn't mean she would stay there. I wanted to give her a sense of stability, you know?"

"Yes, that's so important."

"That's why I'm living here for now. Maybe later when she's handling her grief better, I'll suggest moving to Portland where job opportunities are greater. And my grandparents and extended family live in the area, so she would have family, and I would have some support. But I won't even suggest it until I think she can handle a change."

Which meant he might never be in the same city as Ryleigh. At least not in the near future, and a potential relationship, if she would ever consider one, was out of the question.

She frowned but then smiled but it looked forced. "I applaud your sacrifice. Especially when it sounds as if you don't much like the job."

"I don't hate it, but I have to keep telling myself something my grandpa taught me when I took my first job in fast food." The memory was as fresh today as it had been back then. "He said no matter if I liked the job or not, to give it my all. To remember I was working for God. That way, others will see Him through me."

"Good advice."

"It was the only thing that got me through that job. Now *that* one I hated." He grinned. "One good thing about civilian life is I get to see him and my extended family more often."

"I could never be separated from mine," she stated as emphatically as he would expect.

Okay, time to dig in. *Help me, please.* "Which is why I knew, when we were together, that you could never move to California. We would be at the mercy of a long-distance relationship, filled with times that I couldn't even communicate with you. Not a word. Not one."

She lifted her shoulders. "Other SEALs have relation-ships that work."

Okay, that didn't sit well with her. "They do, but all the wives of the guys I know live in Coronado, and they've formed a tight-knit support group to get them through these tough deployments. You'd have been in Portland all on your own. Sure, you would've been with your family, but they really couldn't understand your problems. You'd begin to feel isolated and blame me. Things would've ended anyway, and it would've been ugly."

"You could be right, but just leaving with a phone call to say you were going—and we were over—was ugly too." She eyed him, and the hurt lingered in her gaze. "More than ugly."

"Yeah, that I regret. I should've said goodbye in person, but we spun up so fast that I had to catch a flight with barely enough time to call you. Still, I could've come back when I was stateside again to talk to you."

"So why didn't you?" The words came out on a whisper of pain.

Oh, man. Man. He'd hurt her more deeply than he'd thought, and she might never forgive him. "I didn't think I could end it if I had to look you in the eyes. I would just keep postponing it, making it harder on us, and taking us down that freight train to ugliness."

"Finn Durham a coward?" She crossed her arms. "Never thought I'd see that."

"A big one when it came to saying goodbye to you." He met her gaze. "If it matters, once Avery and I were on a more solid footing, I did plan to look you up. To explain. Can you forgive me?"

She eyed him for long pain filled moments. "Yes. God calls us to forgive, and I want to live my faith, so it's not an option to hold this against you anymore. But I don't think I could ever consider dating you again, if that's on your mind."

He'd take that. It was a start. But he resisted pumping up his hand because this wasn't really a win. She was following her faith, but was she letting go of the hurt? Didn't seem like it.

"Is that what you were thinking?" she asked.

He had to be honest with her no matter what. "I would like that, but we're in the same place again, aren't we? Different cities and neither can or will move."

"Then we'll be friends."

Friends. Great. She'd put him in the friend zone. Was there a worse place to be?

She held out her hand.

Formal and reserved. He gripped it and shook, but he wanted to draw her close and kiss her instead. How was he going to handle the remaining time he spent with her?

Her phone rang. She quickly grabbed it as if glad to have an end to their discussion.

"It's Russ." She tapped the screen. "You're on speaker, Russ, and Finn is with me."

"Warrant's in for Eckles's place." Russ's deep voice boomed into the silent night. "I want you to join me in serving it in the morning."

"How about after I meet with the Veritas team, if that works for you?"

"It does. Durham, you'll need to sit this out. I don't want anyone outside of law enforcement present. Don't want to give Eckles something to hold against us."

Finn didn't like being left out, but he got it and wouldn't fight. "Understood."

"Just got the background report on Eckles from Colin," Russ said. "Have you read it?"

"Not yet."

"Eckles seems clean, but his wife was involved with ecoterrorism about twenty years ago. The Sovereign Earth group."

"Sovereign Earth, for real?" Finn asked. "Her husband is a logger."

Ryleigh blinked a few times. "Something worth checking into for sure."

"We'll interview her when we serve the warrant," Russ said. "If we think she's holding out on us, we'll bring her in for a more formal interview."

"Sounds good."

"See you tomorrow." Russ ended the call.

"That's really strange about Eckles's wife," she said.

"I've gotten to know Eckles a bit, and I can't see him being our bomber or helping anyone else plant a bomb." Finn bit the inside of his cheek, a habit he really needed to kick.

"Could be," Ryleigh held his gaze. "But if they don't have a good explanation for her ties to ecoterrorism, they could very well be our bombers."

Ryleigh both hated Russ's interruption and was thankful for it. Anything to bring her back to a professional connection with Finn and hide the personal. Things had been getting way too intimate for her liking.

Question was, what would he do now? He'd gained her forgiveness so she hoped he let go of his thoughts of dating again. For her heart's sake. With the sun having set, stars twinkling above, and a soft breeze blowing a sweet jasmine fragrance, the setting was too romantic to resist any attempt he might make to flirt with her.

He sat back and crossed his ankle over his knee. "You

never told me about your search of Shadow Lake Logging. Is that because I'm an employee?"

Phew. He stuck with professional. So why did she feel disappointed? Didn't matter. She would ignore that and answer his question. "I can fill you in. The explosive inventory doesn't jive."

His big brown eyes flashed open, "Man. I'd say it might be a mistake, but I know my inventory was accurate. I even had the office assistant count with me and double-check."

"We saw her signature on the form. So we have to assume the inventory is correct and someone with a key took the explosives."

"And you know it wasn't me, right?" He thrust his chest out.

"I know, but we don't have any proof."

Finn shook his head. "If I planned to steal explosives, I could've fudged the inventory so it didn't look like anything was missing. I can't see any of the key holders stealing them either."

She sat up in her chair to add force to her statement. "But explosives *did* go missing, and the building hadn't been broken into—the lock is intact."

Finn frowned, drawing down full lips she vividly remembered kissing. "Means the bomber had to have a key. Don't ask me how, but he got it. Maybe he stole one of the other guy's keys."

"Then they wouldn't have their key, right?"

"Right. Except Tobias. He could issue one to himself and sign for it."

"He said he didn't have any made, but he could be lying."

"We need to call the locksmith and ask if he cut any new ones in the last few weeks."

"Good idea. Or it could be Gates's key. We haven't recovered any of his keys yet."

"Or if he's our bomber, he might not have cared if the inventory came up short because he planned to take off after the explosion."

"That makes sense." She hoped that was the case, as it would be so much easier to accept Gates's death if he were the bomber.

"Were both kinds of explosives missing or just one?"

"An equal number of both," she said. "Why are there two kinds anyway?"

"It's all about saving money. The red tubes are cap-sensitive sticks that react well with the blasting cap, but are expensive. White is booster sensitive so the loggers pair a red and white together. Red ignites the white and they keep costs down that way."

"Does the team blast a lot?"

"From what Tobias said, it's become more and more common as the days of felling trees on flat ground is pretty much gone. Now they work hilly sites that are more dangerous to the men and using explosives helps save lives."

"Tobias explained how dangerous it can be." She shook her head. "I'd heard it was, but never to the extent I'm learning now."

"Thankfully, Tobias has a solid safety record. He's a stickler for maintaining OSHA's standards. He allows his supervisors to *supervise* instead of being responsible for a log quota like a lot of logging companies require. I was impressed most with Eckles and Gates too. They both thought of safety first. I wouldn't have taken the job if I'd gotten a hint that they weren't all aboveboard."

Good information to have. "Which makes it seem odd that one of them could blow the place up at a time of day when lives could be at stake."

"Yeah."

"We're assuming these missing explosives were used, but that might not be the case. It'll be interesting to see if the Veritas team finds bits of the red and white plastic wrapping."

Finn nodded. "Still, I'm sure other companies use the same explosives."

"Yeah," she said, thinking. "Could the supervisors have taken more tubes than they need for a job, and then stash it away somewhere?"

"Not likely. Tobias really watches the usage and would notice if it went up."

"But it is possible, right? Like over a long period of time."

"Yeah, it's possible." He looked away and gnawed on his cheek.

"What's wrong?" she asked.

He rolled his shoulders. "I need to make sure Russ doesn't publicly suspect me of stealing explosives and setting off a bomb. Social services could get wind of it and take Avery. They'd put her in foster care, and I just promised that would never happen again."

"Then we have to prove it wasn't you before you become an official suspect." She tried to put her sincere desire to help in her tone. "We got the video for the exterior cameras and visitor sign-in log from Tobias, and Russ is combing through all of it tonight. Maybe he'll figure out who accessed the building and this will be all over by morning."

Finn's gaze traveled around the area. "I won't be on those videos, but if I need an alibi, Avery is with me most of the time when I'm not at work."

"But not during driving times or even after she goes to bed at night. You could've snuck out."

He shot to his feet. "I would never leave her alone here."

"I know, and Russ plans to keep this quiet for now," she

said to Finn's back as he paced across the patio. "We didn't even tell Tobias that explosives were missing. And we won't until after we meet with the task force and talk about a plan of action."

He stopped pacing and looked at her. "You're thinking you can use this info to somehow smoke out our bomber?"

She nodded. "Especially if we see him on the video and can ID him."

Finn came back to sit down, but his knee bounced. "Then we have to get through the video stat."

"Problem is, it's been quite some time since I had the cameras installed. Even if Russ starts in reverse order to see the most likely feed, reviewing all of it will still take time."

"Then Russ needs to get more people on it."

"He will, as soon as he can."

"What about you?" Finn's tone skated high for him, sounding unusually desperate. "Can't you work on it tonight too?"

She met Finn's gaze. "Russ prohibited me from going anywhere near it."

Finn stared at her. "Why on earth did he do that?"

She didn't want to answer, but had to. "For some reason, he thinks you and I are an item."

His mouth flopped open. "You denied it, right?"

"Yeah, but I must not have been very convincing." Not a surprise. She couldn't hide her developing feelings for this wonderful man, who save one big mistake would still be in her life.

Especially not after tonight.

11

Inhaling the sizzling scent of frying bacon, Ryleigh slathered raspberry jelly on a slice of toast that was a shade shy of burned. She set it on the plate next to the eggs cooked over easy to pick up her coffee brewed stronger than she liked.

So what if it was all a tad off? The breakfast cooked by Finn touched her more than many other things ever had. He didn't know how to cook. He'd told her that many times when they dated. And yet, he was trying to be the best dad by making Avery's breakfast.

Avery scooped up her last bite of egg and washed it down with orange juice, then looked at Finn. "Your burgers are much better than your eggs."

Ah, the honesty of a child.

"Sorry, Peanut." Finn ruffled Avery's hair. "I try."

"I know," she said. "Maybe cereal tomorrow."

"Maybe." He grinned.

She smoothed her rumpled hair.

"Let me grab a brush to fix that." He raced from the room.

Ryleigh took a bite of toast and savored the hearty wheat

flavor and texture. She imagined Finn wearing an apron in the kitchen baking bread, bringing a smile to her face.

"What's so funny?" Avery pushed her empty plate away.

Ryleigh told her.

Avery wrinkled her nose. "I don't think I'd want to eat that bread."

They laughed together.

"He does some things real good." She leaned closer. "But the kitchen is kind of bad."

Ryleigh nodded in silent agreement.

He returned with the brush and stepped behind Avery to start on a tangled mess.

The little girl glanced up at him. "I can't believe you don't know how to do braids. Especially French ones. Mom did them all the time."

"In Finn's defense," Ryleigh said. "He's never had much hair, so he hasn't needed to learn."

Finn ran a hand over his short hair and made a funny face.

Avery giggled and looked at Ryleigh. "Do you know how to do braids?"

"I do, but I haven't done it in a long time."

Avery's eyes scrunched together. "You have short hair too. How come you know?"

"My hair hasn't always been short. It was long the entire time I was growing up, so my mom and gran braided it all the time."

"You have a gran?"

"I do. And a grandad who live very close to me."

"Lucky. Finn has grandparents but they live way in Portland. That's a long way away."

Finn continued brushing, and her fine hair tangled in the bristles.

"Ouch." Avery's hand flew to the brush to stop him.

Finn flushed red. "Sorry, Peanut. I didn't mean to hurt you."

"I know." Avery looked at Ryleigh. "Can you braid my hair?"

Oh, gosh. That must've hurt Finn. But Ryleigh would hurt the child more by saying no, so she nodded. "I can try, but like I said, it's been a long time so no telling how it'll turn out."

Finn nearly threw the brush to Avery as if he was glad to get rid of it. He offered her an apologetic smile.

She shrugged it off. Braiding hair really wasn't an imposition. She got up and carefully cleared the tangle then set to work separating segments of the soft hair into manageable strands. Once she started, the process came back to her, and she soon had one side neatly braided.

She held out her hand. "I'll need a rubber band to finish this."

Avery shot a look at Finn. "In the pink box that Mama gave me on my shelf."

"Be right back." He bolted from the room.

Avery looked up, her eyes narrowed. "He really doesn't get girly things so much."

"I can see that." Ryleigh smiled at Avery. "But he's trying really hard because he loves you and wants what's best for you."

Avery frowned. "I know, but sometimes I can't help it and I'm mean to him."

"I know you don't want to be, and he knows that too. It's normal and part of grieving the loss of your mother."

"Is it?"

"Uh-huh, and you know what?"

"What?"

"If you have a chance to talk to that counselor, you'll

figure out how to handle it better. If you don't want to do it for yourself, maybe think about doing it for Finn."

"I didn't like going to the counselor. Now maybe I will."

"That's great." Ryleigh heard a noise behind her and found Finn standing in the doorway. He mouthed, "Thank you."

She smiled up at him, and her heart flung wide open to wrap around her growing feelings for him.

Oh, no. She was smitten. Totally and completely smitten again. How had she let that happen?

They couldn't start dating. Not long-distance. He was right about that when they dated before. Long-distance wouldn't work. And honestly, if they didn't have the distance issue, dating could lead to marriage. All well and good if he wasn't now a dad. Ryleigh liked Avery and all, but was she prepared to be a ready-to-order mom?

Finn parked on the road near the mill, now nothing more than a soggy pile of black and charred lumber. Whispers of smoke still rose from the wreckage. If he didn't know a bomb had been detonated in the back building, the wood scattered over the area as if someone dropped a box of burnt toothpicks would tell him an explosion had occurred.

Ryleigh had been quiet for the drive. Maybe she was disappointed by the mechanics' call saying they had to order parts for her car and it would take a few days to return her vehicle to her. So she was stuck with Finn for sure.

She sat unmoving next to him, gaze fixed out the passenger window. Today she'd dressed in dark navy pants along with a white button-down shirt and a blue suit jacket. She appeared both professional and comfortable. She'd gone to Ryan's place to get her suitcase from her sister late last night, and Finn hadn't seen Mackenzie before she headed back to Portland. Exactly as Ryleigh had planned. Hide him away from her family at all costs. He'd be lying if he said it didn't hurt.

"This place looks awful." She glanced at him. "I'd love to poke around in there, but better to sit tight until the Veritas team arrives."

Finn killed the truck engine. "Do you know all of them?"

She shook her head. "Never met Trent or Chelsea. They're new to the team. And I don't know the assistants either. So I guess I know a little more than half of the ones coming today."

"A big team like that will cost them a pretty penny."

"I'm so thankful they said yes."

He looked at her. "And I'm thankful for your help with the hair issue this morning. Avery was *so* happy with her braids. Maybe you could teach me."

"Sure."

"That along with the soccer pointers solidified you as a good guy in her book."

Ryleigh frowned.

"You don't like that?"

"I do, but if this investigation drags on, she has to know I'm just passing through and not to expect me to be around." Ryleigh clutched her hands in her lap. "Maybe I should move out so she doesn't get attached."

"No need." He hated even thinking about that. "I'll have a talk with her. Make sure she knows you'll be going back to Portland when the investigation is over."

"You sound irritated."

"Do I?" Of course he did. He didn't want Ryleigh to leave, and he let it creep into his tone.

As if saving him from saying more, three white vans

rolled slowly down the road, giving them something else to focus on.

"They're here," Ryleigh announced with gusto. "Let's get them started so we can move this investigation forward."

She hopped out and directed the driver of the first van to park on the roadside.

Finn got out too, and despite the bright summer sun shining down on them, he felt a chill. Could be because he knew a woman in one of those vehicles was here to recover the body that Russ protected from the elements overnight with a small bottomless tent.

A man and woman climbed out of the first vehicle that had a Veritas logo on the side. The guy's dark hair was cut short, and he wore black tactical pants and a black polo shirt with a gold logo on the chest. The sheriff, Blake Jenkins, Finn assumed. The woman had red hair and glasses, and she'd dressed in jeans and rubber boots.

Ryleigh held her hand out to the man first. "Blake. Emory. Thank you so much for coming."

So Finn was right. This was the guy they'd been talking to, and Ryleigh had mentioned that he was married to Emory.

Finn joined the trio and introduced himself as the security manager.

"He just retired from the SEALs to take care of a little girl who lost her mother," Ryleigh added, actually sounding proud of him this time.

"Good to meet you," Emory said, but gave Ryleigh a questioning look.

What was that look about? He opened his mouth to ask but the other team members came forward.

"Let me introduce everyone." Blake started by giving background on Ryleigh and Finn. "On the end, we have our anthropologist, Dr. Kelsey Dunbar."

A woman with curly black hair and wearing shorts that looked like a skirt and a frilly top waved at them.

"Next to Dr. Dunbar is her assistant, Shawn Fortune."

A skinny guy with thinning hair saluted.

"Then we have Sierra Rice, trace evidence and fingerprint analysis, and next, her assistant, Chad Powell, and lab tech, Jeremiah Paulson."

Sierra's blond hair hung over her shoulders, and she flashed a kind smile. The guy with thinning dark hair and a slight build was very forgettable. Not so with Jeremiah, who was tall and wiry, and his red hair would've competed with yesterday's fiery flames.

"To his right is Nick Thorn, who I believe you have been communicating with," Blake continued.

Nick's close-cut beard matched his brown hair, and the cocky angle of his head said he wasn't a guy who was used to being forgotten.

"Second row left side we have Ainslie Houston, crime scene photographer, and the guy next to her is her husband Grady Houston, expert in everything that goes boom."

Grady laughed and waved his hand, but Ainslie rolled her eyes.

"Next to him is our latest hire, Trent Ingram. He's a ballistics, firearms, and explosives expert too and works with Grady, but his forte is explosives."

"Good to meet you both," Trent said but smiled at Ryleigh. A smile she returned for the dark-haired guy with a heavy five-o-clock shadow.

"Last but not least, we have Chelsea Vale, our new crime scene photographer."

The curvy woman wore her hair in french braids, resembling Avery's, and had a girl-next-door face covered in freckles.

"That's it," Blake said. "I don't expect you'll remember all the names, but we'll help you out if you forget. We should begin with the recovery of remains." He turned to the team. "Let's get things set up."

The team disbursed, including his wife, heading for the vans, but he remained in place. "I'd like a quick tour of the property while they unload supplies and set up a command center that I will pilot."

"We'll be glad to show you around," Ryleigh said.

"Do you need protective gear?" he asked.

"We're good." Ryleigh dug blue booties and gloves from her suit coat and handed a set to Finn.

"Then let's get after it." He started down the incline.

Finn didn't have a hard time believing this guy to be a former sheriff or as someone who could coordinate this high-profile team. And he could easily understand why Ryleigh suggested bringing in this team. No doubt they could cover a lot of ground and get answers far faster than any government agency with limited resources could do.

At the bottom of the incline, Ryleigh held out her hand toward the destroyed structures. "Finn, why don't you lead the tour. You know the buildings better than I do."

"Start where the bomb detonated," Blake said. "That way I can get Kelsey going first thing."

"That would be the back." Finn paused to put on his booties as did the others.

He skirted well around the first two buildings, memories of the hot flames from yesterday coming back. He didn't really fear death. A guy who deployed as a SEAL couldn't and do his job well. He could have a healthy respect for staying alive though. And he did have his list of ways he would never want to go. Number one being tortured by the enemy, and number two, in a fire where the smoke didn't kill him before the flames took over.

He stopped next to tall stacks of unprocessed logs that

had survived the fire. "Understanding the process here should help you see why the bomb was set where it was. It starts with the loggers. They cut the trees to size in the field, but when they arrive here, they go into the de-barker, which is the big green machine you see just down the road."

"What do they do with all the bark?" Blake asked.

"It's turned into wood chips and sold." Finn pointed at a collapsed conveyer belt. "The log then goes via this conveyor belt if it were still standing inside this back building. If the crew isn't ready for the log inside, it's stacked in these piles until they are ready. However, they don't keep a massive inventory of logs on hand as they dry out when sitting here."

He gestured at the collapsed structure. "First step inside the building is for the worker to square off the log using a computer-aided machine. Then it moves on to building two, where a laser is used to make sure they're the right width. Then they move on to building three, where they're graded and sorted into stacks that are ready to go off to the supplier. Gonna cost the owner a pretty penny to replace those computer-aided machines."

"So the bomber started in the back building because if the equipment was destroyed it would stop the entire process," Blake said. "And the victim is in that building?"

Finn nodded. "Follow me."

Blake looked at Finn as they walked. "From what you told me, no one was supposed to be onsite. Do you have any idea why this person was here?"

"No, but if he's the night supervisor, as we suspect, he could've come here instead of going out to eat with his men. Not sure why, though. Unless he was setting the bomb."

"Sounds like a good possibility."

"He's new to the team," Ryleigh said. "So we don't know much about him, but our task force computer expert is digging into his past. We hope Kelsey can search for the victim's keys and cell phone before she removes the remains."

"I'll ask her, but if it in any way threatens the integrity of the bone structure, don't be surprised if she says no." Blake got out a small notepad and pen. "What's the guy's name? I'll have Nick look into him too."

Ryleigh shared Gates's name. "It would be helpful too if Nick could analyze the computer parts that we believe controlled a photoelectric cell bomb."

"Photoelectric cell, huh?" Blake blinked a few times. "Didn't expect that. I'll get the guys back here as soon as Kelsey clears them to be in the area. Knowing for sure the type of bomb could lead to the bomber, and I know you'll want that info as soon as possible."

"Exactly," Finn said, his respect growing for this man. "That's it for me. You have anything else to add, Ryleigh?"

"We have another scene we would like processed if possible." Ryleigh told him about Uri Gates's home.

"Sierra and her team can do it first thing while we wait on Kelsey to give the all clear back here." Blake took off for the rear building and glanced over his shoulder. "Grady and Trent will want to talk to eyewitnesses to the explosion, if there are any, and to the firefighter who was first on scene. And they'll also want to get a look at the explosives used by this company."

"The firefighter is Ryan Maddox, who is also on our task force," Ryleigh said. "He has a shift here later today. When Grady and Trent are ready to see the explosives, I can arrange access. And as far as eyewitnesses, the day supervisor was here, but I need you to hold off talking to him until after the sheriff and I question him."

Blake furrowed his forehead. "He a suspect?"

"Could be."

Finn wasn't surprised that she didn't provide details

such as Eckles's name as Blake could just look the guy up and not follow her lead. Not that Finn thought Blake would do that. But as a law enforcement officer, she knew to keep quiet. So did Finn. His days of sharing on a need-to-know basis had taught him well in that area.

12

Ryleigh left Finn at the destroyed building to finish their shift and drove Finn's truck to Uri Gates's house. Sierra and Chad followed in their company van. She pulled over to park and bumped the tires over the curb. She cringed. She hoped Finn didn't notice she'd scraped his tires. The truck was far bigger than anything she'd ever driven other than tractors on the family farm, and she didn't have to worry about curbs there.

Sierra and Chad parked behind her and put on white protective suits. Sierra held blue booties and handed a set to Ryleigh.

Ryleigh took them and wrapped her arms around her as the sun slid behind threatening clouds. The forecast didn't call for rain today, and she prayed it would hold off for the forensic recovery at the bomb scene. Sierra and Chad grabbed portable kits that resembled large tackle boxes, and Ryleigh led them to the back door.

"The door doesn't lock, but thankfully the seal I added yesterday is intact." She sliced down the tape and put on gloves before touching the door to open it.

Chad set down his kit on the cracked patio. "I'll get this door printed while you check things out."

Sierra smiled at him and then looked at Ryleigh. "I can't begin to tell you how great it is to have an assistant who can read your mind."

"I've worked with partners like that." Ryleigh put on her booties and then led the way into the room.

Sierra slipped hers on too but stopped just inside the door to scan the room. Her eyes lit up, and she turned to look at Chad. "Make sure you bag the Roomba."

"Will do."

"The Roomba?" Ryleigh asked. "Why do you want to bag a robot vacuum?"

"They're frequently scheduled to run on a regular basis. Often daily. So it could've swept up valuable evidence."

"I never owned one so didn't know you could schedule them."

Sierra nodded. "Plus, we need to check out the model to see if it's a preproduction test version. Early on, Roomba had beta-testers who agreed to let the vacuum collect all sorts of data to help improve its artificial intelligence and provide feedback to iRobot."

"How will that help?"

"The device takes pictures to transmit to Roomba. It might've captured something or someone you'll want to follow up with."

Ryleigh shook her head. "You all never cease to amaze me with your knowledge base."

"What can I say? We love our jobs and like to stay current. Guess you might say we're nosey." Sierra grinned. "We'll process the usual areas and the items dumped from cabinets to see if we can recover prints. Other than that, is there anything else you want us to focus on?"

"Nothing in particular," Ryleigh said. "Just everything you might think will help identify our intruder."

"Right, all the things, just like a true law enforcement officer would request." Sierra laughed. "Let me get a look at the second story."

She picked her way through the rubble and headed for the stairs. Ryleigh followed, careful not to disturb anything on the floor.

Sierra stopped on the third step to squat down. "Some sort of vegetation here. We'll bag it and give it to Winter Fox to review. She's our new forensic palynologist."

Ryleigh stared at the object not bigger than a pea. "Okay, that's a new one for me. What does she do exactly?"

"Forensic palynologists analyze pollen, grains, spores, etcetera from crime scenes. They can use this data to determine what's out of place or unusual in the scene." Sierra started back up the stairs. "An example might be finding pollen at a scene that isn't normally found in this area of the country. That would tell us that whoever was present brought it in from another place, giving you something to go on."

"Most interesting." Ryleigh toured the upstairs with Sierra until her phone rang. She didn't want an interruption right now, but the call was from Russ. "It's the sheriff. I have to take this."

She stopped at the door to the main bedroom and answered.

"One of my deputies found Gates's truck," Russ said without a hello.

Her heart started beating harder. "Where?"

"On an abandoned logging road about a mile from the mill. I hear Sierra Rice is with you. I need to know what she wants us to do with it."

"Hold on." Ryleigh put the call on speaker and asked.

Sierra frowned. "Don't touch it until after I can give it a quick assessment."

"Did you hear that, Russ?" Ryleigh asked.

"Roger that. How soon do you think you can get over there?"

"I'm about done here." Sierra looked at Ryleigh. "Give me the address, and I'll head out from here."

Russ rattled off directions. "I want you to accompany her, Steele."

Ryleigh didn't have to be told twice. "Of course."

"Call me the minute you're done, and we'll go interview Eckles and his wife."

The call went dead.

"The team I brought is too small to handle multiple scenes." Sierra got out her phone. "I need reinforcements."

She made the call and ordered three additional techs to make the drive down to the site, then hung up and looked at Ryleigh. "They'll leave as soon as they can."

"Just like that?" Ryleigh blinked at Sierra. "They'll drop everything and race down here."

"We get callouts all the time. It's part of the job that we all accept when we take it on." Sierra started down the stairs. "Not too much different than your life was as an agent, I assume."

She had a point. So many people in law enforcement gave up much of their private lives to do their jobs. Not only the sworn officers but all the people behind the scenes. Analysts. Crime scene staff. Forensic technicians. And on and on. She'd seen the cost in her family with her dad, grandad, and uncle missing family events. Then her generation dealt with the same thing. But the loving support of others brought them through.

She prayed that the Veritas staff had such understanding and loving support.

They reached the patio door, and Chad looked up from where he was swirling black powder on the glass.

"Pay attention to the third step for particulates to mark for Winter's review," Sierra said. "Other than the Roomba, we have a straightforward B&E evidence collection."

"Will do." He stowed his brush and got out a long strip of wide tape.

Sierra told him about Uri's vehicle and the other team members that would be coming. "I'll find a local garage to have the truck towed. I'd like you to take charge and tear it apart."

"Sounds good." Again no questions asked as he pressed the tape over the powder to lift a clean fingerprint.

"I'll want our van at my disposal at the bomb scene," she continued. "Do you have everything you think you'll need here?"

"I should have." He placed the prints on a white card and got out a pen.

"Call me if anything comes up and when you're ready for pickup."

He nodded and started noting things on the back of the card. Sierra had been right. Her assistant pretty much read her mind and didn't have to stop working to take directions.

Out in the fresh air, Sierra ripped off her gloves, and at the van, she balanced on one foot to climb free of her protective suit and booties. "I'll follow you if you don't mind."

"Don't mind at all." Ryleigh climbed into the truck and got on the road, her mind going on autopilot and wishing Finn was with her.

As much as she hated to admit it, she had to say she'd enjoyed his company. And seeing him with Avery last night allowed her to see a whole new side to the man. She still didn't like the way he'd ended things back in the day, but he'd had good intentions, and it would be churlish not to forgive him. And unchristian. Not something she wanted to be.

Honestly, it felt good to let it go. She'd carried it too long, when she knew God always meant for her to forgive. Now she had peace. About that, at least.

She turned onto the rutted and winding logging road. Many of the trees abutting the gravel were about chest high but others towered over them. The smaller ones, she suspected, were replanted by Tobias's men at some point. A deputy had parked his patrol car next to the lime green vehicle with Oregon plates sitting cockeyed on the edge of the old road. The midsized pickup looked more to her like a large SUV with the back roof cut off for a pickup bed. Thick mud coated the bottom and a heavy layer of dust covered the remainder of the body.

She stopped short and pulled off to the side of the road to give the deputy space to leave if he needed to. Sierra parked behind her, and they both started for the young deputy who was climbing out of his car. He was short and stocky and looked to be in his twenties, but he had a confident stride as he marched their way.

Ryleigh introduced herself and Sierra.

Sierra slipped on gloves. "We need a garage where my team can dismantle the vehicle and process it for evidence. Can you arrange a location while I take a good look at it?"

He ran a hand through glossy black hair. "I can make some calls and see what I can do."

"We'll also need it towed there on a flatbed."

The deputy scratched his neck. "Only one garage I know of in the area with a flatbed truck. Their availability might be a problem."

Sierra raised her shoulders and gave the deputy a no-nonsense look. "I'm sure you can impress upon them the importance of getting this vehicle under cover as quickly as possible."

"Sure thing, ma'am." He spun and charged back toward his car.

Ryleigh stepped up to the truck. "It's clear you're used to dealing with law enforcement."

"I come from a family of them just like you, so yeah. Learned at an early age." She chuckled and walked around the outside of the truck. "Nothing unusual at first blush, but a closer look will be needed. Maybe I'll have Winter come down too."

"You'll soon have everyone from Veritas on the scene."

"Not everyone by a long shot, but most of the department heads for sure."

"I can't imagine how much this must be costing your company."

"Tax write off." She met Ryleigh's gaze. "And even if it wasn't, you can't put a price on catching a bomber who has no regard for human life and could strike again."

Ryleigh left Sierra to arrange Gates's vehicle towing and drove Finn's truck down the long driveway toward Eckles's home to meet Russ. She wasn't surprised that the guy lived in the country. A lot of people did in these parts, but he also seemed as if he liked to be in charge of his life and not have to deal with other people. Made country living perfect for him. And a perfect place to construct bombs without anyone looking over his shoulder.

She found Russ leaning against his patrol car outside the four-car garage, tapping his foot. So he was antsy and impatient. Not new. His behavior could be irritating, but was a bonus for an investigator. He worked quickly and got results, so she couldn't fault him.

She quickly parked and got out to join him.

"Eckles owns three acres," he said. "It'll take some time to properly search the property. After we talk to Eckles and his wife, I'll call in a couple of deputies to help out."

She looked at the house with the curtains drawn. A red flag at this time of day. "You think we'll find her home?"

"She's a stay-at-home mom, which makes our odds better."

"But she's also pregnant, and she thought she was going into labor yesterday."

"She didn't check into the hospital. I called before I came to confirm."

Of course he did. The guy was thorough.

Ryleigh walked through the sunny morning. The temperature had warmed in the past hour, and she didn't doubt they would hit the predicted ninety-five-degree day. Far warmer in southern Oregon than in the Willamette Valley today, and not a pleasant day to have to recover a body burned beyond recognition. But then the team worked in all conditions, and they would persevere.

She led the way up the stone steps to a narrow porch and rang the doorbell. Russ stopped next to her and started tapping his foot again. He wore the same basic uniform as yesterday. Tactical pants. Boots. County shirt and badge clipped to his belt. Sidearm at his side.

She was free to openly carry too, as Oregon law didn't prohibit it. But her gun was concealed under her suit coat. It was one thing to go around carrying in full view when you wore a uniform, another when in plain clothes. A special permit was needed to carry a concealed weapon in the state, which she'd applied for long before she'd even become an agent. Still, in her deputy role, she could carry any way she saw fit.

A dog barked behind the door, and a man told it to pipe down. The door opened, and Virgil Eckles stood looking at them. "Sheriff. Ms. Steele. What's going on?"

"Can we come in?"

"Someone hurt?"

"No," Russ said quickly. "Nothing like that. We just want to talk about yesterday."

"Sure. Okay. Come in." He stood back. "Seems odd that none of us can go by the site to check it out, but Tobias said we aren't allowed on the property until you give us the all-clear. What with the baby coming and all, if I have to be off for any time, being short on pay will hurt."

"Your wife didn't have the baby, then?" Ryleigh asked.

Eckles shook his head and closed the door behind them. "Was just those false contractions. Braxton something."

"Is Pauline here?" Russ asked.

"Yeah, why?"

"We'd like to talk to her too."

Eckles squinted at them. "Why in the world would you want to do that?"

"I have a few questions," Russ said, his wording vague enough not to worry Eckles.

"Oh, I get it. You need to confirm my story of why I didn't go to lunch."

Not really, but...

Eckles pointed at the old blue plaid couch. "Have a seat, and I'll get her."

Ryleigh sat next to Russ and tried to ignore the over-flowing laundry baskets, the dusty tabletops, and the carpet that could use a good vacuum. The place was otherwise organized, and the mess could simply be from being too pregnant to care or even comfortably do the tasks.

"He doesn't seem worried about our visit," Russ said. "But then some people can lie easily and don't get nervous, even around law enforcement."

"I've met my share of people like that. I don't think Eckles is involved. And his wife, as pregnant as she is? Also doesn't seem likely, but then I've seen stranger things on the job."

Pauline lumbered into the room resting her hands over her distended belly. She had dishwater blond hair that fell straight to her shoulders and dark circles hung below her eyes.

Russ introduced himself and Ryleigh.

"Please sit," Russ said.

She plopped down in an armchair. "You want me to tell you I called Virg yesterday to come home?" Her soft southern accent flowed like honey. "Well, I did. Can I get back to the laundry now? Got so much to do before this one comes, and I have two kids to take care of."

"We appreciate you confirming that," Russ said, seeming unusually polite for his gruff nature. "But we really wanted to talk to you about Sovereign Earth."

"Oh, interesting." She blinked long lashes in rapid succession. "What about them?"

"You're a member."

"Was a member way back in the day. Before Virg. Before becoming a mom."

"And you've cut ties with them?" Russ asked.

"I mean not officially cut like resigning or anything, but I just sort of drifted away."

"Why's that?" Ryleigh asked.

"I inherited this place from my uncle, and when I got here, I tried to kick Virg's logging crew off the property." Pauline looked up at Eckles. "But he explained logging to me. Told me how companies are now logging responsibly. I could see the issue from both sides, and when the group turned more radical, I just couldn't get behind the cause anymore."

She smiled at her husband. "And maybe it was a little bit about meeting this guy and falling out with the guy I was dating. He was the group leader, and I ended it when I got serious about Virg."

"Did things end amiably?" Ryleigh asked.

"Mostly." She arched an eyebrow. "Does that matter?"

Ryleigh ignored her question. "Have you communicated with group members lately?"

"No."

"So if I look at your phone I won't see any calls or texts to members?" Russ asked.

Pauline twisted her hands and chewed on her lip.

Eckles placed a hand on his wife's shoulder. "You'd need a warrant to do that."

Russ took the warrant from a cargo pocket. "Just so happens I have one. For electronic devices and the entire property."

"This is ridiculous." Eckles breathed deeply, flaring his nostrils. "You have no basis to get a warrant. What do you expect to find anyway?"

"Maybe you should sit down and tell me what I *am* going to find," Russ said.

Eckles crossed his arms. "Nothing to do with bombs if that's what you're thinking."

"You were at the site at the time of the explosion," Russ stated.

"Just a coincidence."

"I don't believe in coincidences," Russ said firmly.

"Well, I do." Eckles waved his hand over the room. "Go ahead and search. We have nothing to hide."

"But Virg." Pauline shot him a pointed look.

"Doesn't matter. We did nothing wrong."

Russ honed his gaze on Pauline. "What don't you want us to find?"

"My phone. I—"

Eckles came around the chair and squatted by his wife. "Don't say another word, Pauline. Make them work for everything they find."

"I don't know you well, Mr. Eckles," Ryleigh said. "But you seem to be a decent man. Your coworker was murdered. Don't you want to help find the killer?"

"Find the killer, yes, but that's not either one of us. You're wasting your time here."

"And if you have something we might question and have to research it, you're wasting more of our time," Ryleigh quickly said. "Telling us everything you know will help us eliminate you and turn our efforts in the right direction."

He didn't move, the old grandfather clock on the wall ticking down. "Fine. Pauline kept in contact with a woman named Carla Nye. She married the guy Pauline broke up with but didn't take his name. A Dean Keenan. He's a big wig in the group in Alabama, where she's from. He got abusive and Carla ran. Came here to stay with us for a month or so until she could get on her feet."

Russ shot forward on the cushion. "When was this?"

"She left on Wednesday," Pauline said. "But she didn't set a bomb. She was never really one for the group's cause. She only got involved after she met Dean at a bar."

So she'd been gone for three days and could still be in the area. But more importantly, she could be involved with the bombing.

Ryleigh needed more details. "Do you know where she went?"

Pauline shook her head hard. "We didn't want to know.

That way if Dean came looking for her, he couldn't get it out of us."

"But she's on foot," Eckles said. "So I doubt she's gone far by now."

Pauline looked at her husband. "Unless she hitched a ride, which she's been known to do."

"What about her phone number?" Ryleigh asked, feeling as if she was pouncing like a salivating dog.

"I can give it to you," Pauline said. "But she buried her phone out in the pasture so it won't do you any good. She replaced it with one of those prepaid ones. Didn't give us the number for the new one either."

"Do you know the location where she buried the old one?" Ryleigh asked, her hope fading.

The couple shook their heads.

"Again, we didn't want to know," Eckles said.

"When's the last time you saw this Keenan guy?" Russ asked.

"Dean?" Pauline shrugged, but cut her gaze to her husband. "It's been years."

"I need you both to come into the office," Russ said. "To file an official statement."

Pauline nodded. "Does that mean you're done here and won't search?"

"Oh no." Russ stood. "We'll be searching. Make no mistake. I don't intend to stop until I find Carla's buried cell phone and other pieces of evidence you might be hiding."

13

Russ's deputy arrived to keep tabs on the couple, and he tasked Ryleigh with searching the spare bedroom where Carla had stayed during her visit. Pauline claimed she didn't have the energy to clean the space after Carla had departed, but Carla had left the room neat and tidy, and Ryleigh had struck out so far.

She made her way to the deep closet and ran her fingers over the floor in the back. The lip of a board protruded a fraction of an inch above the others. Ryleigh got out a small penknife she kept in her jacket pocket and poked the blade between the boards. A section lifted.

Yes! A secret compartment.

She slid into the closet on her belly and pried it completely open, then focused her flashlight into the hole. A shoebox sat in the small space. Her stomach fluttered with excitement.

Calm down. Record the location.

She snapped both close-up and distance photos for scale. Already wearing gloves, she lifted the box out and took several more snapshots, then carried the box to the bed.

She sat and opened it. Schematics for a bomb lay on the top.

That flutter of excitement turned into a rapid beating of wings.

"Russ!" she yelled. "You'll want to see this."

His footfalls pounded down the hallway, but she didn't wait and dumped the contents onto the bed.

"What do you have?" His voice came from nearby.

"Bomb schematics and copies of the threats sent to the mill."

"Let me see the schematics," he demanded.

She thumbed through the pages and gave him the ones he asked for. As he studied them, she looked through the others. "Emails are between Carla Nye and Dean Keenan." She scanned the top one. "He talks about bombing a logging company to end the news media's lack of attention to clearcutting."

Russ looked up. "Schematics aren't for a photoelectric cell though."

"Yeah, I noticed that. The plans could've changed for the bomb, but she was in possession of the threats. Demonstrates intent. And they both can be brought up on charges for the threats alone."

Russ dug out his phone. "I'll get a statewide alert out on both of them. Secure and log this information as evidence, then take it to Nick from Veritas and get him looking into Keenan. Also request the team send someone over here to print the room. This information too. Never know if Carla or Keenan are going by an alias, and prints could reveal their true identities."

"Will do."

"I'll see if Colin has found anything else about Sovereign Earth. Maybe he can get us a phone number for Keenan. Or even Carla's burner. A long shot at best, but why not have him run it?" He strode from the room.

She gathered up the documents to place them in a large evidence bag. Her shoulders rose and she felt lighter. Maybe, just maybe, she'd found the lead that would take them directly to their bomber and prevent her family's company from getting a bad reputation. Even clear Finn's name.

But more importantly, prevent another explosion and loss of life.

~

Finn waited near Dr. Dunbar as she and her assistant worked to recover the body. The petite woman looked nothing like someone he would expect would work with skeletal remains. He'd seen men and women badly burned in his SEAL days, and the gruesome sight never got easier, but she seemed to be oblivious to it. Or maybe she was very good at compartmentalizing or looking beyond the fact that this was a human being to concentrate on the bones.

Finn checked his watch. Three hours since Sierra had returned from her visit with Ryleigh to Gates's place and from viewing his truck. Ryleigh texted to say she'd gone to Eckles's house, but that was the last Finn had heard from her. He was jonesing to know what was happening. Their shift at the crime scene was nearly over, and he thought they were going to chase down leads together. But without any additional word from her, he didn't know what she was planning.

A vehicle rumbled to a stop at the road, sounding like his truck. Ryleigh? He hoped so. He poked his head around the still-standing wall to find her walking down the incline toward the buildings. She was carrying what looked like a large evidence bag, and she stared down at her feet so he couldn't gauge her mood, but her shoulders were rigid.

He stepped out of the building to meet her.

She looked up. "We may have a lead."

She told him Pauline Eckles was connected to a woman named Carla Nye and a Dean Keenan, both tied to Sovereign Earth.

"Is Keenan still in a leadership role with them?" Finn asked.

"As far as we know." Ryleigh lifted the bag. "And I recovered bomb schematics along with copies of the bomb threats sent to Tobias in emails between Nye and Keenan."

"Whoa, the motherload."

"Exactly." She grinned. "I'll ask Nick to track the pair down and look into these emails."

Finn jerked his thumb over his shoulder. "He's inside collecting computer pieces."

She frowned. "And the remains? Still here?"

He nodded. "Looks like Kelsey and her assistant are about ready to transport them to her lab, where she'll examine the bones."

"So she'll be leaving then?"

Finn nodded. "Not that evidence collection will stop. Sierra will take over processing the forensics in the area near the body, but Russ wants Kelsey to determine cause of death ASAP. He wants to be sure it was the explosion or fire, not something else that killed him. There's no hope of fingerprinting the victim, and she can also get the victim's DNA running."

Ryleigh arched a brow. "I had no idea he thought we might have another cause of death."

"Guess he figures if the victim died before the explosion, then he can't be our bomber."

"Good point."

"Did you locate anything else at Eckles's place?"

She shook her head. "Not yet, anyway. But Russ and his deputies are really just beginning, and we'll send someone from Sierra's team over there too. I'm here to get Nick going on this and get a progress update to report at a task force meeting Russ said he would call."

"You'll want to talk to Blake for that. He's been running around here like mad and compiling information from everyone."

"First, I need to get Nick started on searching for our suspects." She looked at the building, but didn't move.

Finn understood her hesitancy. She didn't want to go in. No one wanted to see such a horrific sight. He was glad to be out of that building for a while and didn't really want to go back in either, but if it made Ryleigh more comfortable, he would gladly tag along. "I'll go with you."

She gave him a tight smile and led the way inside. Nick held a plastic bag and dropped a minuscule item held by tweezers inside. Ainsley was taking pictures nearby as Trent and Grady looked at an item in another plastic bag.

Ryleigh picked her way over to Kelsey, stepping over hunks of debris in her booties.

Kelsey was bent over the victim's head and spraying something into his mouth. She looked up and held up her bottle. "Spray glue to help stabilize the remains. Sets a virtual cast over the victim's jaw. It can help prevent damage during transport, perhaps giving us a better chance at dental identification."

"If you can get dental x-rays for the suspected victim, right?" Ryleigh asked.

"Right," she said. "Shawn will begin hunting those records down."

"Were you able to locate Gates's keys or phone?"

"Definitely no phone, but keys are still a possibility. I

didn't find any keys under the remains. Some of the fabric from his jeans were fused to the bone so they might be caught up in that. I'll get back to you as soon as I know anything."

"And I'll let you know if we find keys here," Sierra said.

"Thank you." Ryleigh moved over to Nick. "I have a top-priority job for your team."

"Spoken like a true law enforcement officer. Everything is priority. Good thing I have a big team." He chuckled.

She smiled as if she knew he was right, and she deserved to be called out. She told him about Eckles, Nye, and about Dean Keenan and the documents. "Can you try to locate them?"

"Absolutely, but with Carla having just gone underground, she might be hard to find."

Her expression fell. "You don't think you'll find anything?"

"I said hard, but not impossible." He grinned as he closed the bag in his hand. "I'll give my team a head's up and get them moving on it. They'll get the basics going, then I can tweak what they come up with, and we'll go from there."

"Thanks." She held up her evidence bag. "What do you want me to do with this?"

"Give it to Blake for safekeeping. He can start a log for the other scene, and I can review the documents in a cleaner environment. When I'm done, Sierra can run prints."

"Thank you." Ryleigh smiled at the team, her genuine thankfulness evident to all.

"You'll want to see this." Grady stood and held his bag up to the light, Trent looking on.

Ryleigh stepped over to them.

Finn followed and got a clear look at the bagged item. "The photoelectric cell?"

"It's a photoelectric cell all right." Trent's dark eyes

gleamed with interest. "There's enough here to ID the make and model. Don't know if that'll help us, but a bomber who uses photoelectric cells might have a preference for this brand, and this bit could lead to him or her."

Ryleigh patted her bag. "The schematics we recovered don't use a photoelectric cell."

"We need a look at those," Grady said. "Trent can get cleaned up to examine them while I keep at it."

"And here I thought you'd give the newbie all the scut work." Trent grinned at Grady.

"Hey, I happen to enjoy the scut work." Grady laughed. "But seriously, man. Don't expect a break from it all the time."

"I still don't get why the bomber chose a photoelectric cell," Ryleigh said. "We have abundant sunshine this time of year, but he couldn't predict the weather. And he had to place the cell near the window and account for any temperature difference it might provide too, right?"

"Yeah," Grady said. "It's odd, I'll give you that. I've never seen or heard of anyone who used this method for detonation and I've seen a lot of devices in my time. What about you, Trent?"

"Nope, never." He snapped off his gloves. "And I agree this is odd. If I planned to use a photoelectric cell, I wouldn't use one in a situation like this. It would be far more effective as a package or briefcase bomb. That way, when the item was opened, light would hit the cell and kaboom."

"Maybe the bomber chose this method because they're not commonly used for bombs, and he hopes it'll throw us off track," Ryleigh said. "Or even point to someone else."

"That seems possible," Finn said, letting the implications settle in. "With the unpredictability of the device, we have to assume whoever built this bomb was okay with a loss of life."

"At least he chose a maintenance day when there would be a limited crew onsite," Ryleigh said. "But yeah, he had to be good with the potential of killing people."

"Doesn't sound like most ecoterrorists I've read about," Trent said. "They're all about preserving life and restricting their efforts to damaging the property."

Ryleigh nodded. "Have you found any evidence of the white or red plastic from the company's explosives?"

"Nothing yet," Grady said. "But anything that survived the blast could've melted in the fire."

"Determining the type of explosive is very important for us to move forward," Finn said.

Grady worked the muscles in his jaw. "Understood, and chemical analysis will give you that. But we might never be able to tell you if it's from this company's stash."

"What about any sign of an accelerant used for the fire or chemicals left behind?" Ryleigh asked.

"Nothing," Trent said. "But we'll take samples back to the lab to be sure."

"Let me look at that bag." Sierra joined them and took the evidence from Grady. She turned it in her hands and held it up to the sunlight. "Minimal soot and should be easy to clean for fingerprinting. Plus, we've had success in getting better prints lately on difficult objects with a new technique we're piloting called vacuum metal deposition."

"How does that work?" Ryleigh asked.

Sierra gave the bag back to Grady. "VMD involves the thermal evaporation of metals—mostly gold, silver, and zinc —inside a special chamber. The controlled high vacuum conditions cause the metals to form thin films, developing all fingerprints present so we can see them."

"And you can do that on a burned item like this?" Finn asked.

Sierra nodded. "If we can safely remove the soot first. Which we can often do."

"How long will the process take?" Ryleigh asked.

"Hmm, well." Sierra tilted her head. "To use the custom-built chamber, I first have to get this back to the lab. But once there, it should move along fast. Again, depends on the cleaning process."

No matter how long, it was too long for Finn's liking. Each minute they didn't know the bomber's ID was a minute his own name could be linked to it. "Can others at your lab run it?"

"Sorry, no. Just me." She held up a hand. "And before you suggest I take off to do it, I'm not leaving here until I'm certain the rest of my team can properly handle the remaining work without me."

An answer Ryleigh's tight expression said she didn't seem to like. "I don't mean to be difficult, but getting the bomber's ID is crucial. I know you used a helicopter when you recently helped Mackenzie. Would you consider flying back on that, running the test, then returning if needed?"

"I don't know." Sierra glanced around the space. "There's a lot of work to do here."

"The evidence isn't going anywhere," Finn pointed out. "And with the bomber at large, he could strike again."

"They have a point." Kelsey looked at Sierra. "The clear weather is supposed to hold for days with no risk of rain. Besides, you had them fly in for me due to my pregnancy. It's the least we can do for you in yours."

Ryleigh gaped at Sierra. "You're pregnant?"

"Yes." Sierra eyed Kelsey. "But I'm only four months along and wasn't announcing it yet."

Kelsey blushed. "Sorry. I forgot. Forgive me?"

Sierra gave her coworker a good-natured roll of the eyes. "You know I will."

"Then let me make that call." Kelsey smiled. "As a bonus, your techs and Winter can come down on the chopper instead of driving. They'll get here sooner, and I can fly back with the remains and get them started sooner too."

"Perfect!" Ryleigh clapped her hands, and the sound echoed through the ruins.

She might be excited about this development, but Finn knew they still had an uphill battle. Sure, they might soon have the victim's ID—even the bomber's ID. That would be great. Still didn't mean they could run right out and find him.

More likely, a manhunt would ensue, and that could turn deadly.

14

Russ called the update meeting at noon, and he instructed Ryleigh to grab sandwiches, chips, and bottles of water that Reid served to the Veritas team. So she and Finn had loaded up and brought meals back to Russ's conference room, and Ryleigh had dug in with everyone else. She was famished. Stress did that to her. Others couldn't eat when stressed, but she could consume a side of beef and still have dessert.

She'd chosen a thick slab of roast beef on a melt-in-your-mouth bun. It was so delicious, she wanted to know where it came from so she could get it again when she was back in town. *If* Tobias didn't fire her company.

She set down her bun. "Anyone know where Reid got the lunch?"

Colin swallowed. "Now that's something I can answer. Reid had his cook make them. She not only cooks for Reid and the staff, but she makes meals for campers the first few days while we teach them how to fend for themselves. She backs off once they get their own meals together, but she still feeds us." He patted his stomach. "I've had to work out more to get rid of all the homemade rolls and bread since I came here."

"Her name's Poppy." Russ smiled fondly. "She's worked for our family for years. She lives with Reid and his daughter."

"She's a strict vegetarian, but she'll even serve meat," Ryan said. "But if she's around when you eat it you get an earful."

Ryan and Russ laughed together, showing a softer side of Russ that Ryleigh knew existed. Too bad she hadn't seen much of it so far.

He balled up his paper napkin and shot it toward the trashcan. "Kills her to use disposable products too, but her heart for helping others does at times transcend her drive to recycle."

Ryan nodded. "Her grandparents came to Oregon in the sixties' hippie movement. That's where she met our mom, and she's still involved with the group."

"Might she know about ecoterrorists in the area then?" Finn asked.

"Maybe," Ryan said. "I can ask her, but if I don't get a meal for a month, I'm coming for you."

Ryan laughed, and Finn joined him. Ryleigh liked seeing the two men getting along when they'd had a tense beginning.

Russ fired an intimidating look at Finn. "In light of the recent findings, we need to talk about your continued involvement with the task force."

Finn didn't even blink an eye. "You know I'm not involved in the bombing, and the evidence will bear that out."

"I know you had means—a key to the explosives' depot. Opportunity—access to the building and explosives."

"What about motive?" Finn fired back. "Why would I want to blow up my place of employment? Makes no sense."

"I don't know." Russ continued to stare. "But I'll figure it out."

Finn's hands curled on the table, but that was the only indication of his irritation. "Sounds like you want to kick me off the team."

"I would like you to voluntarily remove yourself."

"No."

"Figured you'd say that."

"Remove me from the group, and I'll go off on my own to investigate." Finn fired a challenging look at Russ. "Is that what you want? A rogue investigator messing in your case?"

"You know I don't."

"Then there has to be a compromise that we can both live with."

Ryan cleared his throat and both men shot their attention to him. "Finn, you and Ryleigh are basically working as one right now, right? Russ, why don't you insist that Finn doesn't investigate without Ryleigh at his side?"

Russ's shoulders relaxed. "I can live with that."

"Me too," Finn said.

"What about me?" Ryleigh fired a look between the men. "No one asked if I could live with it."

Ryan shifted his attention to her. "Well, can you?"

Could she? Meant more time with Finn. Honestly, it hadn't been a hardship to be in his company most of the time. And if continuing to partner with him moved the investigation forward, she owed it to the victim to do her best to help. "I can do it for the good of the team and to find a resolution."

"Good. That's settled then." Russ eyed Finn. "Don't make me regret my decision."

"I won't."

Russ stood and looked down the table at his assistant. "Pass out those packets, Allison."

She got up and walked around the table, handing out a thick packet of stapled papers to each team member.

"Allison is giving you background documents Colin prepared for Gates, Eckles, his wife, and for Dean Keenan too. Take a good look at them as you finish eating, and I'll get started on listing the latest developments on the boards."

Colin set down his sandwich, turkey on hearty wheat bread, that had been Ryleigh's second choice. "I'm still working on Nye and have algorithms running on everyone. They could turn up additional info from more obscure or difficult sites to access, like the dark web, but I thought you would want to have some background to start with. I should have details on Nye by the end of the day."

"Great work, Colin." Russ crossed the room, grabbing a blue marker as he passed the smaller board, and started to write below the To Do list from the prior day.

Ryleigh slowly chewed her last bite to savor the rich flavor and dug into the report, starting with Uri Gates. He was born and raised in Adamsville, Alabama. Went to work as a logger right out of high school. Married Greta. Worked his way up to supervisor. Then a logger on his crew was killed by a tree, and Gates sunk into a dark period in his life. That's when his wife divorced him. No red flags other than his depression. Contents of his medicine cabinet proved he still took the meds, but it seemed as if he was functioning well except for being overly careful as a supervisor.

Ryleigh turned her glass of iced tea and moved on to Virgil Eckles and his wife, Pauline. His report was even less helpful. Nothing at all to draw attention to him. He became a logger at nineteen and worked for Tobias ever since then, a supervisor for ten years now. No serious accidents. And he was well-liked by the crews. He met and married Pauline ten years ago. She was born and raised in—*wait, what?*

Adamsville, Alabama.

Ryleigh looked up. "Anyone else see Pauline Eckles and Uri Gates grew up in the same town?"

"Me." Finn peered intently at his phone. "I'm looking up the town population now to see how likely it is that they could know each other."

That would've been Ryleigh's next move, and she was glad he'd already started.

His head came up. "A little over two-thousand people."

"A city that small and they're a year apart in age," Russ said. "They could well know each other."

"But if Eckles told her about Gates when he started," Finn said. "Why didn't she say something about knowing him from back then?"

"They could have something to hide," Ryan said.

Ryleigh looked at Russ. "We didn't ask her about Gates. We need to question her again."

"Indeed." Russ wrote it on the whiteboard under his name.

"A good lead for sure," Ryleigh said. "Thanks, Colin."

"All in a day's work." He drained the last of his water bottle.

Ryleigh couldn't drink a thing right now. Not with her heart beating fast. She returned to the reports and looked at Dean Keenan. He too lived in Alabama, but in Birmingham, where he led Sovereign Earth. He'd been arrested several times for minor charges at protests and paid fines. That was until he'd assaulted an officer and served five years in prison. He'd continued to lead the group from his cell.

"This Keenan guy's a piece of work," Finn said.

"Seems like he wouldn't be opposed to killing people." Colin crinkled his empty bottle and pitched it at the recycle bin. "I couldn't find any phone numbers for him. No surprise. These guys are all often paranoid and only use virtually untraceable prepaids."

She turned to the Sovereign Earth packet and learned the group was suspected of several bombings and violent protests, but they hadn't been charged with any crimes.

"Looks like Sovereign Earth isn't such a peaceful group," she said. "But no one has ever been able to prove it, including me."

"Yeah," Colin said. "They don't take responsibility for their work. At least not in so many words, but if you read between the lines, it's clear people who claim group membership are behind a lot of the violent events."

"Are you looking into other members?" Finn asked.

Colin nodded. "I've got searches running on everyone I found. After it completes, I'll cull down the list to people who could be related to this incident."

Ryleigh looked at the other details for Sovereign Earth. "I see Pauline Eckles still shows up on the group's Alabama roster."

"Yeah," Colin said. "That's where she first started appearing. Then she moved to Atlanta. From what I can tell, she was trying to move away from Keenan after a contentious breakup. She still continued to work with the group but later moved to Oregon, and then she disappears from any of their other details."

"Any reason given for her Oregon move?" Ryleigh asked to try to confirm her statement.

Colin nodded. "Her uncle died, and he left his property in Shadow Lake to her. Good timing as it appears as if Keenan was still bothering her. Shadow Lake Logging had a contract to log her uncle's property, and that's when she met Eckles."

"That matches her statement to us." Russ looked around the table. "Any other comments on the background reports?"

"Nothing for me, except I'm eager to see Carla Nye's

report." Ryleigh looked at Colin. "Especially to see if you can track her down."

"I'll make sure you know anything the minute I find something." Colin smiled.

Ryleigh tapped her stack of papers. "With your ecoterrorism background and these reports, what's your gut telling you?"

His smile wavered. "Sovereign Earth could be behind the bombing. Not sure I buy it yet though. Not when I haven't gotten any hits on a photoelectric cell bomb."

"Looks like they keep changing their MO over time," Ryan said. "Could be why they haven't been caught. If you don't leave patterns, investigators can't link the dots."

"It could also explain why they might've used a photoelectric cell on this bomb," Finn said.

There had to be something they were missing, and Ryleigh wished they had more data right now. "Still doesn't explain why Keenan had schematics that didn't show the cell, though."

"Hopefully, Colin's additional research will give us more to go on." Russ tapped his marker on the board. "Let's run down the To Do List and get caught up."

He swiped his marker through getting a warrant for Tobias's office and tapped the words deep dives on Gates, Tobias, and Eckles. "We have preliminary reports, but let's leave this open for now. Colin, you mentioned photoelectric cells? Have you struck out only on Sovereign Earth or a wider search?"

"Countrywide and nothing's come up." Colin frowned. "But the algorithm continues to run."

"Nick at Veritas is also searching," Ryleigh said. "Sounds as if it's not common. Grady and Trent said they've never seen one used."

"My search of ViCAP bears that out too," Russ said. "We

struck out in Oregon. My deputy is searching other states now. Unless that turns something up, we might not be able to connect the method to the suspect unless we can pin it down through the Veritas team's evidence recovery." Russ listed Grady as the responsible party for getting more information on the actual photoelectric cell.

"Sierra was confident she could fingerprint it too," Finn said.

Russ put it on the board and added hotel guests. "My team is working on looking for anyone from out of town who is involved in ecoterrorism. We collected guest lists from local motels and hotels, and they're clearing the guest's names now." He fixed his gaze on his brother. "What have you learned about competitors?"

Ryan snapped his chair forward and it squealed. "My research doesn't point to anyone who might want to hurt Tobias's operation. None of the other businesses are in dire financial straits. One of them is closing next month because he couldn't make a go of it anymore and is getting out before he goes into the red. Still not a red flag as he's calling it quits. I also did some asking around. Sounds like the other loggers think of Tobias as the grandfather of the logging industry in the area and respect him."

"I could dig deeper online on the owners if you want," Colin said.

"I doubt you'll find anything but it would be good to be thorough," Ryan said.

"It's all yours, Colin." Russ added it to the board. "Okay, let's move on to new items, starting with forensics. Anyone have any questions about these items I just added?"

He tapped the top item he'd jotted down.

- *Nick Thorn - Deep dive on Carla Nye and Dean Keenan and try to trace emails*

- *Sierra Rice - Process forensics located at Gates's house, especially fingerprints, the Roomba, and particulates*
- *Sierra Rice - Process DNA and fingerprints on photoelectric cell and Nye's documents*
- *Sierra Rice – Process Nye's bedroom at Eckles's place and Gates's truck*
- *Kelsey Dunbar - Identify victim and determine cause of death and look for Gates's keys in his pocket*
- *Emerson County deputies - Find Carla's cell phone*
- *Emerson County staff - Review video from explosives' depot.*
- *Grady and Trent - Talk to eyewitnesses to the explosion and the first firefighter on scene*
- *Grady and Trent – determine type of explosives used for bomb*

"I called the logging company in Alabama and confirmed that Gates did indeed work there," Ryleigh said. "Thankfully, his former wife didn't answer, and I was able to confirm he was well-respected. The manager I talked to said he left due to a dispute with his former wife, just like he told Tobias."

"So he didn't lie," Russ said. "Good to know."

"And I'll need a key to the explosives' depot so I can let Grady and Trent take a look at the explosives Tobias's team uses."

Russ got a key from his pocket and slid it down the table, then glanced at Finn. "Unless of course you have one you're not telling me about."

Finn rolled his eyes. "You know I don't, and I got ahold of the locksmith who's in charge of making the depot keys. No one has asked him for a key, and he hasn't made one for anyone since I hired him."

"Then only four people had a key." Russ locked gazes with Finn.

"Unless one of the other guys found another locksmith to cut a key," Finn said. "But they would have to be dishonest to do it."

Russ continued to stare at Finn. "Barring that, if we confirm the explosives were the same type as stored in the depot, that would mean only four people could have set the bomb."

Finn sat up higher. "Only three. You know I didn't do it."

"We'll see," Russ said. "We're through half of the video feed from the depot."

"And?" Finn demanded.

"Nothing yet except legit access as noted on the log."

"The explosives could've come from anywhere," Finn said. "We have no proof to the contrary."

"I've also got feelers out in the state looking for any missing explosives," Russ said.

Ryan tapped the table, taking his brother's attention and immediately lowering the tension level in the room. "I've also asked the other logging company owners to check their inventories and get back to me if there's anything missing."

Russ spun and wrote the information on the board.

"The last to do item would refer to Grady or Trent talking to me," Ryan said. "That hasn't happened. I'm guessing they'll interview me on my shift."

Russ nodded and ran his gaze over the group. "A lot has happened in a short time. Have I missed anything?"

The others shook their heads.

"Jenkins will do a daily report for us, but he'll also have the experts notify us right away of anything they think needs immediate action." Russ capped his marker. "Let's talk prime suspects at this point. Theories?"

"Eckles doesn't have motive," Ryleigh said. "But he had

access to the explosives and the site, and his wife's connection to Sovereign Earth could tie him to a bomb."

"I'm not liking him for it." Russ leaned against the wall and crossed his feet at the ankle. "But I can't rule out a possible connection to it through Nye and Keenan. The sooner we locate them the better. With the alerts out on both of them and Colin's algorithms, hopefully we'll see success on finding her."

"I also think Eckles and his wife are holding back," Ryleigh said.

"Agreed." Russ stood. "Let's bring them in for questioning this time. Put the fear of the law in them."

Russ set down the marker. "Anyone have anything else to add or are we ready to get back at it?"

"Ready for sure." Ryleigh got out her phone to call Eckles and his wife and demanded they come in for an interview. She couldn't wait to get back to questioning them and unearth whatever it was they seemed to be holding back.

Finn didn't like being excluded from another interview, but at least Russ had allowed him to watch through the one-way glass in the interview room. Ryleigh sat next to Russ at a small table, and Pauline Eckles had slumped into a seat across from them. Russ had separated the couple to interview them one at a time to see if he could trip them up in a lie.

Pauline rubbed her belly. "You know this stress isn't good for a pregnant woman."

"I'm sorry for that," Ryleigh said, sounding sincere. "But if you don't have anything to hide this shouldn't be stressful at all."

"Come on now." Pauline rolled her eyes. "You know being called in here is stressful. Likely why you did it."

"Then let's get to our questions so you can go on home." Russ sounded surprisingly gentle. "When we last talked you didn't mention knowing Uri Gates."

"Uri? Oh, wow. That's a name from the past. I went to school with him." She blinked several times. "What's he got to do with anything?"

"He's the night supervisor at Shadow Lake Logging."

"Are you sure?" She scratched her cheek. "There's only one night supervisor, and Virg said the new guy's name is Smokey."

Finn watched for duplicity in her expression, but she looked at Russ and Ryleigh with a level gaze. Finn had learned how to read people and it looked like she hadn't been hiding the fact that she knew Gates.

"That's Uri's nickname," Russ said.

"Okay, wow. Just wow. That's crazy that he would end up working with Virg. Uri was a year behind me in school, so we didn't hang out, but he was on the wrestling team and I was a cheerleader, so I knew him." She flashed her gaze to Russ and held on. "Don't think I'm involved because of this. I haven't seen Uri or talked to him since high school. After he graduated, I'd heard he went off somewhere to start logging."

"What did you do out of high school?" Ryleigh asked.

"Me?" Her eyes flashed wide open. "I couldn't wait to get out of that stinking little town, so I moved to Birmingham with my best friend. We took minimum wage jobs as file clerks and shared an apartment."

"How did you get involved with Sovereign Earth?" Russ asked, his tone more direct now.

Pauline frowned and hunched over the table. "Same way Carla did and the way a lot of the females in the group did. I met Dean in a bar. Started going out with him and he brought me in."

Ryleigh leaned closer to Pauline. "Where did Dean and Carla hook up?"

"Georgia." The word came out on a spit of disgust. "Dean got more and more radical, and that just wasn't me, so I broke up with him. I tried to leave the group then, but he hounded me. So I lied and said I got a job transfer to Atlanta, figuring he'd finally leave me alone. I didn't really get a transfer, but I did move there. I met Carla at work, and one night when we were out, Dean showed up. He started by begging to get back with me, but when I told him to take a hike, he hit on her. No matter how much I warned her, she fell for his charms and got involved with him."

"Did she remain in Atlanta and have a long-distance relationship?" Russ asked.

"Stayed in Atlanta, but no long-distance for Dean. He moved in with her and sponged off her. His true MO for women." Pauline shook her head. "I don't really blame Carla. He's very charismatic, drop-dead gorgeous, and hard to resist."

Finn didn't like to hear that. The guy's charisma and charm could make him hard to find because he could locate women all across the country who would let him hide out with them.

Ryleigh and Russ dismissed Pauline and brought in her husband. Russ's hope for tripping them up in a lie grew slimmer by the minute as a sullen Eckles gave the same answers as his wife.

"Did you ever mention Gates to your wife?" Russ asked.

"Yeah, sure," Eckles said. "We called him Smokey at work, so that's the name I would've used."

"Did you know Gates was from Alabama?" Ryleigh asked.

"Is that so?" His tone rose. "Wonder if he knew Pauline."

"They grew up in the same town."

Eckles shook his head. "Now isn't that something? I mean, I knew he had a southern accent, but we never got into personal details."

Russ planted his palms on the tabletop. "Don't you find it a coincidence?"

"Well, yeah, sure. A big one. Wait!" He shot up in his chair. "If you think this means Pauline or I had something to do with the bomb, then you're still way off base."

Finn was starting to believe the guy, but until they had proof he or his wife had nothing to do with the bombing, they couldn't officially rule them out. Russ might not feel the same way as he continued to pummel Eckles with questions, but the guy held up under the onslaught.

Russ stood. "I'll give you one last chance to tell me anything you haven't shared."

Eckles blinked up at Russ. "There's nothing. At least not that I know of."

Russ glared down at the guy. "If I find out you and your wife are still hiding things from me, I'll throw the book at you both."

"No worries," Eckles said, but his face was tight. "We've put it all out there for you."

Russ turned Eckles over to a deputy to escort them out of the building, and Russ and Ryleigh stepped into the hallway.

Finn joined them, and they all tromped to the lobby that smelled of orange cleaner to retrieve their phones and weapons, then head out to the parking lot. Finn had to admit to being glad to be out of the sheriff's office and in the sunshine, but the warm sun didn't change anything. They still didn't have a solid lead on their bomber's identity.

Finn stopped and faced the others. "Looks like they're a dead-end except for their connection to Carla Nye."

"Yeah, but at least our questions were answered," Ryleigh said.

"Not sure I'm ready to agree with that." Russ frowned. "I get the feeling there's something they're still holding back."

"Hopefully, Nick's or Colin's research will tell us what." Ryleigh started to shove her phone into her pocket but it rang, and she looked at it.

"Speaking of Nick." She tapped the screen. "The sheriff and Finn are with me so putting you on speaker, Nick."

"I've had a chance to interrogate the Roomba during my breaks." Nick's excited tone shot through the phone. "You'll want to see what I found on the machine's memory. Could be the very lead you need to bring in this bomber."

15

Ryleigh stepped toward Nick, where he sat at a portable table near the front of the mill property. Reid had erected tables and chairs in this area to serve the Veritas lunch. The Roomba sat on the table next to Nick's computer. He had his face in his laptop and seemed oblivious to the soft breeze blowing his hair or all the commotion around him.

Question was, was he being overly dramatic in his promise of a lead or did he really have something great?

Finn trailed behind her, and she waited for him to rush past and pounce on Nick, but he didn't. Another oddity that she couldn't explain.

Nick looked up and a broad smile crossed his face. "Thanks for coming."

"What do you have that you couldn't send to me?" Ryleigh didn't mean to sound like she was put out for coming here. She was going to meet Grady and Trent at the explosives' depot anyway and would've driven right past the mill.

"Well, I could've emailed it, but thought if you had any questions, I'd be right here to answer them." He pointed at the chair next to him. "Besides, it's always nice to see when an investigator gets excited about a lead, and this is a good one."

"Okay, stop tormenting us and show us what you have." She took the chair next to Nick.

Finn stood behind them.

Nick clicked his mouse on a video displayed on his screen. "This is a snippet from the Roomba."

The screen filled with a pair of boots in motion. Not like Gates's work boots, but very unique black leather boots with crisscrossing leather straps starting at the instep and held in place with silver buckles. The straps, placed about an inch apart, continued up the boots as far as she could see. The shiny silver heel glinted on the screen.

"Those don't belong to Gates," she said, her excitement piqued just like Nick claimed would happen. "Or at least, he only had work boots in his closet, and these weren't found in his truck either. Plus, the boots don't have a lift, and the guy isn't limping."

"Looks like he had a visitor," Finn stated.

Nick nodded. "An earlier video shows these boots followed by the work boots walking past the camera. It was recorded the day before the bomb went off around one p.m."

"Right before Gates was due at work." Finn gripped Ryleigh's chair and leaned closer, his scent of minty soap enveloping her. "This guy could be the last person other than the mill workers who saw Gates alive."

"And the guy who trashed Gates's place," Nick added.

"He ransacked the townhouse?" Finn asked. "You see that on the video?"

"I did. Let me fast forward to show you." Nick sped up the video to later in the day at four p.m. The unique boots appeared, but then moved out of view and items hit the floor in the kitchen. Dishes. Pans. Canned and boxed foods. Spices. Silverware.

"That's it for now." Nick stopped the video. "He moves out of camera range, and the next time we see the boots, the guy is walking out the front door a couple of hours later."

"I imagine Gates came home from work to find his place trashed," Finn said. "Maybe he knew this guy did it. Maybe not. Either way, he didn't report it to the police."

"The big question is why," Finn said. "We need to get more information on these boots."

"Way ahead of you." Nick grinned. "They're made by New Rock, a company out of Spain."

"Spain," she said. "That could limit the number of people who would own them."

"You'd think so, but look at this." Nick clicked an internet link. "The boots are sold online."

"Well, drat." Ryleigh stared at the Amazon page Nick had brought up.

"Still, the description says it's a vintage style." Finn lifted his hands from the chair and moved back. "And the boots look worn so maybe someone knows who has a pair around here."

Ryleigh nodded. "We can ask around. Local gossips are bound to know if anyone owns boots like these."

"Give me a minute to isolate and enhance a still shot." Nick's fingers slid over the computer trackpad. "And I'll text it to you."

"Perfect." Eager to move forward on this lead, Ryleigh got up. She came face-to-face with Finn.

Something flared in his eyes, but it quickly evaporated, and he stepped back. "You have a plan?"

"Seems like a boot for someone who cares about their appearance," she said, her thoughts still perking. "Someone like Keenan who thinks he's a ladies' man. We can show the picture to Pauline. She might know if he wears New Rock boots."

"Sounds like a good start."

"And if it's not him, then we can ask locals if they recognize the style." She was already thinking about the shop owners in town who would likely know.

Finn smiled. "We might finally have something, and the bomber's ID could be within reach."

She returned his smile and got lost in the warmth flowing her way. The urge to touch him was strong. Very strong. But the wind kicked up, whipping the stench of burnt materials in the air and snapping her back to task.

"Ryleigh," Grady called out from down the hill where he and Trent were trudging toward them. "Ready to check out that explosives' depot?"

"We good to go?" she asked Nick.

"Have at it. I can text the still shot so off you go." He flicked his hands as if they were bugs he was swatting away.

"Ready," she told Grady, but wished she was going to see Pauline instead to ask if these fancy silver-heeled boots belonged to Dean Keenan.

Finn had parked on the road just shy of the deputy standing at the top of Shadow Lake Logging's driveway. He forbid them from driving down the hill. In fact, he'd insisted on calling Russ to ask if they had permission to access the place at all.

Not that Finn could go into the explosives' depot anyway, but he could head down the hill with the men and Ryleigh to answer any questions they might have about the inventory or procedures.

The deputy gave them a thumbs up, and Finn pushed

open his truck door. He met Ryleigh by the hood. Trent and Grady had gotten a phone call before leaving that they'd had to take, so they hadn't arrived yet.

"I can at least get the door open for the guys." Ryleigh led the way around the deputy, who eyed them both.

On the other side of the barrier, something set Finn's protective instincts into overdrive, and he caught up to her while scanning the property. He searched the valley and the area around the building. Watched for movement. A flash of a weapon. But saw nothing except grass and weeds swaying in the breeze and a bright beam of sunlight shining down on the building and making it look less institutional.

Was he missing something and someone was hiding on site? Someone the deputy hadn't seen?

Not likely. But Finn got a hinky feeling when approaching situations that could possibly go wrong and the feeling was creeping over him. He eased closer to Ryleigh. She didn't seem to notice and kept moving.

Boom!

The ground shook, and the office erupted in front of them.

Finn didn't think. He grabbed Ryleigh and took her to the ground, covering her with his body.

A concussive force hit him hard and thundered over his back. Building shards shot through the air, skimming over his shirt. Sharp, needle-like pain stung the back of his neck. The building rumbled. Groaned. Metal twisted with wails of pain.

He hazarded a look down the hill. The building's upper floor wobbled and collapsed. A billow of debris-laden dust swirled up the driveway.

He turned his head to let the cloud pass over them.

"You okay?" he whispered.

"Other than being crushed by you, yeah." Her terrified tone cut him to the core.

"Sorry." He lifted on his elbows but remained in place to stop any additional flying shrapnel from harming her.

"No worries," she said. "You got me to the ground faster than I would have done on my own."

His gut hadn't failed him. He let out a long breath of relief and looked up the hill. "The deputy's down."

"You okay, Deputy?" he called out.

No response or movement.

Concern rising, Finn lifted higher. "I've got a first aid kit in my truck.":

"I'll call 911 and Russ while you get it."

Finn rolled free and came to his feet, breathing as shallowly as possible to keep from sucking in dust particles.

He charged up the hill and grabbed his kit from the back of his truck. He saw Ryleigh on the phone, then they both ran toward the deputy. Finn was trained in combat emergency treatment, and he'd had to administer his share of emergency aid to fellow SEALs, so he was confident in his skills, but the deputy wasn't moving and that was never a good sign.

Ryleigh beat him to the injured man, tossed her phone to the ground, and felt his neck for a pulse. The deputy stirred and rolled to his side.

"Don't move." Ryleigh placed a hand on his shoulder. "You have a large piece of shrapnel in your back, and you've lost a lot of blood."

"What happened?"

Finn glanced down the driveway to see if the building had caught fire, but he didn't see any flames. "A bomb took out the office."

"How's that even possible?" He brushed off Ryleigh's

hand and tried to sit up but failed and fell back to his side. "We've had eyes on this place twenty-four/seven."

"We'll figure that out," Ryleigh said. "But for now, rest and don't move or you might make your injury worse."

"This is my watch. I can't just lay here. You both okay?"

"We're fine," Ryleigh said.

"I doubt anyone could be in the building, but if someone got in to set a bomb without us seeing it, a person could've gotten in the same way."

"Let us worry about that," Finn said. "I'll help stop your blood loss, then assess the damage."

"Plus, I've already called 911 and Sheriff Maddox," Ryleigh said. "And I know he would want you to listen to us."

The deputy sagged against the gravel. "Fine, but hurry up and get down there."

"Will do," Finn said, but the bleeding had to be stopped or Finn wasn't going anywhere. He had special blood clotting gauze in his kit, and he applied it to the wound, his fingers immediately coated in sticky blood.

"Hold these in place," he instructed Ryleigh.

She didn't flinch but took over the job and didn't back down even when the deputy moaned in pain.

"What's your name?" Finn asked to distract the guy.

"Eddie."

"Well, Eddie, this is going to hurt a bit but hang with me." Finn grabbed rolls of gauze and secured the projectile to Eddie's back so it didn't continue to move, pushing Ryleigh's hands out of the way when he no longer needed her to hold the quick-clotting gauze.

Finished, he sat back to assess. The gauze didn't darken with blood. *Good.* At the very least Finn had slowed it down.

He stood. "That should hold until the medics get here.

I'm going down there to see if others are trapped or injured. Call out if the bleeding starts again."

Ryleigh peered up at him, her gaze unreadable. Did she want to go with him? Want him to stay here while she investigated? He shouldn't just assume it was up to him to go to the building, but he had more experience with this kind of debris and destruction.

She swallowed. "Be careful."

He nodded and took off, picking his way down the driveway cluttered with shards of concrete and wood from the building. At the bottom, he had a good view of the explosives' depot. The little building stood strong amidst the debris. If it had exploded, none of them would've likely survived.

Thank You for that!

But Finn wasn't foolish enough to approach the depot. Not when another device could be set. The good news was that the camera was still intact too, meaning they might have video stored in the cloud. And if they could safely get into the building, they might be able to recover footage that captured the bomber stealing explosives.

Finn took a good look at the main structure. The back wall still stood but the second story had collapsed as he'd watched. Twisted metal rebar stood as jagged spears along the perimeter. The concrete smothered the first floor and anyone who potentially had been in the building. Dust and pollutants still lingered in the air, but so far fire hadn't broken out.

A small blessing. Maybe a big one if the surrounding area didn't catch fire.

"Anyone in there?" Finn yelled. "Call out so we can help."

He leaned closer and listened, bringing back all kinds of unpleasant memories from his deployments. He didn't have

PTSD as a lot of guys suffered from, but he still didn't like to recall missions that ended in similar situations. Especially where innocent lives were lost. Most horrifically, children's lives.

He waited. Waited some more. Bending forward. Craning his neck.

No response.

Please, if there's someone inside, let me hear them.

He called out again and listened.

Nothing.

If someone was trapped in the rubble, they didn't seem to be alive or at least they weren't conscious.

A siren sounded at the road. Either Russ or an ambulance or both.

Finn turned to climb the hill, careful not to trip over debris. Swift movement in the distance caught his attention. He spun, drawing his sidearm, ready to charge after whoever was out there.

A large buck sprang away in the thicket surrounding the property. The majestic animal moved fast and disappeared from view. The poor fella was likely scared to death.

Finn let out his breath and climbed the incline, but adrenaline continued to course through him. Russ's patrol car pulled to a stop behind Finn's truck, and an ambulance screeched to a halt beside it.

Russ rushed over to his deputy, dropped to his knees, and placed a hand on his officer's shoulder. "How you doing, Eddie?"

"Don't worry about me." Eddie offered a wavering smile. "Just a scratch, and I'll be fine."

Russ looked at his deputy's back, his face pale. He seemed to battle a wave of emotions by gazing into the distance. The sheriff's hand shook. So the strong lawman was a softie after all. At least when it came to one of his deputies getting injured.

"Ambulance is here," Finn said, trying to bring hope to the situation.

Russ let out a long breath, his chest deflating like a punctured tire. "I'll ride along with you and call your wife, Eddie, so she can meet you at the hospital."

"Stay here." Eddie shot a look at Ryleigh. "She might temporarily be one of us, but she was a fed, and feds don't know how to do a thing." He tried to laugh but it turned into a deep agonizing cough. "They need someone who knows the real law enforcement world to keep them in line."

Russ chuckled, but it was forced.

A female medic with long blond hair in a ponytail rushed up to them. "What do we have, Sheriff?"

Russ moved out of the way. "Puncture wound in the back."

The medic looked at the wound. "You dress this?"

"Nah," Russ said. "I..." He looked around as if finally noticing Finn stood over him.

"I did," Finn stated. "I had first aid training in the Navy."

"Great work." The medic flashed Finn a smile and then took Eddie's vitals. "Pretty good for someone who's trying to shirk his duties." She chuckled.

Eddie tried to laugh again but gave up.

The medic looked up at her male partner. "Let's get him on the stretcher and out of here."

"Stand back," the other medic said, moving in with a backboard.

Russ took a few more steps back, and Ryleigh and Finn joined him.

"You're both fine?" Russ's voice caught.

"Thanks to Finn's lightning-fast reflexes." Ryleigh looked at him, her eyes wet with tears.

183

"I'm good to go," Finn said though he knew he'd suffered some minor cuts on his neck which weren't even worth mentioning.

"Thank God for that." Russ stared down the hill. "Anyone look at the building damage up close?"

"I got a good look," Finn said. "The explosives' depot is still standing, but the office has totally collapsed. We need to get someone out here to clear it so we can search the rubble for anyone who might've been injured."

One of the Veritas vans pulled up and parked on the road. Finn had forgotten all about Trent and Grady coming over here.

They strode down the road as if they were arriving to take charge of the crime scene.

Grady pointed at Eddie as the medics loaded him up. "He gonna be okay?"

Russ shrugged and planted his hands on his waist. "If you're here to get a look at the explosives, that'll have to wait now."

If Grady was upset over Russ's terse tone, he didn't show it. "We were, but looks like you can use our services again."

Russ rubbed his forehead. "We haven't even determined if anyone was in the building, and we're a long way off from processing forensics."

Trent took a step closer. "We can do more than forensics. We've been testing something new that could help search for victims and other explosives without risking lives."

Russ widened his stance. "Tell me about it."

"Not an it, but them. Robobugs." Trent bounced on his toes. "They're rechargeable, remote-controllable cyborg cockroaches."

"Say what?" Ryleigh gaped at Trent.

"They're just what they sound like," Grady said. "Cyborg insects—part insect, part machine. These remote-controlled cyborg cockroaches are equipped with tiny wireless control modules. They're powered by rechargeable batteries attached to solar cells."

"So they what?" Russ raised his eyebrows. "With something strapped to their backs, they can move around?"

Trent nodded. "A backpack is 3-D printed to conform to the insect's thorax. Despite the mechanical devices and ultrathin electronics, the insects can still move freely."

Ryleigh shook her head. "That sounds unbelievable."

"It does," Grady said. "But we've been testing them for some time, and they transmit the information we need to safely clear buildings like this one."

Finn was impressed. More than impressed if that was possible. Something like this would really have helped on deployments in war zones, but he didn't think it would be practical to try to keep the bugs alive on a mission.

Still, today, the bugs could do everything they needed on this scene, and Finn wanted to know more. "The explosives' depot is still standing. Could we send them in there to determine if it's been booby-trapped?"

Grady nodded. "As long as we can get them inside, we can get a good look at the area."

"I'm guessing you didn't bring them with you, though," Ryleigh said.

"No, but we can transport them on the chopper coming to drop off additional staff," Trent said.

Russ looked at the departing ambulance. "Get those bugs on that chopper now. We need to know if this bomb took anyone else out."

16

Ryleigh was thankful Grady caught the helicopter before it took off and arranged for the team to include the bugs. They should arrive any minute. But she wasn't a do-nothing person and standing at the edge of the property and waiting for the cyborg bugs to arrive was tantamount to torture.

Sure, she'd removed shards of debris from Finn's neck with tweezers from his first aid kit, but now she did nothing but swing her gaze to the road every time a vehicle drew near. Then when the vehicle wasn't a Veritas van, a sinking feeling settled into her gut. That was when she wasn't feeling Finn's antsy fidgeting as he waited too.

Her phone chimed, and so did his. They both grabbed them like lifelines out of boredom.

"It's the picture of the boot from Nick," she said. "Let's show it to Russ to see if he recognizes it." She started toward Russ's car, where he was sitting and talking on his phone. Finn followed.

Maybe Russ had also received an update on his deputy. Ryleigh approached the car, offering another prayer for Eddie and his family. Russ looked up from his phone and then slid out.

"Any word on Eddie?" she asked.

He shook his head.

"We just got the pictures of the boot I told you about." She held out her phone to him. "Ever see anyone wearing this style?"

Russ studied the photos. "Nah, and it's not a boot I'd forget. Make sure I get the picture, and I'll distribute it to my team so they can ask around. If a local has boots like these, someone is bound to remember them."

His phone rang, and he grabbed it. "Russ Maddox."

He plunged a hand into his hair, messing up the usually neatly combed strands. He started to pace, then stopped and stared at his feet. "You're sure?"

He listened. His hand went to the hood of his car to steady himself, and he sagged against it. "Thank you. Thank you so much."

He ended the call, his face pale, and he looked like he might be sick. "Eddie will be fine. Doctors safely removed the stake in surgery. It missed his heart by two inches and didn't hit any other internal organs."

Russ kept his hands on the car and took deep breaths. The big strong man had nearly been brought to his knees. She never doubted his loyalty to his team, but he cared more deeply than she'd imagined, and this injury had thrown him for a loop.

Coming from a law enforcement background, she understood his deep emotions more than most people could. Officers were not only coworkers, but they were family too.

He stowed his phone and turned to lean against the hood of his car. "You never want to see one of your people hurt. It happens, but you have to do everything you can to make sure it doesn't happen needlessly."

"You couldn't have stopped this," Finn said.

Russ's eyebrow rose. "Maybe. Maybe not. We won't know until we figure out how our bomber got into the building to set the device with my deputy on duty."

"Maybe it was set the same day as the first one," she suggested. "Then for some reason, it only detonated now."

Finn chewed on his cheek, his gaze tight. "Could be possible, I suppose, but why wait to detonate it?"

"What if this one had a photoelectric cell too, and wasn't connected to a computer?" Ryleigh asked. "It could've been in a closet or other dark place and the bomb wouldn't detonate until they opened the door and the light hit it."

Russ frowned. "Except no one was in the building today when this went off. Unless someone came in without my deputy seeing them. Either way, it's just like the other bomb, and the bomber didn't care if the explosion hurt or killed someone."

Ryleigh nodded. "Once the bugs confirm no one is in the building and there's no remaining danger, then the Veritas staff can look for residue from the bomb. What they find could not only tie it to the other explosion, but provide a lead that the fire destroyed at the mill."

As if the mention of the Veritas team brought them to the scene, their van finally pulled to a stop by the barrier. Grady, Trent, and Blake slid out and marched around back, purpose in their steps.

Good. Their eagerness to get this show on the road was just what Ryleigh wanted to happen.

"Let's see what these cyborg cockroaches are all about." She raced for the van and didn't care if Russ or Finn caught up, but they did.

The Veritas guys were slipping into white Tyvek suits.

"I wondered who would control these bugs," Ryleigh said. "Guess it's you guys."

"Most of us are trained." Grady expertly slid his other

188

hand into a disposable glove. "But since this involves a bomb, Trent and I are best skilled in searching for bomb fragments."

"Of course the priority is to search for survivors first." Blake tugged up his zipper. "As sheriff, I worked my share of collapsed buildings and know how to find trapped people."

Russ planted his feet, his forehead wrinkled. "I almost lost a deputy in this explosion, and I hope you all can give me what I need to bring the perpetrator to justice."

"We'll do our best," Trent said. "And our best is better than most investigators give you."

Russ's phone chimed, and he looked at it. "As much as I hate to leave before you do your thing, something urgent demands my attention." He looked at Ryleigh. "Keep me updated."

"FYI." Blake picked up a pair of gloves and shook them to free the fingers. "Sierra and Kelsey are flying back on the chopper with the victim's remains. I also sent the evidence we've collected so far. Sierra will run her tests on the photo-electric cell and then return."

"Excellent work," Russ said, his admiration for Blake's skills in his expression. He strode toward his car.

"Showtime." Trent gloved up and reached into the van. He withdrew a small closed container with tiny holes in the lid and sides. He lifted out a Lucite container from inside. Two-inch-long roaches scuttled around in the clear plastic box.

Never did Ryleigh think she would be happy to see roaches. Yet she was—sort of.

Trent opened the container and used tweezers to remove one and hold it out for them to inspect. "As you can see, on the front end of the thorax is a tiny wireless control module powered by a rechargeable battery attached to a solar cell."

The bug's entire body was covered with plastic and wires ran to the legs.

"The wires stimulate the leg segments." Trent placed the roach back in the box and secured the top. "Allows us to send the bugs where we want them to go. And the solar panel on top keeps everything charged. With just a handful of roaches, we can thoroughly scour a building in record time."

"Disgusting yet very interesting." Ryleigh wrinkled her nose.

"I concur." Finn pretended to shudder.

"Let's put these bad boys to work." Grady quirked an eyebrow and smiled. "Someone grab the controllers."

Blake reached into the van and opened another bin to reveal handheld controls that resembled video game controllers with a computer screen mounted on the side. He handed one to Trent and Grady, then took one for himself.

Trent held his out to display it for them. "This device works on Bluetooth and is basically the same system as you would use to control a robot."

Grady picked up the roaches and started for the driveway, where he held up his hand. "End of the road for you all. Stay up here for your safety. We'll keep you updated."

Ryleigh didn't want to be left behind. She wanted to watch the camera feeds from the bugs, but she also didn't want to get hurt. Nor did she want the three men continuing down the hill and toward the building to be hurt either. She offered a prayer for their safety and that they wouldn't discover that someone perished or was injured in the building.

The guys halted near the crumbled structure.

"Anyone here?" Blake called out and paused to listen.

No sound. Not even a squeak.

The sun broke through puffy clouds, blinding Ryleigh.

She cupped her hand over her eyes to get a better look at the action below. Trent went to the far end of the building, and Blake stopped near the middle. Grady joined Trent, took out a roach and called out an ID number.

Trent tapped his screen a few times. "Got him. Let him rip."

Grady placed the roach at the edge of the building, and Trent started moving his controller. "We're good to go."

Grady joined Blake and called out another number.

Blake studied his controller's screen. "Yep. I see him. Ready."

Grady took one out and followed the same procedure as the other two men.

"This is so cool." Finn stood on his toes and held a hand over his eyes. "I mean it would be if they weren't looking for survivors or victims from a bomb."

"Agreed," Ryleigh said, but it really wouldn't do to be too excited until the men cleared the building. Only then would they know for sure if someone had perished in this explosion.

Hanging back like this wasn't Finn's idea of a good time. The stakes were so high. The team could locate someone who hadn't been able to call out. Who was seriously injured or dead. Lying in tangled and twisted wreckage. From his SEAL days, Finn could easily imagine having to go down to the wreckage to free someone, and his gut was tight with concern.

Stop. Visualizing a traumatic scene doesn't help.

He looked at Ryleigh. "We should start considering that if the bombs were set by the same person, then whoever perished in the first bomb might not be our bomber."

"Yeah, he wouldn't be alive to set this one unless they were both placed on the same day." She locked gazes with Finn. "We could be looking for two people, but if Gates died in the first blast, and he isn't the bomber, why was he at the mill at that time?"

"This is so frustrating." Finn curled his hands into fists. "We should have an answer to that by now."

He watched as Trent moved over to Blake, and Grady joined them. They held a brief conversation.

"They must know something." Finn's heart started to pump wildly.

Grady looked up the hill. "We're all clear. No additional devices, victims, or survivors waiting for rescue."

Finn let out a long breath. "Finally, some good news."

Ryleigh kept her gaze pinned down the hill. "Now we can pick this building apart and look for evidence."

"That'll be a big job. Even if we pulled in the entire Veritas team from the other site, it could take days." Finn looked at the rubble and pondered the search. "What if Russ let Tobias's workers help move debris? That could speed things up. Under the Veritas team's direction, of course."

Ryleigh looked at him. "Russ wants evidence before Monday. Means he'll likely approve it, and so will Tobias."

"I have something," Grady shouted. "Finn, you'll want to look at this."

Finn charged down the hill, dodging debris on the way. He heard Ryleigh coming after him.

Grady looked up from his controller. "My roach is in the front left quadrant of the building. Glass says it's near where a window had been located. The extensive damage and the outward placement of the glass tells me the concussive force originated there."

"Any evidence of a computer or photoelectric cell?" Finn asked.

"Not yet." Grady held up his controller and tapped the screen that displayed the video recorded by his roach. "But see this? Looks like the same plastic wrapping from explosives Shadow Lake Logging uses."

Finn leaned closer and shaded his eyes from the sun. "It does indeed."

"I want to get excited about this," Ryleigh said. "But don't other loggers use the same explosives?"

"But I'm not sure they all write the received date on them like Tobias insists on." Finn glanced between her and Grady. "When new explosives arrive, the receiving clerk uses permanent marker to date each tube. Looks like part of a date on that wrapper."

"Yeah." Grady grinned at Finn. "Yeah, it does."

Finn jerked a thumb over his shoulder. "So it very likely came from this depot."

"Then let's get this roach inside the building to see if we can safely enter it to check the inventory." Grady used his controller to bring his roach out of the building.

As much as Finn appreciated this technology, he had to admit to being creeped out by the roach.

Grady picked up the bug. "You two stay here. I don't want you close to the building until I make sure it's safe."

He crossed the property and bent to set his roach in the space under the door then moved his controller, his focus intent on the screen. He maneuvered his controller, and the bug disappeared. Finn knew Grady was not only looking for devices set with a photoelectric cell, but for boobytraps too. He would search the door area, especially around the frame, where a tripwire could've been placed to trigger a device when the door opened.

Thankfully, the depot was a small building and could easily be searched. Or at least Finn thought it was easy. He'd never controlled a live bug, but he'd played his share of video games to know eye-hand coordination was the key to success.

Grady looked up from his controller. "Place is clear."

Finn charged over to Grady. "Then let's get this lock open and get inside."

"This is a crime scene now, so if you're going in, you'll have to suit up," Grady said.

"I'll get dressed and come right back." He didn't wait for permission to take a suit from the van but charged up the hill, his legs fueled with adrenaline. If they discovered missing explosives, it could mean the security video could have captured images of the thief.

He chose the largest size of one of the ugly white suits from the box, but he barely fit, and the suit stretched tight on his body. He looked much like the other guys, but he was taller so the legs were even shorter on him.

He jogged back down the hill, put on the booties, and looked at Ryleigh. "Do you remember the inventory count?"

She nodded. "Seventy-two white ones and seventy of the red tubes."

Grady looked up at the building. "Looks like the security camera is intact, and we could get our bomber on video. I didn't see a computer inside. Is it stored in the cloud?"

Finn nodded. "Same is true of the cameras on the office building. So we should have footage right up until the explosion took the cameras out."

Finn looked at Grady and then at Ryleigh. "I know Grady cleared this place, but I want you both to step away. Just in case the roach missed something."

"It's not necessary." Grady moved his roach out of the building and held it up. "I have full confidence in this little guy, but I appreciate your caution."

Ryleigh lifted her chin. "I have faith in Grady's assessment and will stay put too."

"Then you have the key," Finn said.

Ryleigh slid it into the lock and twisted. The arm dropped open, and she let it fall to the ground.

"Okay, step back." He trusted the roach—to a point. And really wished Ryleigh had moved away, but he couldn't force her to go.

He took her spot and held his breath. He slowly eased the door open. Nothing happened. No explosion. No sound, save the groaning door hinges.

He stepped inside.

A few items had fallen to the floor, likely due to the reverberations from the bomb, but the explosives all remained in their boxes on the shelves.

Grady put on booties and stepped inside too, and Ryleigh hung by the door. Maybe she was watching Finn as Russ was going to pitch a fit when he found out Finn had gone into the depot. But he had witnesses here to prove he didn't take anything.

"I got the red ones." Grady began running a finger down the tubes.

Finn moved to the white tubes and started counting.

Grady looked back at Ryleigh. "Seventy-two of the white ones on my first count, but I'll double-check."

"That's a match for the inventory," Ryleigh confirmed.

"Seventy of the red tubes," Finn announced and tried to keep his disappointment out of his voice.

"Looks like no one accessed the depot then since I was here with Russ," Ryleigh said. "And the bomber won't likely be on the video."

Finn was disappointed. Sure he was, but... "We had two cameras on the main building. One is focused on the door. The other had a wider range. Both are motion activated.

The wide-angle device could've picked up someone outside the office."

Ryleigh looked at Finn. "Then let's get to reviewing it. We should go to Russ's office to download files if there are any. Chain of custody and all of that."

Finn snapped off his gloves. "We both might have access to the files and can download them, but we'll need Tobias's approval to cover our bases. You call Tobias while I drive."

Grady stepped outside. "I'm sure Blake will split the forensic team with the mill site and get the forensics going here. I can start by recovering that packaging, and we'll go from there."

"Thanks, man." Finn bumped fists with Grady and followed Ryleigh, who was already racing up the hill as if a fire chased her.

She really was invested in finding out who was behind these bombs. She was desperate to keep bad publicity from ruining her family's company and also find the bomber. Finn had added motivation now too. Not only did he need to clear his name so family services didn't take Avery from him, but he too wanted to help save the Steele family's reputation along with bringing in the bomber.

They climbed into his truck, and he maneuvered around the other vehicles to get them pointed toward Russ's office.

Ryleigh took out her phone and made the call. "Tobias. Good. I'm glad I caught you."

She explained the reason for her call. From what Finn could hear of the conversation, it didn't seem as if Tobias was fighting access to the video files.

"Thanks, Tobias," she said. "Also, if Russ approves, do you think your crew would like to help the forensic team move the rubble at your office?"

Tobias's raised tone came through the phone, but Finn couldn't make out his words.

"Okay, good. I'll let you know." She ended the call and smiled at Finn. "We're good on the videos."

"Sounded like Tobias objected to his men helping with the debris," Finn said.

"Only that he would have to pay them when the company isn't bringing in any income." She tapped her phone screen. "I'm texting Russ to update him and let him know to expect us."

He glanced at her when she was too focused to know he was watching. He was getting used to having her at his side, and he liked it. Liked her. Maybe more than liked.

She laid her phone on her lap and looked at him. "Since the Eckles's place is just down the road, we should stop on our way to show the boot photo to Pauline."

"Good idea. She could very well ID the person who trashed Gates's place, and he could be our bomber."

"True, but we have no proof of that." She stowed her phone and tapped the clock on the dash that read four-thirty p.m. "Only an hour before you have to get home to Avery. You sure we have time to do both things?"

"I can wait until five forty-five, but Russ probably won't let us review the files anyway."

"You could be right." She sat back, a pensive look on her face. "Can I help with dinner tonight?"

"Saturday night we make personal pizzas from scratch, so we'll each make our own."

"Oh, okay," she said. "Sounds good."

"It's another one of Felicia's traditions. Avery hasn't seemed to really enjoy it, but maybe with the way she's opening up, tonight will be different."

"As long as you don't try to brush her hair." Ryleigh laughed.

Finn should laugh too, but his failure over braiding was

a sore spot with him. "Maybe after dinner, you can teach me how to do those braids."

"Of course. But I have to warn you." She paused and cast a serious look his way. "It's probably the hardest thing you'll ever have to master. Even harder than becoming a SEAL."

She laughed, a full-throated sound that made him wish they were on a date, and she wasn't forced to be with him in a hunt for a deadly bomber. But she *was* forced to be here, and he had to remember that. Even if she was fitting in. Even if she was great to be with. And even if he was falling for her big time.

He forced his mind to the drive and that alone, enjoying the wooded area until the Eckles's metal mailbox, dinged with buckshot, appeared at the road. He turned down their drive. Gravel crunched under his tires, and tall grass and weeds swished against the wheels. Two vehicles were parked in front of the small and unimpressive house.

"Looks like they're both home," he said as he killed the engine.

"That baby is taking its sweet time in arriving." Ryleigh slid out.

He followed her up to the door and pounded hard.

Eckles opened it and glared at them. "You ever gonna leave us alone?"

"Yes, if you've done nothing wrong." Ryleigh met his gaze, her shoulders back. "Can we come in for a minute?"

"I'd rather not." Eckles crossed his arms, a strong whiff of Italian spices and garlic drifting out of the house. "We're about to sit down for supper. We'd like to eat in peace and have some alone time before the baby is born."

"This will take just a second," Finn said. "We have a photo to show you and Pauline."

Eckles sighed and dropped his arms. "Fine. She's in the kitchen. Wait here. I'll get her."

He took off, stomping in exaggerated steps.

"He isn't happy to see us," Finn said. "You think that means anything?"

"Maybe or he could just want his life to return to normal and be left in peace as he said. At least, that's what I would want. Especially with a baby on the way."

Finn imagined Ryleigh pregnant with his child, and the vision was not at all unpleasant. In fact, he liked it. He didn't even know the guy he'd become since he'd left the SEALs and spent a couple of months caring for Avery. Changed him and his priorities, that was for sure. And he liked the new guy better.

Talk about a shocker.

Pauline lumbered into the room, slapping oversized fuzzy pink slippers on the linoleum floor. The old floral apron covering her belly was dotted with spaghetti sauce, the cause of the aroma that had made Finn's mouth water.

Eckles trailed her. They stopped by the door, and he took her hand.

She gave them a defiant stare. "You have a picture to show me?"

"Do you know who might wear boots like this?" Ryleigh displayed the photo for Pauline, and Eckles looked over his wife's shoulder.

"Oh. Oh! Yeah. Yeah. Dean has a pair like that. Dean Keenan." She rolled her eyes. "He thought he looked so cool with those and his leather jacket from New Rock."

"You're sure he wears them?" Finn asked.

"Positive. Saw it with my own two eyes when I was in the group." She freed her hand from her husband's hold and planted both of them on her back. "And when Carla was here, she said he's still wearing them. The matching jacket too. Like he couldn't let go of the past or her."

"I can confirm that," Eckles said. "I never saw the boots

but heard Pauline and Carla talking about them. Laughing too."

Ryleigh looked at Pauline. "Do you know anyone else who wears this make of boot?"

"Nah, who would want to wear them?" She grimaced. "Maybe they were cool at one time, but that time has passed."

Ryleigh stowed her phone. "Would you both be willing to testify to the fact that Keenan wears this style of New Rock boots?"

Pauline looked at her husband, and they both nodded.

"And you're sure you haven't seen him in years?" Finn asked.

Pauline bit her lip.

Okay, what was up with that? Had they lied again?

"As Russ told you, if you hold back, he'll bring you up on charges." Ryleigh shared her gaze between the couple but let it land and sit on Eckles. "And I don't doubt he'll do it."

"Dean was here." Pauline glanced at her husband. "I'm sorry. I had to tell them. I don't want to go to jail. I just had to."

"That's okay, honey." Eckles took his wife's hand again but peered at Ryleigh. "He showed up here the day after Carla took off. Demanded to know where she was. He threatened us. Said if we told anyone he'd been here, he'd come back and kill the baby."

Pauline rested her free hand on her belly. "I shouldn't have told you. Now this little one is in danger."

"He won't come back." Eckles rubbed her back. "He's forgotten all about us and is focused on tracking Carla down."

"God help her when he finds her as no matter how careful she is, I'm sure he will." Pauline shivered.

"Hopefully we'll find him first," Finn said.

"Okay, for the last time, is that everything?" Ryleigh eyed them both. "You're not holding back again."

"No, no," Pauline said. "That's all. Honest."

Finn didn't know what to think. They seemed sincere, but they'd lied very convincingly.

"Thank you for your time." Ryleigh turned to leave.

"Wait?" Pauline called out. "Did Dean set the bomb at the mill?"

"We're not at liberty to say anything at this point." Ryleigh headed down the stairs.

Finn followed, processing the news. After the door closed behind them, he faced her. "This is our best lead so far."

"You're right." Her words were upbeat, her tone not so much as she quickly strode toward his truck. "But it's only a lead. Still doesn't tie Keenan to the bomb."

Finn opened the passenger door for her and met her gaze. "Then let's hope the video from the depot or logging office does just that."

17

Finn trailed Ryleigh into the conference room that smelled of popcorn, and his mouth watered. He was looking forward to pizza night more than usual. Not only because he was hungry but because it would be good to chill out for a while when things had been so tense today.

He pulled out a chair for her when Russ marched through the door and eyed them both.

Oh boy. Here it comes.

"Neither of you will be touching those video files." He planted his feet as if expecting an argument.

"Figured you'd say that." Finn dropped into the chair next to Ryleigh. "But you do need one of us to give you the login information."

Russ grabbed a notepad and pen and fired them across the worn laminate table toward Finn. "Write it down. I'll do the rest."

"Will do." Finn tried his very best not to sound irritated. "But could you at least log in before we leave and check for files? There might be only a couple to review, and you could look at them and tell us what they contain."

Russ frowned. "I suppose I can do that."

Finn grabbed the pen and scribbled down the web address for the cloud site along with his username and password.

Russ snatched up the paper. "Be right back."

He departed as swiftly as some of the RPGs Finn had launched during his service days.

Finn looked at Ryleigh. "You didn't tell him we identified Keenan as the one whose boots were on the Roomba video."

"Neither did you."

Ah, turn it back to him. Nicely played. "I didn't want to prejudice him on the video. If he knew about Keenan, he might try to see the guy when it isn't him."

"Same for me." Ryleigh's phone rang. "It's Sierra."

Ryleigh tapped the speaker button and set her phone on the table between them. "You're on speaker with Finn. Please tell me you have news for us on the photoelectric cell."

"Sorry, not yet," Sierra said. "I just got to my lab and will begin processing it as soon as we get off the phone. But I got a call from my guys dismantling Gates's vehicle, and they've finished their work."

"And?" Finn prodded.

"And most interesting is they found blood in the back. Not a large quantity so could be from a simple cut. Or someone bled out in the vehicle and it was cleaned up well."

"Blood," Ryleigh said. "Didn't expect that."

"Don't read too much into it just yet. Could be from an on-the-job injury. Anything really. But we'll run it for DNA and that might tell you something."

"We'll wait for further news, then," Finn said.

"My team also found Gates's phone, which Nick will image and review, plus they recovered multiple sets of fingerprints along with some additional particulates that they gave to Winter. They also located Gates's vehicle keys hidden under the driver's seat. Looks like a house key on the ring too, but no brass key like you described for the explosives' depot."

So maybe someone had stolen Gates's key and used it to take the explosives.

"Chad didn't find it at the guy's house either, right?" Ryleigh asked.

"No," Sierra said. "So it's still missing."

Now they were tasked with figuring out where it had gone, but Finn didn't know where to start on that until he had time to think.

"I won't get to processing these vehicle prints until I get back to the mill," Sierra said. "But Chad will do a comparison on the ones lifted at Gates's place to eliminate those. I'll get back to you as soon as I've cleaned and processed the photoelectric cell for prints. I'll send an email to everyone to update them."

"Okay, thanks for the update." Ryleigh ended the call and turned to discuss this latest news with Finn, but Russ rushed into the room carrying an iPad. "We have one video from the depot."

"Can we look at it?" Ryleigh asked.

"Figured you'd ask." He set the iPad between them and tapped the video play button.

Finn fixed his focus on the screen, hoping he could ID the man's face. The night was dark and shadowy. No movement, but something had activated the camera. A large figure came out of the building. A man. In a hoodie.

"He's not carrying anything." Finn stared at the screen. "No explosives so what was he doing in there?"

Ryleigh leaned closer to the iPad. "I'd say he planted something, but we didn't see anything out of place."

The man turned to lock the door. Finn squinted to get a

look at his face, but shadows cast over his face deep in his hoodie. He spun to go. Taking long steps.

"His boots!" Ryleigh poked the screen. "It's Keenan. It really is."

"Yeah," Finn said. "Yeah, it is! Keenan's our guy."

"Hold up." Russ paused the video and glanced between them. "You showed me the boots but you didn't say anything about Keenan owning a pair."

Finn told him about their visit to Pauline.

Russ went around the table and dropped into a chair. "Ties Keenan to Gates."

Ryleigh nodded. "Keenan had a key in that video, and Sierra just told us that they found Gates's keyring and his depot key wasn't on it. So maybe Keenan stole Gates's key when he trashed his place and stole the explosives that night."

Russ's gaze cut around the room and landed on one of the whiteboards. "Good theory, but we don't have any evidence with him stealing the explosives. No evidence, no proof of his involvement. Except that he went into the depot."

"Maybe he shows up on the earlier videos." Ryleigh leaned forward, her eyes gleaming with enthusiasm. "Have you finished reviewing them?"

Russ nodded and leaned back in his chair. "Since you started requiring all visitors to sign in, we were able to ID everyone in the videos. No Keenan."

"Which means he didn't come to the site before this. Or at least he didn't trigger a camera." Ryleigh sat back. "The question then is, did he steal the explosives or not?"

Finn didn't know the answer either. "He could've been onsite but the camera malfunctioned."

"How likely is that?" Russ asked.

"It can happen," Ryleigh said. "The video goes to the

service provider first before recording on the company account and fails to connect more often than I would hope."

That could be their answer. At least Finn hoped it might be. "Did any of the videos display a static or a black screen?"

"I remember a couple of them in the middle of the night," Russ said. "Figured it was an animal or leaves moving that triggered the camera, but it didn't pick up the animal."

"Keenan could've visited in one of those times," Finn said. "Can you look at them again to see how long the videos lasted? Maybe he had time to get in, take the explosives, and get out while the camera was trying to connect."

"That could very well have happened," Ryleigh said. "Though he couldn't have planned for an outage unless he had a signal jammer."

Russ planted his hands on the table. "Sadly, thieves are using those more often to block signals on home doorbell cameras."

"You can buy one online for ten bucks," Ryleigh said.

Russ shook his head. "Policing these days isn't what it used to be."

"It's a challenge for sure," she said. "But the technology has also helped catch tons of bad guys and put them away."

"True." Russ shot to his feet. "I'll get with Colin on this. For now, Keenan looks like our top suspect."

"Agreed," Ryleigh said.

"I'll have my team go back through those video lapses," he said. "See if we missed anything. And I'll ask them about the silver-heeled boots."

She also told him about the blood in Gates's truck and Sierra's take on it.

"Interesting twist, but she's right," Russ said. "We should wait for the DNA. Keep me updated on any developments, and we'll meet again first thing tomorrow."

He spun and departed without waiting to see if they had any questions. He was clearly used to being a leader, something Finn could respect.

Finn glanced at the clock. "We should get going."

Ryleigh sat for a moment before getting up and heading for the door. "I wish these videos had provided answers—not more questions."

"Agreed." He walked by her side to the lobby. He wanted to be the one to give her those answers, but he couldn't. At least not yet, and that grated on him. He was a fixer. A doer. The past two days had been more waiting and pondering than doing. Not his wheelhouse at all.

He held the exterior door for her and opened the truck door too. He should be spoiling this woman. Pampering her on a nice date. Not helping her find a killer.

"We should review Colin's reports again." She climbed up on the seat, her mind obviously still on the investigation. "Especially the ones on Keenan, Carla, and the other Sovereign Earth members. Maybe we'll see something we missed."

"We can do that right after Avery goes to bed," he said, closing her door. He jogged to his side of the vehicle, wishing that they could spend quiet time together instead. Recouping. Refreshing. And getting to know even more about each other.

Yeah, he'd changed all right. For the better he hoped, but what if once Ryleigh got to know the softer, more relaxed side of him, she didn't like him?

She buckled her belt with a solid click. "Can we make time to play a little soccer with Avery? She's really talented, and I'd love to give her more pointers."

"We'll have to ask her what she wants to do. Pizza night is usually movie night too, but she might make an exception for you."

"Either way, some downtime sounds good." Ryleigh sat back and looked out the window.

She was done talking. He didn't mind the silence between them, but he wanted more. Maybe the easiness they'd once shared. Talking. Joking. Laughing. Finishing each other's sentences. She'd been much more lighthearted than him, and she brought that side out in him too.

As a SEAL, he'd been constantly on edge. Waiting for danger. Planning and prepping for the worst so it didn't come to pass and take out anyone on the team. But he'd honestly felt more balanced around her. Relaxed and content.

Could they ever get that easiness back and find a way to be together even with hundreds of miles between them?

He hadn't changed his mind about moving Avery before she was ready. No compromise on that. None at all. And just like he couldn't see how Keenan got the explosives from the depot, he couldn't see a way around a long-distance relationship.

So stow it. Stow your feelings.

Ryleigh was off limits.

Remember that. Don't hurt her again.

Something else that he couldn't compromise on either. No matter how painful it was for him.

The drive to Finn's house where Avery was being cared for by her babysitter was short, but Ryleigh had relaxed and sleep beckoned. She would love to take a quick nap before dinner, but she also wanted to spend time with Avery.

What a surprise. Ryleigh had never thought of herself as mother material. She doubted Finn considered himself father material either, but here he was raising a child by himself. And from what Ryleigh had seen, he was putting that can-do SEAL attitude into his every move and doing the best job he could do.

Ryleigh understood. The child's terrible loss really spoke to Ryleigh's heart, and the desire to help Avery find joy in life again ate at Ryleigh. Much like she'd seen in Finn. So tonight, she would relax and forget about the bomber. At least until after Avery had gone to bed.

Finn pulled into the driveway. Avery sat on the porch steps. She waved wildly at them and then came running.

Finn stopped shy of the garage. "Something's up."

Ryleigh looked beyond Avery to movement on the porch. "Come on, now. What are *they* doing here?"

"Who?" Finn shifted into park.

"My grandparents." Ryleigh had to work hard to get the words out over her rising unease. "They're rocking away on your porch."

He glanced at her. "That's odd."

"For most grandparents," she said. "But not mine. They don't know what boundaries are in the lives of their grandchildren. It's sweet but can sometimes be over-whelming."

Irritating too, but she wouldn't speak badly of them. It was love—so deep that Ryleigh only hoped to emulate it one day—that motivated their every action.

Still, she dreaded this upcoming conversation and sat watching until Finn opened her door.

He gave her a pointed look. "Coming?"

Ryleigh got out. She had to believe they arrived to butt into her life. Thankfully, she'd only told Mackenzie about Finn and had sworn her to secrecy or her grandad would give Finn an earful.

Avery rushed up to Ryleigh and Finn, excitement burning in her eyes. "Your gran and grandad are here. I like them. They're nice. They brought cookies and other good stuff. I wish I had grandparents as nice as them."

Avery grabbed Finn's hand and dragged him toward the porch. He cast Ryleigh a plea for help, so she somehow got her feet moving, and the three of them reached the steps together. The situation in so many aspects would be idyllic. The sun shone warm and a soft breeze played over the yard, carrying the scent of roses from bushes dividing the next-door property. She was with the man she was falling for and his sweet little girl.

But then, her grandparents stared at her from the rocking chairs creaking with each move.

Her gran pushed ruby red glasses up her nose and smiled. "We knew you and this wonderful man would be working hard on the investigation and could probably use a home-cooked meal."

"Actually," Ryleigh said. "Finn cooked a fabulous dinner last night."

"He grilled burgers." Avery thrust her chest out. "They were really good."

"Thanks, Peanut." Finn held his hand out to Ryleigh's grandmother. "Finn Durham."

She clasped his hand firmly and shook. "Eloise Steele, and this is my fine husband, Artie."

No way her grandad, who was a former lawman, would sit for an introduction. He stood to shake hands and look Finn in the eye. "Nice to meet you, young man. Were you in law enforcement before your job with Shadow Lake Logging?"

Finn shook his head. "Retired SEAL."

"Impressive," her grandad said. "Thank you for your service."

"Ditto from me," her gran said. "We should probably get dinner going. Bring the basket, Artie."

"Wait," Ryleigh said. "Saturday night is pizza night. Avery's tradition."

"It's okay," Avery said. "She's making spaghetti, one of my favorites. Your grandad said it was the best spaghetti in all of the world, so I want to have it." She took Gran's hand. "Besides. She made her own bread. Can you imagine? Making your own bread. It must be really good."

"Avery does like bread," Finn said.

Ryleigh's gran looked down at Avery. "Ryleigh can bake bread too."

Avery's gaze flashed to Ryleigh. "You can?"

"Yes. Gran taught me."

Avery switched her focus to Gran. "Can you teach me too?"

"Of course. You're about the same age as when I taught Ryleigh, her sisters, and cousins."

Avery shot Ryleigh a wide-eyed look. "You have cousins too?"

"Three of them. All girls."

Avery frowned. "Man. You've got it all. A mom and dad, grandparents, and cousins."

"I am most blessed," Ryleigh said, trying to sound convincing while her wayward grandparents stood on Finn's porch where they really didn't belong.

"For now, why don't we start with teaching you how to make my spaghetti," her gran said. "Then tomorrow, maybe we can tackle the bread. If not, then on my next visit to see the Maddox family."

"You're staying the night?" The words flew from Ryleigh's mouth before she could control them. "But where?"

"The Maddox family kindly offered us a room."

"I know Russ and Ryan are bunking there too, so you could stay here if needed," Finn offered.

Ryleigh wanted to swat him, but she shoved her hands

in her pockets and held her breath as she waited for her gran to answer.

"Thank you for the kind offer, but we're looking forward to catching up with the Maddox family. We'll be glad to join you for church in the morning though." She clasped Avery's hand and marched inside.

Ryleigh wanted to argue. To ask her grandparents to go home before they figured out she had feelings for Finn and really settled in to their favorite pastime. Matchmaking. Which had intensified as she was the only granddaughter without a match. But she loved them with everything she was made of. She would never want to hurt them when they believed they were doing what was best for her.

It was just like the way God dealt with her—doing what was best for her even though she didn't see it. Or like it. So many things in her life that seemed like disasters or trials, and she could see God's hand in them. See how He had used the situation to grow her into the person she was today. If she'd never suffered, she wouldn't have the compassion she felt for Avery. Or even the compassion she needed to show Finn after the career he loved had come to an abrupt end.

So she would go with the flow. Let her gran make the meal and hope that things didn't get too uncomfortable during dinner.

Finn picked up a box of groceries.

Her grandad took the cooler next to it and then looked at Finn. "You fish, son?"

Ryleigh groaned.

"What?" Her grandad looked at her, a broad smile on his face. "Can't a fella ask a question?"

"Honestly, I'm surprised it took you this long to ask him. Seems like it might be a record." She laughed.

"Hey," he said. "It's been like five minutes since we met.

I'm sure I've waited to ask someone far later than that." He chuckled and went toward the door but turned and looked at Finn. "Well, do you? Fish that is."

"I do indeed." Finn smiled. "I love to go fishing."

"Well, praise be." Her grandad's eyes sparkled, and she knew Finn had just won his heart. "Finally, one of the men in my granddaughters' lives who likes to fish. We'll have to go out sometime. But now, my sweetie needs this cooler."

He entered the house.

Finn looked at her.

"I know. They're something else," she said as she didn't know what else to say.

"They are for sure, but I like them, and Avery seems to as well. So let's forget about the investigation for a while. I'll send Avery's sitter home, and we'll just enjoy your grandparents' company for dinner."

A very generous attitude and it upped her respect for him.

She smiled up at him. Their gazes locked. Time stopped. Heat flashed between them. Sizzling like the fire, but this time warm and lovely. Not harsh and scary. Okay maybe a bit scary too. She shouldn't be gazing into his eyes. Wishing for more. Like maybe a kiss.

She broke the trance and rushed past him and into his house.

She would enjoy the dinner all right. Because she'd officially fallen for this guy again, and she wanted to be in his company.

Problem was, when this investigation ended, and she left Finn and Avery behind, she was in for a world of hurt, and there would be no way around the pain.

18

Finn struggled to eat. Not because the food wasn't good. Not because the company wasn't good. Both were great. He loved being with Ryleigh's family. But most importantly, Avery bloomed in their presence. Coming alive in a way he hadn't seen since her mother's death.

He set down his fork to look around the table. Avery sat between Eloise and Artie across from Ryleigh and him. He'd tried not to look at Ryleigh but could feel her next to him and feel her unease. She seemed to wait for her grandparents to do something she didn't care for. He wanted to reach under the table to take her hand, but that would likely make her jump and draw attention to them.

Besides, Avery was who really captivated him. Her big smile. The joy in her posture. And that was due to the warmth emanating from Ryleigh's grandparents. Eloise's gentle approach combined with Artie's comical antics had Avery beaming. Finn's grandparents were more reserved. Less open. Avery hadn't bonded with them like this.

But the biggest surprise of all?

Finn felt the child's joy to a degree that he thought would be reserved for his own child if he ever had one.

But now what? She was falling in love with the idea of having grandparents like Eloise and Artie. He would have to take her to see his grandparents more often and hope they warmed more to her. They tried, but they were older, and Avery seemed to exhaust them very quickly. He would make a point of visiting his sister, too and make the most of those relationships.

At some point, he would need to begin thinking about a relationship for himself and someday providing Avery with a mother.

He glanced at Ryleigh.

Could he even consider a relationship with another woman or was she the only woman for him?

He didn't know, but he could easily imagine her in his life. To wake up to her each day. Have breakfast with her and Avery. Coming home at night to both of them.

That seemed like something worth fighting for.

As they worked together, he would have to keep an open mind and decide if they could handle a long-distance relationship. Or even if she might be open to temporarily relocating to Shadow Lake. He wouldn't ask, of course. Even if he could sway her that way, she might grow to resent him for it.

He turned his attention back to his meal and put the last bite of crusty white bread into his mouth. He chewed, even enjoyed it, but was thankful when the meal came to a close and he could get up and move. "I'll clean up so you all can get going to visit with your friends."

Artie stood and looked at him. "Appreciate that, but not sure my Eloise will allow it."

She got up and studied Finn. "I would rather clean up, but it's your house so if you want to, I won't stand in your way."

"I want to," Finn said, brooking no argument as he had

to move. "It's the least I can do to thank you for such a wonderful meal and for making everyone feel at home."

Avery flung her arms around Eloise. "But I don't want you to go."

"Sorry, honey," Artie said. "We have to go now, but remember, we'll go fishing together soon if it's okay with Finn."

She spun on Finn. "Can I? Please."

He brushed her hair from her eyes. "Sure thing, Peanut."

"We'll see you in the morning for church and brunch," Eloise said.

How had he and Ryleigh transitioned from watching videos of a potential killer to talking about brunch? Just showed how life could change in a flash. The day Felicia died was the day Finn's life changed forever. In an instant. One minute he was a carefree single guy, and a telephone call later he was a full-time dad. Unbelievable.

Ryleigh moved around the table to her grandparents. "I'll walk you to the door."

She and Eloise turned for the door, and Avery clung to Eloise's hand.

Artie hung back. "Must've been tough to give up your life to come here and raise Avery. How are things going?"

"I have to say they weren't great." He frowned as the past memories of Avery's negative behavior assaulted him. "But I had a conversation with her to assure her that I was never leaving her. I think she finally believes it, and she's started to open up."

"Don't know how much this is worth, but my parents always told me the hardest things we go through in life will turn out to be the best for us in the long run. We can't see it when we're in it, but we can look back and see how it molded us as a person. Or God can often put someone special in our life. Someone we need. Someone like my granddaughter."

Finn didn't know how to respond to the last bit, but the first part he could relate to. "Your parents were very wise. As are you. Thanks for sharing it."

"And my granddaughter?" His gaze locked onto Finn, and Artie's thick glasses did nothing to hide his questioning gaze. "What are your intentions for her?"

"We're not in a relationship so—"

"So nothing." Artie took a firm stance and gone was the cuddly grandfather to be replaced by the retired law enforcement officer. "You both have feelings for each other. It's as plain as can be. You hurt her once before. I'm keeping an open mind on that, but don't do it again."

Finn couldn't help but gape. Artie and his wife had been so pleasant to him, and all the while they'd known he'd hurt Ryleigh. How could they have done that?

"You know about that?" he asked once he got control of his thoughts.

"Whole family does. Not that Ryleigh knows we're in the know, so keep this between us." He ran his gaze over Finn. "From what I can tell at this point, you seem like an honorable man. Be that guy with my granddaughter, and we'll get along just fine. Don't, and you'll not only have me to contend with but Ryleigh's whole family. A force you don't want to reckon with if you know what's good for you."

His gaze clung to Finn for a long moment, then the warning cleared from his eyes, and he held out his hand. "Nice to meet you and thanks for your hospitality. See you at church in the morning."

Finn shook hands but stood staring after the older man as he walked away. What had just happened? Ryleigh's grandad was like night and day. Hot and cold. A chameleon.

Unexpected for sure. But Finn would take the warning to heart.

The investigation might be filled with big fat questions but this one thing was crystal clear—if he couldn't commit to a future with Ryleigh, then an honorable man would keep his feelings to himself. And he was an honorable man, wasn't he?

∼

Ryleigh played a game of Uno at the kitchen island with Avery while Finn finished up the dishes. The silverware clanked as he loaded them in the basket, and the rooms still smelled like her gran's spaghetti. Ryleigh should focus on the game, but she kept thinking about dinner. She'd enjoyed the meal. Actually, she'd loved having Finn and Avery with her family. And her grandparents had behaved. She didn't know what her grandad had talked to Finn about at the end, but they both came out smiling, so no big deal, right? If her grandad was true to form, he'd been comparing fishing stories.

Finn closed and started the dishwasher running. The hum filled the background as he came to the island. "Time for bed, Peanut."

"Aw, I don't want to go to bed yet." Avery's lower lip seemed to grow ten sizes.

Ryleigh smiled at the child. "I'll read the Nancy Drew book with you."

"Okay." Avery hopped down from the stool and bolted from the room.

"She admires you." Finn started to gather the cards together.

Ryleigh looked at the doorway the child had disappeared through. "I admire her too. I guess it might seem weird to admire a child, but she's handling one of the toughest things anyone could ever deal with. I don't know if I could've done it when I was her age. Could even do it now." She faced Finn and found him watching her, a warm smile on his face. "And I admire you for handling it when you were a kid too."

He waved a hand. "That was a long time ago."

"Still, I know it left scars, and yet you're able to open your heart to Avery." She rested her hand on his. "You're a good man, Finn."

He jerked his hand free and busied himself with putting the cards in the box. Okay, what had she said? Done?

Something had changed during dinner, but what?

Avery came running into the room in bare feet and pajamas, giving Ryleigh no chance to ask. Avery flew at Finn, and her arms circled as far as she could reach. His face lit with surprise.

She peered up at him. "I made something for you today."

"You did?"

She stepped back and unfurled her hand to reveal an elastic bracelet made of multi-color beads. "It has my name in it so you don't forget about me while you're working."

She took his hand and slid the bracelet onto his wrist. The pastel beads looked out of place on the athletic man with a rugged build, but his eyes glistened with unshed tears.

He knelt and looked her in the eyes. "This is the nicest gift I've ever gotten."

Avery's eyes widened. "Really?"

"Really." Finn scooped her close for a hug, and a contented smile turned his lips up.

It was all Ryleigh could do not to leap up to hug the pair and share their joy. But this was their moment. A milestone in their relationship and a very special one. Anything she could say or do would spoil that.

Avery pulled back and bit her lower lip. "Promise you'll wear it all the time."

"I promise. Except when I shower."

"Yeah." She nodded hard. "You can take it off then. I made a matching one too, but it has your name on it. I'm going to go put it on right now." She kissed him on the cheek. "Night, Finn."

"Night, Peanut."

She ran to Ryleigh. "I'm sorry I didn't make one for you. I didn't have enough time."

"No worries." Ryleigh smiled. "I loved seeing the one you made for Finn."

Avery grabbed Ryleigh's hand. "Let's go get my bracelet and read."

Ryleigh let Avery lead her to her bedroom.

Avery retrieved the bracelet from her top dresser drawer and slid it on her wrist. "I think Finn liked it a lot."

"I know he did," Ryleigh said. "And I know he'll wear it all the time."

Avery slid under her covers, and Ryleigh sat on the bed to read the book. Avery snuggled against Ryleigh's side, and the warmth of the little body pulled at Ryleigh's heart.

"I like this." Avery sighed. "You snuggle better than Finn. Gran does too. More like my mom."

Ryleigh thought about her mother and gran. Ryleigh was so blessed to have both women in her life, and she needed to be more thankful for them. Her gran was getting up in years, and Ryleigh had to appreciate her even more before she lost her, and she was only a memory like Avery had of her mother.

She brushed Avery's hair from her face. "Mom's do have a special touch."

"But dads are fun," Avery said. "I don't know my real dad, but I think Finn's gonna be a good one."

"I think so too." Ryleigh imagined Avery and Finn's future together and all the milestones they would share.

Avery's first date. Going to college. Getting engaged. Married. Becoming a mom herself.

Trouble was, Ryleigh appeared in all the images that came to mind, and try as she might, she couldn't scrub herself out of them.

She had to get out of that room and clear her head. She returned to the story and read until Avery's eyes grew heavy.

Ryleigh closed the book. "Time for lights out."

"Aw," Avery said. "I'm going to miss you when you go home."

"I'll miss you too," she said and gave Avery a squeeze, then got up. "But for now, I'll see you in the morning."

"Night." Avery grabbed Ryleigh's hand, jumped up on the bed to give Ryleigh a butterfly-soft kiss on the cheek.

Ryleigh hugged the little girl. "That was sweet of you, Avery. Good night."

Avery clung to Ryleigh, but she extracted herself from the hug and felt like she might suffocate from all the emotions flowing through her. She rushed down the hall and out through the French doors onto the wide deck that ran the width of the home. She gasped for a deep breath of the cooler night air and leaned on the railing. Fearing a panic attack, she gazed up at the clear night stars sparkling like diamonds tossed into the sky.

She'd enjoyed dinner and tucking Avery in way too much for her own good. She started imagining meals like this all the time. Her and Finn. And that meant her as a mother. Wow! What a crazy thought to even ponder, much less pull the trigger on. Of course, Finn would have to want that too. Avery as well.

She didn't think he would want a relationship. Especially not now when everything was so fresh between him and Avery, and the child was just coming to trust him. No. That was a dream she had to pocket. For now. Maybe forever.

"You sure bolted." Finn's voice came from behind. "Everything okay?"

She jumped and spun. "You scared me."

"Sorry," he said, searching her face. "Did something happen with Avery?"

It did. Totally. But Ryleigh couldn't tell Finn that she was falling for a child and wanted to help take care of her. To help heal the little girl's heart with all the love Ryleigh's mother once lavished on her. Because Ryleigh couldn't be that mother for Avery. Ryleigh could never move here and leave her family. She'd never even considered such a thing.

Finn's gaze intensified, locking on hers. Digging. Probing.

She started to look away, but he took her chin softly in his hand, and his gaze softened into a blush of warmth. "I shouldn't do this. Told myself I wouldn't do this. But I can't help it. Not with the way you look in the moonlight. Captivating."

He slid his hand into her hair, cupped the back of her head, and drew her close as he lowered his head. He was going to kiss her. Right now. Right here. She should say no. Stop. But she inched toward him and wound her arms around his neck to pull him even closer. His body was rock solid and unyielding.

Time stood still. She waited for the touch of his lips. Knew what it would feel like. But it seemed like an eternity before he settled them on hers. She pressed into him. Into the kiss. Gave into the emotions of the past few days. Deepened the kiss and clung to him.

His arms went around her. Solid, yet he held her like she was fragile at first, then tightened his grip. She reveled in his touch. Wanted this more than anything right now. Wanted him in her life.

She let go of her worries. Of her fears and just kissed him back as if her life depended on it.

Her phone rang. Sounding like a mighty gong in the quiet of the night. She startled back to her senses. He jerked back. She took in long breaths. Not wanting the kiss to end, but wanting it to end at the same time.

She'd seriously fallen for him again. The kiss told her that. Big time.

She caught her breath and dug her phone from her pocket. "It's Russ."

She expected Finn to look disappointed at the abrupt end to their kiss, but he stepped back and appeared relieved. He hadn't wanted to kiss her. He'd said as much, but for some reason had given in. Much like her. Fighting the feelings that just wouldn't let go. Even now as her phone continued to ring.

She forced her attention to the call and answered. "Russ."

"Just thought you'd want to know," he said. "Sierra sent techs to Eckles's place to help look for Carla's phone. They located it right off the bat. Nick is running an image, and then he'll get the information to us."

"Did he say how long it would take?" She stole another long breath, her pulse racing.

"Couple of hours. So keep an eye out for it and for the call logs from Gates's phone too."

"Will do," Ryleigh said, then ended the call to tell Finn about it.

She looked at her watch.

Eight-thirty.

"I'm going to my room to rest so I'm fresh when the information arrives." She didn't wait for Finn to say anything but took off. Ran away—bolted was more like it.

She'd probably just lied to Finn. Not intentionally. She would try to rest, but she highly doubted she could sleep with the crazy thoughts that told her to turn around and throw herself into Finn's arms instead of putting the hunt for a killer first in her mind.

19

Finn sang the last line of the song in the small contemporary church he and Avery had been attending. Felicia had been a member here, and Avery was plugged into the children's ministry. She loved it, another reason why Finn was hesitant to move her. Not that he couldn't find another great church in another city.

If they moved to Portland, he liked the church he'd grown up attending, but they'd never transitioned into contemporary worship, which he favored these days. He assumed wherever the Steele family attended had to be great, but didn't mean it had his favorite form of worship either.

But moving held another challenge.

What job would he do? Military personnel often went into law enforcement. He thought he would like being a cop, but could he do the job while being the sole caretaker for Avery?

Would it be too dangerous? Would the child worry?

He couldn't do that to her. Even if he didn't like the job he ended up with, she took first place. Maybe he should talk to the Maddox brothers about starting his own survival business in Portland. Could he succeed at that? He would have to because, first and foremost, he had to provide for Avery.

The pastor offered his blessing, and Finn turned to the others who'd joined him this morning. The Maddox brothers and their parents, plus Reid's daughter Jessie and their cook, Poppy, who also belonged to this church, were there. Finn hadn't met them as they usually attended the early service. He and Avery came to the later one. Ryleigh and her grandparents had arrived too, and she'd sat with them in the row behind him. The entire visiting Veritas team filled three rows behind everyone.

For an hour they were able to forget about the crime awaiting them and focus on refreshing their souls. At least that was what Finn had been doing. Now he was ignoring his urge to look at Ryleigh to see if she would give him any hint of how she felt about last night's kiss. She'd been nothing but professional with him on the ride to church, but was her usual open and warm self with Avery.

Guess that told him what he needed to know. She might've liked the kiss—that wasn't in question for either of them—but she regretted it just as he did. Nothing honorable about giving in to it. He had to do better. Be the man her grandad expected Finn to be.

He turned the bracelet on his wrist. At least one thing wasn't a bust from the night before. He hoped the bracelet meant things would be easier between him and Avery from now on. He could at least say from his side that the moment brought out every protective instinct in him, and he knew he would do anything to keep his little peanut safe and for her to feel loved and cherished for the rest of her life.

Listen to him, even thinking a word like cherish. Ugh. Not a word that had ever been in his vocabulary, but it was there to stay now.

Eloise approached him. "Nice bracelet. Avery worked so hard to make it for you, and I'm glad to see you wearing it."

He released the beads and smiled. "When a special little seven-year-old offers you a bracelet, you wear it for as long as she wants."

"I haven't spent much time with you, young man, but as soon as I saw that bracelet on your wrist this morning, I knew you were a good man." Eloise smiled. "Ready for some brunch? Barbie and I have everything ready and in warming dishes in the fellowship hall, so we can serve the whole group."

He still couldn't get used to the fact that Barbara, the Maddox brothers' mother, was nicknamed Barbie. All he could think of was a Barbie doll. But from what he'd seen so far this morning, the name fit her free-spirited personality far better than Barbara or even Barb would.

"Thank you for going to all the trouble for us, but we'll have to eat and scram for a task force meeting," he said, his mind going to the information Nick had finally provided for the team this morning. Turned out Carla had a tough password on her phone and cracking it had taken longer than Nick had hoped, and he'd worked through the night.

Eloise waved a hand. "No worries. I live with a family of law enforcement or former law enforcement officers, and I'm used to that."

How Avery might have to deal if he took a law enforcement job came to mind. "How did your children handle the worry of their father potentially getting injured on the job?"

"When they each got old enough, we sat down and had a plain talk. Brought it out in the open and then encouraged them to talk about their feelings whenever they were afraid." She lifted her shoulders. "Every time the news reported an officer injured or slain it would come up. We didn't watch the news much in those days."

He nodded at her logic.

Her eyebrows rose over the large blue glasses she wore that morning. "Are you thinking of going into law enforcement?"

"Maybe in the future, but Avery's so devastated by losing her mom that I feel like I need to do a desk job so she doesn't have to worry about losing me."

"That is a concern." Eloise rested her hand on his arm. "I can see how desperate she is for a family, but I think that existed before her mother died. She told me she didn't know anything about her dad or blood relatives on his side."

Finn nodded. "She was conceived on a drunken one-night stand before Felicia came to faith. She doesn't know much more than the guy's name was Joe Carlisle, but she never looked him up. Told Avery that he loved her but wasn't ready to be a dad."

"So someday the child will want to find him, and you'll have to tell her the truth."

He nodded. "I'd do it now, but I know she either won't believe me or won't be able to handle it on top of losing her mom. But if I wait, will she hold it against me?"

She tsked. "You have a real predicament there."

"What would you do?"

"Me? Oh, I don't know. I suppose I'd wait until Avery's settled in who she is, and then if she mentions her dad, sit her down and tell her the truth."

"And hope she doesn't hate me for keeping it from her."

Eloise squeezed his arm and let go. "But here's the thing, Finn. You didn't create this problem, and I know you'll fix it in the best way possible. With God at your side as you do so, it'll all work out, and all the worry in the world isn't going to change things."

She was right. Of course she was. Worry was just bringing tomorrow's troubles forward to today. Troubles that might never come, but was there a parent alive who didn't worry at some time?

He doubted it. Didn't excuse his worry, but with having been thrust into the position of a single father, he suspected he would always be more prone to worry. He just had to overcome it.

But he had SEAL fortitude and that would never change. He and the guys often said the only easy day was yesterday, and he had to get comfortable being uncomfortable. That's what he had to do. After all, he was all in, all the time with Avery. He could do this.

Would do this.

"Let me go get Avery from the kid's program, and we'll meet you in the fellowship hall," he said and turned to leave, greeting the pastor and the few people he'd connected with in his short time there on the way out.

By the time he reached the gathering room, the kids had finished their worship, and Avery skipped his way. He'd never seen her skip, but then he'd not seen her often in her first seven years. Just occasional visits. More when she'd been a baby when Felicia needed more support, and he'd tried to provide it on his leave.

He smiled at the sweet child. "Looks like you had a good time."

"It was okay, but let's go. I promised Gran I would help serve the food." She thrust her hand into his and tugged him down the hallway toward the fellowship hall.

When she'd gotten so comfortable touching him, he didn't know, but he liked the feel of her tiny hand in his.

Chatter spilled from the room, and the aromas of freshly cooked bacon and onions, coffee, and toasted bread each fought for his attention. His stomach grumbled.

Inside the room, he found two long tables set up in a buffet line and loaded with warming dishes, a large coffee pot, stacks of paper products. Positioned near the food were round tables with white tablecloths, napkins wrapped around disposable silverware, pitchers filled with juice, and chairs butted up to them. Barbie and Eloise had gone to a lot of trouble and must have gotten up at the crack of dawn to pull off such a nice spread on such short notice, if they'd slept at all.

Ryleigh was standing near the front of the line with Colin, Ryan, and Russ, smiling at Colin. Finn didn't like her attention to the man, but they were just friends. That had become obvious. Still, Finn wanted her smiles but had no right to them.

Avery let go of his hand and wrapped her arms around Eloise, who stood at the buffet table lifting off warming lids. "You said I could help."

"And you can, sweetheart." She smiled down at Avery. "I have a very important job for you. I need someone to make sure the juice pitchers on the tables never run out of juice."

Avery let go and lifted her shoulders. "I can do that."

"Maybe you should eat before you start," Finn suggested. "So you'll be ready when your babysitter gets here to take you home."

Avery's lip trembled. "I want to stay here with Gran."

"I'm sorry, sweetheart," Eloise said. "We'll be heading back to Portland as soon as we clean up after the meal."

"But why?"

"That's where we live." She smoothed a hand over Avery's hair and bent lower. "But I have a secret for you if you can keep it."

Avery's eyes widened. "I can. Tell me."

"Grandad and I have reserved all of the Maddox cabins for Labor Day so the whole family can come down for the weekend and then you can meet Ryleigh's sisters and cousins. If Finn says it's okay to join us."

Avery's gaze flashed up to his. "Can we?"

"I hope so, Peanut," he said, being purposefully vague until he talked to Ryleigh about it.

Plus, it probably wasn't a good idea to encourage this relationship between Avery and Ryleigh's grandparents. Maybe as a seven-year-old she would forget all about them a day or so after they left. He could only hope he would too.

$\sim$

Ryleigh avoided Finn as she chewed the last of her perfectly browned bacon—crisp and crunchy in a way that her gran had perfected, but Ryleigh never seemed to achieve on her own. Finn had been ignoring her, too, until he came to the table where she sat with the rest of the task force team.

She was glad to see he wore the bracelet from Avery. They hadn't talked about it, but Ryleigh knew it meant a great deal to him just by the look on his face when he'd received it.

Russ cast a frustrated look at Finn. "Eat up, man. We've got work to do."

"Had to get Avery settled first," Finn said with not a hint of justification in his tone as he attacked the egg casserole sitting next to bacon, sausage, fresh fruit, and toast on his plate.

She was glad he didn't feel the need to apologize for being a good dad, and she smiled her approval.

He returned it with a genuine brightening of his face. She'd been terse with him in the truck on the way to church. She didn't want to be, but when an almost uncontrollable urge to hold his hand took control of her, she'd had to take a firm stance. She'd even had to sit on her own hand so she didn't reach out, and that made her mad at herself.

Russ leaned forward and lowered his voice. "You all look at the data from Carla's phone?"

"Give us a chance, we just got it," Ryan complained around a mouthful of eggs.

"Then let me tell you about it. Nick found a bunch of deleted calls to a Gerry Horne. Guy had a history of ecoterrorism and lives out in the boonies near Round Prairie. Don't know much else about him at this point. Figured Ryleigh and I would pay him a visit when we finish here, and then we'll have that update meeting if needed."

The others nodded.

"We're still waiting on Gates's phone logs." Russ cast a pointed look at Nick.

Nick took a long sip of his juice, not looking the least bit put out by Russ. "You'll have the data as soon as my team finishes."

Colin set his fork on his empty plate. "I culled down the list of Sovereign Earth members who could potentially be related to this incident and emailed the list to everyone. Four names came up that might be worth looking into, but it's marginal at best."

"We can tackle that after we interview Horne." Russ shifted to look at Finn. "You have duty at the bomb scene with Veritas. Any problem with that or are you on daddy duty?"

Finn held a fork with a chunk of ripe cantaloupe in the air. "No problem."

"Good. Good." Russ looked at Colin. "I want you to dig for information on Horne so by the time we get to his place we know everything about him, even how often he sneezes in a day. And I'd like satellite images of his property first. Don't want any surprises."

Colin pushed his chair back and picked up his empty plate and cup. "Then I best get started."

He dumped his items in the trash and took off for the door.

Ryan sipped his coffee. "Grady has some questions for me, so I'll meet with him when we finish up here."

Russ clapped his hands, and the room went quiet as people stared at him.

He shook his head. "Sorry to disturb you."

The others went back to their conversations, but the level lowered to a quiet hum as if they might be listening for what Russ had to say next. He had a very commanding presence. Couple that with the uniform he wore, and he seemed like a force to be reckoned with.

Hopefully this Horne fellow would be intimidated by them and cooperate by giving up Keenan's whereabouts if he knew it.

Russ peered at her. "You about ready to hit the road?"

Ryleigh nodded and grabbed her dishes before looking at Finn. "I'll likely get back to the crime scene before our shift is up."

"Be careful." He held her gaze as if he wanted to say more, then picked up a slice of bacon.

She tossed her dishes but filled her cup with coffee and added a lid. Russ was already at the door tapping his foot.

Still, she stopped to hug her gran and grandad. "Thanks for this amazing brunch."

"Hank and Barbie did their share too."

"But if I know you, Gran, you did all of the cooking."

"'Course she did." Her granddad laughed. When he quit, he pointed at Finn. "Now you go easy on that young man. Give him a chance."

"You're not trying to matchmake, are you?" She grinned. "That's Gran's job."

"Hey, you been married for as many years as we have,

and you don't know where one of you starts and the other finishes." He chuckled.

"And he's right," her gran said. "Finn seems like an upstanding guy. Just look at how he gave up his whole life for sweet little Avery."

But wouldn't give it up for me.

Oh, wow! Was she still holding that against him? She'd forgiven him for hurting her, but had she forgiven him for not letting her take first place in his life? God always came first, but she probably wouldn't come next now either. Not with Avery to care for. That Ryleigh understood. But coming second to a job when he'd been a SEAL? Maybe not as much.

Russ glanced at her and tapped his watch.

"See you soon." She gave her grandparents one last hug and rushed to the door. "Just saying goodbye to my grandparents and thanking them for the meal."

"I appreciate that, but we can't let this Horne guy skate." Russ marched out to his patrol car.

She had to jog to keep up and climb in at the same time as he did while balancing her coffee. She set her cup in a holder and buckled her seatbelt.

Russ tapped Horne's address into a GPS program. He got his belt on and ripped out of the parking lot.

"There are kids around," she said. "You might want to slow down."

"I know what I'm doing," he said, but the vehicle slowed some. "Keep an eye on your email for any updates from Colin."

She took out her phone and laid it on her knee face up so she could see the screen flash with a message or text before it even sounded an alert. She would normally rely on the signal, but she figured seeing her take action might help Russ calm down.

He had the radio on low, and the dispatch calls played in the background. That couldn't be good for his nerves either. She would try to get him involved in small talk until they got closer to Horne's place and had to pay attention.

She glanced at the address. "Why do all these ecoterrorists live out in the boonies?"

"That's a question for Colin, but if I had to guess they're probably free-spirited and don't like the rules of living in a town. Plus, they like to be self-sufficient. Grow organic veggies and free-range chickens. I'm just guessing based on what my mom and Poppy have said, as some of the people they grew up with would probably be called ecoterrorists today."

"Your mom was once part of a commune, wasn't she? But I never knew the details." Ryleigh sat back and picked up her cup. "Tell me about her, and how she met your dad."

"Nothing to tell really," he said, sounding as if he didn't like the topic. "Her parents moved out here in the sixties from the Midwest and joined a hippie commune. She was born and raised there, but when she hit eighteen, she took off to see the world. Met Dad at a Rod Stewart concert one of his buddies dragged him too."

"Really? Your dad doesn't seem like a big rock concert goer."

"He's not. Has always been kind of buttoned down. He followed in my grandpa's footsteps and became an accountant to support the family. But he always loved the outdoors more, so he invested wisely and bought the resort. Then he set up his own CPA business and took as many clients as he could handle while also managing the resort."

"And starting the guide business."

Russ nodded. "By then he only had a few accounting clients he'd kept on for years so he could focus on the outdoors more."

"Why did the resort close?"

"Business got to be too much for Mom and Dad, and we were all doing our own thing."

"And none of you wanted to take over for them?" She took a sip of the coffee. Strong and black just like she liked.

He glanced at her. "Don't take this the wrong way, but after being in the hospitality business all our lives, none of us wanted to do it. Too many demands and complaining campers. But then Reid's wife died, and he decided to leave the FBI to be with Jessie more. Ryan was just next door, so we figured we could get a survival business going and make enough money to at least support Reid. Turned out better than we could've hoped."

"But you really don't want to join in the family business full-time?"

"No." Russ clicked on his blinker. "I'm more like my dad than my mom, and this job suits my personality. Cut and dried with a lot of rules." He laughed and glanced at her. "I'm surprised you left the FBI. A lot of law enforcement officers would do just about anything to get into the bureau."

"Family has to come first, right?" she asked.

"I suppose, but I'm not sure I would be as selfless as you."

"Don't get me wrong, I did it primarily for the family, but it also got to the point that I didn't feel like I was making much of a difference anymore."

"I get that, but I do see the difference I make on a daily basis."

"Cybercrime is a lot different than local policing. You shut one group down and another group can be up and running, creating a huge problem worldwide so quickly your head spins."

"Yeah, I can see that. Our crime is pretty finite. Though the drug trade has gotten to be a big problem that isn't so easily policed. Especially with the fentanyl issues. It's changed everything overnight, and I honestly fear for our future."

The light flashed on her phone. "Email from Colin."

She opened the message. "He included satellite photos and background on Horne. Guy's nearly seventy. Was big in Sovereign Earth in the eighties. Colin couldn't find much since then except one photo of him with Keenan at a logging protest in Alabama about twenty years ago. He was arrested twice for disturbing the peace during similar protests."

"Sounds like he might not be active or our bomber, but he could still know where Keenan is located."

"Yeah." She kept reading but nothing else jumped out at her.

Russ slowed and leaned forward to look in the direction of a mailbox. "We're here."

She looked up to see private property and no trespassing signs alongside signs warning of dogs. "Horne doesn't want visitors for sure."

"Might be all bark and no bite, but I'd like to take a look at that satellite footage before we go in." Russ pulled to the side of the road and got his phone from his shirt pocket. He tapped the screen. "Property's overgrown. Several outbuildings and places he could take cover to evade us. I've got a spare vest in the trunk. Let me get it for you."

He checked his mirror and then slid out.

She didn't like the idea of requiring a Kevlar vest. Russ was likely just being cautious, but still, she needed to take extra care. She pulled out her weapon and popped out the magazine to check it was fully loaded. Not that she really doubted it, but better to be safe than sorry. Besides, seeing the bullets gave her confidence, and she slid the clip back in place with a click that echoed in the empty car.

Russ opened the driver's side door and tossed in a vest. She put it on as he started the car forward. She pulled the Velcro as tight as it would go, but the vest remained too big, leaving vulnerable spots. Still, it was better than nothing.

He turned into the driveway and met her gaze. "Be alert."

She nodded and leaned forward to scope out the area. Maple trees flanked the straight driveway, and vines tangled below, climbing the trunks as if trying to swallow the canopies. Russ followed dirt tracks and tall grasses swished on the vehicle's undercarriage. The driveway opened into a clearing holding a small log cabin and several tiny outbuildings. Horne parked a vintage orange and white VW bus with rust burrowing into the side out front.

Russ pulled up behind the van and killed the engine.

A deep dog growl and bark emanated from inside the house. She searched for any movement but saw nothing. Hand on her weapon, she got out, and the curtains fluttered on the front window.

"See that?" she asked.

"Movement in the window at my three o'clock." He eased to her other side, likely planning to protect her if Horne opened fire.

She stepped through the deep grass next to Russ and kept her gaze moving over the area, letting it settle for longer on the window with each pass.

They reached a small porch with an old green sofa and a black metal tray table. An ashtray and a wine bottle holding a candle with wax dripping down the sides sat on top.

The door cracked open. She and Russ both stopped. She tightened her hand on her weapon.

"Whatcha want?" a gravelly male voice came from the opening.

"Sheriff Russ Maddox," Russ called out. "We're here to ask questions about a recent lumber mill bombing."

"Heard about that. Had nothing to do with it."

"Please step outside, Mr. Horne," Russ said, his tone leaving no question as to whether Horne should comply.

He came out wearing a stained tank top style undershirt and torn bell-bottomed blue jeans that looked as old as he was. "I got nothing to say to you, so you can be on your way."

Russ ignored him and climbed the steps. "We wanted to ask about a friend of yours. Dean Keenan."

Ryleigh followed Russ up to the worn porch and noticed the butts in the ashtray were hand-rolled, likely pot. Not against the law in Oregon, but if she were still an agent, she could hold him on a federal offense, which they hardly ever did.

He crossed his arms, his skin shriveled, leathery, and sagging. "What about him?"

"When's the last time you saw him?" Russ asked.

"Ain't seen him in twenty years, back in Alabama. But I'm guessing you already know I saw him then."

"We do."

"But we also know you saw him recently," Ryleigh said. "And before you answer this time, you should know that if we find out you lied to us, we'll be more than happy to bring you up on charges as an accessory to murder. You'll probably go away for the rest of your life."

He tightened his arms, but his gaze wavered. "I didn't murder no one or even know about someone getting murdered."

"But you said you heard about the bombing," Russ said. "Surely you heard someone died onsite."

"Well, yeah, but that's not murder. Had to be an accident."

Ryleigh locked eyes with the guy. "Setting a bomb is not

an accidental act, Mr. Horne. It's murder, plain and simple, and if you had knowledge of this bomb before it was detonated, you're as guilty as the person who set it."

"Something you would already know from your other arrests," Russ added.

"Look." Horne flipped back straggly long hair the color of the fluffy white clouds above. "I saw him on Friday morning, so what? We talked about old times. That's it."

"What was he doing in Oregon?" Russ asked.

Horne rubbed the stubble on his face and looked beyond them as if he might not answer. He finally lifted his chin and sighed. "He was looking for his old flame. Carla Nye."

"Why?" Russ asked.

"She dumped him, and he'd never let his wife leave him. He's kind of a possessive guy, and he wants to get her back, but she's running from him."

"Why?" Ryleigh asked.

Horne stuck out his chin. "I don't know him all that well so I don't know, and he didn't say."

"Why did you go to Alabama for the protest?" Russ eyed the man. "That's a long way to travel for a protest."

"Not if you like road trips like I used to. 'Sides, it's good to go back and visit your roots every now and again." He smiled in the direction of his VW. "Old Van Gogh's taken me a lot of places over the years."

"But you specifically went for that protest." Ryleigh brought him back on track.

"Yeah, so what?"

"So if we dig into what happened back then, will we find that a bomb was detonated at that protest too?" she asked.

"Nah, Sovereign Earth didn't set no bombs when I was with 'em. Closest we came was to a guy who was with the Alabama group for like a minute. A real radical who liked to blow things up, but we weren't like that, and we kicked him out."

"And what was this guy's name?"

"Pauly—Paul—Wasser."

"You know where we can find this Pauly guy?" Russ asked.

"Six feet under." Horne cackled, revealing stained teeth.

"Did he have a favorite method of detonating bombs?" Ryleigh asked.

"Guy was nuts. Thought he could set them off using some weird device that detonated the bomb when light hit it." Horne shook his head. "Don't know if he ever got one to work that way."

"Do you mean photoelectric cells?" Russ asked.

"Hey, yeah. Yeah. That's it. A photoelectric cell. Crazy right? That's not something that seems like it would even work."

Ryleigh agreed it was indeed crazy. Not because it couldn't work but because it could work and had worked. Leaving them to find the person who might've followed in Wasser's footsteps. Perhaps Dean Keenan.

20

At the original bomb site, Finn waited for Ryleigh and Russ to climb out of the sheriff's patrol car. Eyes alight with excitement, she stepped around the back of the car to join Finn. Russ moved at a slower pace.

"What did you learn?" Finn asked and started them heading toward the area where the Veritas team was hard at work.

"We have a solid lead." Ryleigh updated Finn on the visit to Horne, telling him about a guy named Pauly Wasser who used or wanted to use a photoelectric cell as a bomb detonator.

"We already have Colin looking into him," Ryleigh said, that enthusiasm riding in her tone too. "And searching for any connection he might have to this bomb."

Finn caught her excitement. "Sounds like a promising lead."

"So this Dr. Fox has a lead for us?" Russ asked, direct and to the point as usual.

"She does," Finn said.

"Great." Ryleigh smiled. "Not only will we have even more to go on, but it'll be good to meet her too."

Finn led the way to the back of the site where Sierra had returned to recover additional forensics, and Winter stood next to her. They both wore protective white suits, blue booties, and white masks, all dirty with black soot and grime. During Finn's shift, he'd found Winter interesting to watch. She had dark hair to her shoulders that she'd almost angrily pulled back when she'd set to work, and a very intent stare. Not just when she was observing evidence, but Finn had noticed she seemed intense all the time, even during breaks.

She looked up, as did Sierra, who nodded a greeting. Winter didn't nod, but she lifted her mask and stepped forward. She ripped off one of her gloves and held out her hand to Ryleigh. "You must be Ryleigh, who Finn has told me all about. I'm Dr. Winter Fox. Veritas Center's forensic palynologist."

"Thank you for coming." Ryleigh shook hands and then stepped back.

"Are you kidding?" Winter said. "I'm glad to be here. This kind of scene challenges my skills."

Russ introduced himself, and they shook hands as well. "What do you have for us?"

Sierra joined them. "Before Winter shares her findings, I wanted to tell you that we were unable to lift any full finger-prints from the recovered bomb fragments, including the photoelectric cell. We did find a partial, but not enough to search the database."

Ryleigh frowned. "I was hoping for prints."

"As were we," Sierra said. "And I promise you we did our best. We did however recover DNA from the partial print, and Emory started running it last night. We should have the results sometime tonight."

"That's hopeful, then." Ryleigh smiled.

Sierra nodded. "We *did* recover fingerprints from Carla

Nye's documents. Hers, which are in the database from a protest arrest. And another set of prints lifted from the bomb schematics. Those prints were also in the system from protest arrests for a Dean Keenan."

"No other prints?" Ryleigh asked.

"No."

"And Keenan's and Carla's prints both matched to their names?" Russ asked.

"Yes."

"Then we know they weren't going under assumed names," Russ said. "That could've changed though. We need to be open to the possibility that they're both now using assumed identities to fly under the radar."

"But we now know for sure that Keenan touched the schematics," Finn said, his mind awash with the possibilities. "They could be his plans, and she stole them from him. But what I still don't get is why she didn't take the items with her."

"Maybe she left them behind as an insurance policy," Ryleigh suggested.

Russ cocked his head. "You mean like if he wanted to kill her, he couldn't until he had the plans in hand that could implicate him in a bombing."

Ryleigh nodded, her gaze locking with Russ's. "We really need to find her."

"We will." His shoulders rose. "You can count on that. Maybe the alert will help."

"Nick and Colin are working on getting additional information on both of them," Sierra said. "It's nearly impossible today to live without at least one connection on the web, and she's bound to slip up somehow. When she does, one of them will catch her in their algorithms."

Ryleigh's expression brightened, likely excitement from her IT background. Finn honestly found all the internet searching boring, but the data Colin and Nick provided was priceless in today's electronic world. Plus, this kind of surveillance was very efficient. With some keystrokes, Colin or Nick could provide information that would take a person weeks, maybe months, to locate with boots on the ground. If they found the data at all.

Finn had never been sent on an op as a SEAL without detailed analysis of intel found in the cyber universe, but he also personally surveilled his target or their allies whenever possible.

"Thank you for making the extra trip to your lab to process the items," Ryleigh said.

"Gave me a chance to see my hubby." Sierra looked at Winter. "You're on."

"Before you start, Dr. Fox." Russ took a step closer. "I've never heard of a palynologist, so give me the low down."

Winter explained her job.

Russ frowned. "That's clear as a bell. Give me an example."

Winter shifted on her feet, and her booties whispered on the rubble. "I have a perfect one on this investigation. I reviewed the evidence collected from Mr. Gates's house. The item recovered on his steps is a white prickly poppy seed."

"And that means something significant?" Russ questioned.

Winter gave a sharp nod. "This plant can be grown here in Oregon under ideal conditions, but it typically grows only in the South and requires dry conditions, which we definitely don't have here in the winter months. The plant would rot in our wet clay soil."

"You're saying someone carried a white poppy seed on their footwear to his house," Finn clarified. "Does it grow in Alabama?"

"Absolutely."

Russ flicked his hand in the air. "That's a long way for a little seed to stick on a shoe."

Winter nodded. "It could've been caught in a tread and dislodged somehow when the shoe flexed or something like that. Or the footwear might not have been worn until arriving here. Could've also hitched a ride on socks or pants. Even a jacket. Any article of clothing, really."

"And that tells us someone from the South, maybe Alabama, was in Gates's house," Finn said, but he didn't get too excited as they already knew from the Roomba that Keenan had been in Eckles's place.

"Exactly." Winter's deep blue eyes lit up. "And a similar seed was recovered from the passenger floor of Mr. Gates's truck and in the bedroom at Mr. Eckles's house where Ms. Nye stayed."

"We think Keenan has been in two of these locations, so he could be our seed carrier," Russ said. "I need to ask the Eckles if he went into the bedroom where Carla slept."

Ryleigh looked at Russ. "Or Carla could be the seed carrier."

Russ nodded. "Could be. Still, I'll stop by Eckles's place to ask if Keenan went into that bedroom."

"Couldn't you just call them?" Finn asked.

"I could, but each time we talk to the couple, they suddenly remember something they left off before, and an in-person visit might gain us additional information." Russ looked at Winter. "Great information. Thanks. Have you located anything here?"

"I have." Winter smiled broadly, and her face came alive. "Near the bomb site, I located a partial footprint most likely from a boot as it had a lug sole pattern. I've determined the particulates are comprised of ninety-three percent pure calcium carbonate."

"And that means what?" Russ asked.

"Some might think it means limestone, but limestone is purer. I suspect this is marble dust."

Ryleigh's long eyelashes fluttered. "Where would *that* come from?"

"Several places," Winter said. "It's commonly used to add texture to oil paints so perhaps an artist who mixed his own paints and got it on his sole from that. Or it can be used in mortar. There are other uses too, but not as common."

Russ planted his hands on his waist. "Means we could be looking for someone who paints?"

"Yes," Winter said. "The concentration was small so it could've been picked up elsewhere too."

"Like?" Finn asked.

Winter shifted on her feet. "In this general area, I'd say the Oregon Caves."

Russ cocked his head. "Oregon Caves."

Winter nodded. "The caves are made of marble, and a person could potentially pick up dust from touring the caves. Especially if they went on the off-trail caving tour, which I did once. It's a requirement to wear lug-soled boots on this tour because you crawl over boulders. You have to belly crawl, and squeeze through spaces as small as eleven inches high and only nineteen inches wide." She shook her head. "The spaces were so tight, I'll never forget those numbers our guide shared. I didn't think I'd make it through them, but I did."

"But why would you?" Ryleigh shuddered. "I'm slightly claustrophobic, and it makes my skin crawl to think about it."

"I don't know if my shoulders would even fit," Finn said. "But I wouldn't mind going on a tour like that."

"I'll leave it to you guys to try." Russ shook his head. "Crawling around in a hole in the ground isn't my idea of a good time. I'll take the wide open outdoors, thank you very much."

"We have a far different idea of a good time." Winter laughed. "But seriously. Since the caves are so close, I think you have to consider them as a possible source."

"We could be looking for someone who visited the caves or even works there," Ryleigh said. "I'm leaning toward visiting, which Keenan might've done since he's from out of state."

"Or even Carla Nye," Russ said. "We can't rule her out yet."

"I think the size of the boot print might do that," Winter said. "We haven't determined a size yet but we're leaning toward a male boot due to the width of the print."

"Did you find this dust in Gates's house?" Finn asked.

Winter shook her head. "We analyzed the debris the Roomba picked up and no sign of it. If it's important, I can go back and do more samples. I could even sample boots if you would like. Just let me know."

"The boots we saw Keenan wearing in the Roomba video weren't lug soles," Ryleigh said. "He would've had to wear different footwear on the cave tour."

"Not unlikely," Russ said.

"I don't know anything about your suspects," Winter said. "But reservations are required for the off-trail tour, and I'll bet they keep records."

Russ pulled his shoulders back. "I'll get a subpoena for their records. With any luck, that list will contain the name of our bomber."

The clock hit noon, and Ryleigh and Finn still had to finish their shift at the crime scene while Russ left to talk to the

Eckles on his way to his office to arrange the records subpoena. Ryleigh wanted to use the last hour until Ryan arrived wisely, so she was looking for Blake to get an update, and Finn came along with her.

She found the former sheriff at the small command center he'd set up near the first building. He looked up from his seat behind a white folding table and laptop screen. "I saw you talking to Sierra and Winter, so I assume they updated you on their findings."

"They did," she said.

"If you want to take a seat." He pointed at two folding chairs across the table from him. "I can give you a quick rundown on where we stand on the various scenes."

"Thank you." Ryleigh sat in the metal chair, warm from the sunshine.

Finn turned a chair next to her to straddle it and rest his arms on the back.

"We have fully completed Mr. Gates's house. His vehicle is complete too, and I know Sierra told you about the keys and phone. Her team back at the lab are running the many prints that were lifted." Blake tapped a key on his keyboard and looked at the screen. "A text from one of our techs at the Eckles's property asking for clarification. They've completed the bedroom where Carla Nye stayed, and of course, you know they found her cell phone. But he wants to know if we want the entire house processed or just the bedroom."

Ryleigh looked at Finn.

He shrugged.

Ryleigh wished Russ were here to weigh in, but this was a detail she was fully capable of deciding. "If the team keeps working on the bedroom, will it alter things here?"

Blake leaned back and put his hands behind his head. "We could move faster here if they were on site."

That could be a big factor in meeting Russ's deadline

that night. He didn't want the feds called in, and despite having been a fed herself, she didn't either. It was a matter of pride now to solve this investigation before needing their help. "We're more apt to get a lead here than in the Eckles's house so bring them back here."

"You got it." Blake dropped his chair to the ground with a thump and typed a reply on his keyboard using a fast two-finger method. "Also of interest is that Grady and Trent have determined the make and model of the photoelectric cell and are tracking down the locations where it's sold. That might bring news sooner rather than later."

"Perfect." Her phone rang, and the caller ID announced the Veritas Center.

"Someone at the center," she said and quickly answered.

"Hey, Ryleigh, it's Kelsey," she said. "I have some information for you."

"Hold on while I put you on speaker so Finn and Blake can hear." Ryleigh tapped the speaker button. "Go ahead, Kelsey."

"I've found what I think might be your missing key for the explosive depot next to the remains. There's a lump of brass in a scrap of denim fabric attached to white fabric that looks like material used in jeans pockets. The heat from the fire melted the brass, so it's not recognizable as a key. Still, you have to think it would be the most likely brass item he would carry in a pocket."

"The fire was hot enough to melt brass?" Ryleigh asked.

"Seems so. The nearby bone was severely burned too and bone doesn't burn at the typical lower temperatures of a routine house fire. Of course, this fire wasn't routine as we had an ample supply of fuel from the wood and sawdust. So short answer is yes, the fire in this particular location was at least hot enough to melt brass."

"And I take it from what you're saying, you can't tell it's a key for sure?" Finn clarified as he was known for doing.

"True," Kelsey said. "And I can't even say for sure that he was carrying it in his pocket. It could have been something nearby made of brass that then melted and stuck to the fabric. If you bring in a key, we could do a metal analysis to compare this lump to it."

Ryleigh glanced at Finn. "We'll get a key to you if we find it's crucial to have it analyzed."

Finn nodded his agreement.

"On another note, I have an answer you've been waiting for," Kelsey said. "I've confirmed that the explosion was the cause of death."

"Way to bury the lead." Blake smiled.

"I like to go out with a bang. Oh wait, no. That's bad isn't it? What with the bomb and all. I better stick to the facts." She chuckled. "I found trauma to the bones that I believe came from shrapnel, but it's all superficial. However, none of those wounds were life-threatening. Not even close. But he sustained a wound to the skull. I believe it's from a metal shard that the bomb turned into a projectile and that *was* fatal."

Finn shared a quick glance with Ryleigh that she couldn't interpret. "Could it also have come from someone hitting him with something metal?"

"No." Kelsey's firm tone discouraged any discussion. "The concussive force left a specific fracture to the bone that a human couldn't have inflicted from a blow. The only thing that might have the same concussive force would be a bullet, but the diameter of the wound is too large for a bullet, and the shape is wrong as well."

"Did he die immediately?" Ryleigh asked.

"I can't say for certain, but the shard would've pierced his brain so it's likely."

Not that it mattered, but Ryleigh hated the thought of any prolonged human suffering, especially if he wasn't the bomber.

"And what about ID?" Finn's eager tone mimicked Ryleigh's feelings. "Were you able to confirm the victim is Gates?"

"Not yet." Kelsey let out a long breath. "But Emory is running DNA and should have results later today. We could know sooner if my assistant can locate Gates's dental records, but he's struck out so far."

"Thank you, Kelsey." Ryleigh worked hard not to let her disappointment show through her tone. "Please let us know as soon as you have confirmation on his ID."

"Will do." Kelsey ended the call.

Ryleigh pocketed her phone and looked at Finn. "Not sure that helps us. We've always thought Gates had a key to the depot, so if he's the victim, then the key makes sense to be there."

"Exactly, and knowing the bomb killed him isn't a surprise either," Finn said.

"It does rule out other foul play, though," Blake said. "Maybe not important to your theory, but important to the investigation."

Ryleigh's phone rang again. She dug it out. "It's Russ."

She answered, but before she could put him on speaker his tone shot through the phone.

"We just had a sighting of Carla Nye in a cheap motel in Grants Pass." Ryleigh hadn't heard him sound this pumped since the investigation began. "I'm going to get eyes on the building ASAP and thought you might want to come along."

"Finn too?" Now why did she feel the need to have him join them?

"The guy has to know how to run a stakeout, so sure,"

Russ replied quickly. "Meet me at my office, and we'll pick up an unmarked vehicle."

"Roger that." She ended the call to loop Finn in.

"A stakeout." He grinned as he came to his feet. "Now that's right up my alley."

21

Finn took a long look at the two-story older motel painted white with blue doors and a flashing neon vacancy sign at the road. The parking lot faced the swimming pool, surrounded by a chipped wrought iron fence, and the rooms overlooked the far side of the pool. They could easily see Carla's room number. No action. Not yet.

Still, Finn didn't like not being behind the wheel and in charge of the op. Sure, he was simply sitting in the backseat of Russ's plain sedan, the faint odor of a prisoner having hurled keeping him company. Russ was at the wheel, and Ryleigh sat in the passenger seat. They weren't moving. Weren't in hostile territory where Finn might have to take quick action to protect Ryleigh.

Nothing they'd learned about Carla provided even a hint of her being a weapon-wielding militant. But when someone thought they were cornered, they could react far out of character. If she carried a weapon, she could draw and fire on them.

At least Russ had provided both Finn and Ryleigh with Kevlar vests. Good, but not perfect. Give him a tactical vest with armor plates to be most effective against a wide variety of ordnances, not one of these lighter versions.

He touched his chest by his left armpit. Yeah, he knew their failure all right. Took that bullet when an insurgent was cornered and got off a lucky shot that went a few inches wide of the vest. That situation had been much like this one, except he'd been facing enemy combatants in a war zone where emotions were amped up all the time.

"By the way," Russ said, taking a swig of the can of soda that he'd bought from a machine when they'd completed a walk-around of the building, "the Eckles claimed that Keenan never went into Carla's bedroom. I tried to pin them down on it in several different ways, but never tripped them up. I figure they're telling the truth."

"Then if the seeds were from Keenan," Ryleigh said, "he had to have gotten into the house when they were gone or sleeping in the next room."

"Seeds could be from Carla," Finn said, reminding them of that point.

"Yeah, could be." Russ set his can in the holder. "Also, Grady called to say he found part of a photoelectric cell in the rubble at Tobias's office."

"The same type of bomb as the mill," Ryleigh stated, sounding more like a mutter.

Finn sat up. "That's a big discovery, right? Bomb one is detonated on Friday afternoon. Bomb two goes off Saturday afternoon. Grady said the explosion occurred near a window. I remember noticing the sun hitting the building before the bomb detonated. Friday was a sunny day and if it had been there that day, it would've gone off then."

Ryleigh glanced at him. "So it would've had to be placed on Friday after sundown."

"Right," he said. "Because if someone had turned on a

light or something to expose it, it would've taken them out, and we would've found their body in the wreckage."

She nodded. "Then whoever died in the first bomb couldn't have set the second one."

"Great. So we're looking for two bombers, or the guy who died isn't our bomber." Russ shoved a pistachio into his mouth. He'd been eating them and spitting the shells into a drink cup from a fast-food restaurant since they'd settled into the car after the tour of the motel property.

The cracking noise got on Finn's nerves. He was about ready to grab the bag and chuck it out the window when a woman fitting Carla's description walked across the busy road, dodging traffic and crossing the lot toward the motel.

"Could be her." Russ pitched his pistachio bag and cup into the console to lift his binoculars. "Yeah, yeah, I think it's her."

Finn leaned forward and strained to get a better look, but she was too far away for a clear view. He'd never been so unprepared for an op in his life, and people got hurt when the team wasn't prepared.

Unease swam in his gut as he leaned almost into the front seat for a better view of the woman. "She carrying?"

"Not that I can see from this angle." Russ kept watching. "We need to be ready to act. We'll let her get into the room, so she can't make a break for it. Ryleigh and I'll knock on the door and announce ourselves. Finn, you have the back in case she tries to shimmy out the bathroom window."

Ryleigh looked over her shoulder. "I'll text you when you can come inside."

"I'd appreciate that." Finn made sure to keep his frustration from his tone.

He didn't want to be at the back and likely out of any action. He wanted to be right by Ryleigh's side, but that hope ended when they'd scoped out the property and discovered the room had a possible secondary exit in a window. He'd agreed then that as the only non-law enforcement officer in the group, he should leave the direct approach of Carla up to the others.

Finn wanted to take back his agreement, but he was a man of his word, and he would do his job, even if it wasn't as commander of the group. Yet another reminder of what he'd left behind.

He waited for the pain to twist his gut again, but it didn't. He turned the bracelet on his wrist to read Avery's name, and her little face came to mind. He would make the same decision again. Leave the SEALs. No questions asked. Maybe he really was learning to live with the pain and not let it control him.

Thank You.

Carla headed down the side of the pool toward her room and kept looking over her shoulder.

"She's acting scared," Ryleigh said. "Which makes sense since she's on the run and further helps cement that it's her."

"It's her all right." Russ handed the binoculars to Ryleigh. "Take a look for yourself."

Finn wanted to grab the binoculars but sat back as she lifted them to her eyes.

"You're right," she said. "No doubt it's Carla."

"Get ready to go," Russ said. "We move as soon as she opens that door but not a second sooner."

Finn put his hand on the door handle and made ready to fly. He really was too big to be sitting in the back and had to be careful not to get his feet tangled up on the exit.

Carla inserted the key in the motel door.

Finn's adrenaline kicked in. He gripped the handle tighter.

She pushed the door open.

"Go. Go. Go." Russ bolted from the car.

Finn made it out almost as fast as the sheriff, and he beat Ryleigh. They traveled left for the walkway to the room, he charged right, skirting the pool and a few landscape shrubs. He headed down the other side of the rooms until he reached the fourth from the end. In case someone passed by, he leaned casually against the concrete block wall serving as a fence for the property but kept his gaze sharp behind his sunglasses.

He watched the window and started counting down in his head.

One, one thousand.

Two, one thousand.

Three, one thousand.

On and on until he'd hit two-hundred-fifty. The window opened.

Hello. Game time.

He came to his feet. Ready for action if needed.

Carla got the window all the way open, punched the screen onto the ground, and tossed out a backpack. She slid her feet into the opening.

Finn stepped out of the shadows, silently making his way across the lot. He searched her for the telltale bulge of a weapon but saw nothing. Still, he retrieved his pistol from his ankle holster.

She came out feet first, her back to him.

He crept closer, only three feet behind her.

"Oomph." She landed in a crouch but was on her feet in an instant and bending for her backpack.

"Hello, Carla," he said, his adrenaline now flowing like a cold stream in Alaska and putting him on high alert. "Going somewhere?"

Ryleigh peeked through the window and into the slit in the curtains. Carla's back disappeared into the bathroom as she bolted with her backpack into the space.

"She's running. Stay here. I'm going to the back." Ryleigh was glad she beat Russ to the punch and took off toward the back of the building. She hadn't been on an op like this in too long, and her adrenaline was nearly swamping her. A run around the property would help burn some of it off.

She kicked it into gear and rounded the corner. She came to a screeching stop. Finn was approaching, holding Carla by the elbow, her backpack in his other hand. The woman's face was narrowed and oozing frustration.

"Carla Nye?" Ryleigh asked.

She lifted her chin. "Yeah, so what?"

"So, I'm Deputy Ryleigh Steele, and I have some questions for you." Ryleigh retrieved the handcuffs Russ had issued to her. "And these are in order since you've already tried to run."

Carla frowned but didn't argue when Ryleigh pressed the woman against the wall and slapped on the cuffs. Her jacket reeked of marijuana, and her hair was dirty and stringy.

She wasn't under arrest, but Ryleigh wanted to know if she was armed. She patted the woman down and found a knife in a sheath at her ankle, which Ryleigh removed. She also took the room key from Carla's pocket.

Ryleigh held up the knife. "Worried someone is going to hurt you?"

"Maybe."

Ryleigh gave the knife to Finn and took hold of the cuffs to direct Carla toward her room, where they would question her. She glanced at Finn. "Thanks for the backup."

"You ever need backup again, I'm your guy." He smiled and it was intense and, might she say, possessive.

She didn't need to be looked after, but she'd be lying if she didn't admit she liked the look because it meant he cared enough to want to protect her.

Russ peered down the walkway at them, lips clamped closed.

"Finn had things in hand," she said, the pride she felt for this fine man in her tone. "But I decided to cuff and search her. Found a knife at her ankle."

"Armed, Ms. Nye?" Russ raised his eyebrow. "I'm Sheriff Russ Maddox, and I'd like to ask you some questions about Dean Keenan."

"That creep," she spit out. "Haven't seen him in a month and don't know what he's done. So might as well let me go."

Ryleigh held onto Carla and gave Russ the key to unlock the door. It groaned open as if tired from frequent use. Ryleigh ushered her charge into the room that held a simple queen bed, boxy nightstand, and matching desk with two wooden chairs. She pulled out a chair and settled Carla onto it.

Ryleigh dragged the other chair over the wild blue and green patterned carpet that held a heavy perfumed scent as if the maid had doused it with something to hide another odor.

Ryleigh faced Carla and took a seat. "Tell us about your relationship with Dean Keenan."

"I'm married to him as I'm sure you know. But we split up when he took a swing at me." She lifted her shoulders and thrust out her ample chest covered in a vintage Grateful Dead T-shirt. "Ain't no guy, no matter how much I love him, gonna deck me."

"You left him, but he doesn't want to let go." Russ stood next to Ryleigh.

"No." Carla looked up at him. "Which means I need to get out of here before he finds me again."

"You weren't easy to find," Russ said. "Even with our statewide resources looking for you."

"Yeah, but I had to use my credit card for this room, and we have a joint account. He could see the charge."

Finn stood on Ryleigh's other side, his feet planted wide. "What are the odds that'll happen?"

She shrugged. "He's not the brightest bulb, you know? He's a cash only guy. Doesn't trust banks and never used the card. Never paid attention to our finances either. I'm hoping he doesn't figure out he can call and ask about any recent charges."

"He nearly found you at the Eckles's place," Ryleigh said.

"He did?"

Russ nodded. "Showed up the day after you left."

"Which is exactly why I didn't tell them where I was going." She let out a long breath. "Did he hurt Pauline or Virg?"

Ryleigh shook her head.

"Thank goodness for that." Carla lifted her hand to her chest and let out a long breath. "I would've hated to hear he smacked Pauline around in her condition. Or maybe she's had the baby by now."

"No to that too," Ryleigh said. "At least not as of this morning when Sheriff Maddox talked to her."

Russ rested his hands on his hips. "You seem like a good friend to the Eckles."

"I am. So what?"

Russ looked Carla directly in the eye. "So, just because Keenan didn't hurt them on his first visit, doesn't mean he won't go back."

Carla's eyes darkened, and she shot a panicked look around the room.

Russ stepped closer. "And you can help stop that from

happening by telling us what you really know about Keenan's whereabouts."

Carla gnawed on her lower lip and looked down.

"I would hate to have Keenan show up at their house totally frustrated and a newborn in the house," Ryleigh added to try to appeal to her sense of decency.

"I don't know a lot," she finally said. "He's been getting increasingly bizarre. Talking a lot about setting off a bomb. He'd gotten frustrated that no one, not even the news media, pays any attention to him or the group anymore. He sent threats to Shadow Lake Logging. That much I know because he shared them with me in emails. One day, he packed a bag but wouldn't say where he was going. I snooped before he left and found bomb schematics in the bag, so I took them to try to stop him from setting one off."

"And then what happened?" Russ asked.

"Then when I tried to pin him down on what his plans were, he took a swipe at me to stop picking at him. So I shoved the plans in my bag and took off. Not sure where I thought I was going. I knew if I left and took the plans with me, I'd better end up somewhere he wouldn't find me."

Finn perched on the edge of the credenza. "And you thought that was the Eckles's house?"

"Yeah, I mean, Dean pitted me against Pauline all the time. Of course that meant we never got along real well. At least not around him, but we were once friends and could both relate to living with the creep." She shifted in the chair, her cuffs rasping against the wood. "But either he figured it out or he was coming to Oregon to set the bomb, because he showed up at Uri's place out of the blue."

"Uri Gates?" Finn leaned forward. "You know him?"

She nodded. "We dated back in the day. So I'd looked him up while I was staying with Virg and Pauline. He knew I was trying to avoid Dean and called to give me a heads-up."

"When was that?" Russ asked.

"The morning before I took off."

Ryleigh felt like they were getting a lot of answers, but they didn't really help them discover if Keenan planted the bomb or not. "Did Uri say why Keenan was at his place?"

"Kind of." Carla rolled her neck. "He was asking a lot of questions about Shadow Lake Logging. Dean went out of the house the morning Uri called me, and Uri said he'd found components for a bomb in Dean's bag. Uri was afraid Dean planned on blowing the place up. Last I talked to Uri, he was going to keep a close eye on the company explosive inventory. Dean too, for as long as he was in town. So Uri could stop Dean if he needed to."

Okay, now they had some answers that might help, but... "Why didn't you report it to the police?"

"Dean didn't have any experience with bombs, and I still had the schematics so I didn't think he could build one." She twisted her fingers together. "Besides, Uri assured me he had things under control."

"Looks like you were wrong." Russ told her about the explosion at the mill and the victim.

Her mouth dropped open. "Someone died? But who?"

"We're waiting on confirmation," Ryleigh said, not wanting to give her Gates's name without an official identification. But now it was looking more like Gates got caught trying to *stop* the bomb rather than set it.

"I'll bet Dean did it." Carla's eyes filled with tears. "I hope you find him." She sat forward. "And if he did it and killed this person, then he goes away for a long time, right?"

"If he goes away, he quits bothering you." Russ eyed her. "You could help us with that."

"Me?" Carla flashed her gaze up to him. "But how?"

"Simple," Russ said. "Get word to him that you're staying

here, and we'll be waiting for him to show up and collar him."

Carla shook her head hard. "If I called him, he'd know it was some sort of a trap."

"You have a point." Russ stepped back, running a hand through his hair. "We'll have Virgil Eckles call Keenan, and tell him he doesn't want any trouble, so he's ratting you out to protect his family."

"Yeah. Yeah." Carla gave a vigorous nod. "That should work."

"We were never able to find a phone number for Keenan," Finn said.

"He uses prepaids." Carla fixed her rapt attention on Russ. "I have his latest number. I can give it to you, but I'm not sure if it's still in service."

Russ got out a notepad and pen. "Go ahead."

She rattled off the number.

Russ jotted it down and then looked up, his jaw set as he looked at Ryleigh. "Give me a minute to arrange for backup. Then we set the trap and finally get our hands on Dean Keenan and bring this investigation to a close."

22

Finn paced his living room, waiting for Russ to call from the motel and say Keenan had picked up his phone. Eckles had tried to call, but got Keenan's voicemail and had to leave a message. They couldn't even be sure Keenan would get the message. He could very well have dumped that phone and gotten a new one.

"You're making me nervous with all the pacing." Ryleigh patted the couch cushion next to her. "Come sit by me instead."

He didn't want to sit, but he also didn't want to add to her anxiety. After all, she'd come here to be with him when he'd had to take over Avery's care. She'd wanted to stay with Russ to arrest Eckles. That had been obvious, but she'd returned to the house with him, likely to support him. He appreciated her consideration and letting everything go so they could enjoy time with Avery during dinner.

The house still smelled like the tangy pizzas they'd each made for the delayed pizza night. Ryleigh had put her all into it, then read to Avery and tucked her into bed. He really would be blessed to have her at his side. He regretted ever breaking things off with her.

He sat next to her and put his feet up on the glass coffee table holding a layer of dust that he never seemed to find time to take care of. The grime bugged his need for orderliness instilled in the military.

"This is Keenan's opportunity to find out where Carla is," Ryleigh said. "I'd think he'd jump at the chance to call back."

"Maybe he knows it's a trap," Finn said. "I saw it often enough in ops when subjects wouldn't bite on bait we dangled for them."

She looked at him intently. "You miss it, don't you?"

"I'd be lying if I didn't say I did."

She frowned.

He didn't want to be the cause of her unease. Not now. Not ever. "But I'm coming to accept the change."

She lifted her hand as if she wanted to touch him, but then let it drop to her knee. "But accepting isn't really living, is it?"

"No."

"What do you think it will take for you to find the enthusiasm you used to have for life?" She held his gaze, digging deep. "Your passion for everything you tackled was one of the things I always loved about you."

Loved about me? As in loved me? He had to ignore that point for now, but he could still answer her question. "With the way Avery is starting to open up, I think it's already happening."

But for how long? Would Avery shut down again when Ryleigh left?

He clamped his mouth closed to keep from frowning at the thought of her leaving and drawing even more of her attention.

She grimaced.

Great. He'd failed to hide it. Big time.

"What is it?" She leaned closer, and he caught the sweet scent of her coconut shampoo. "What's bothering you?"

"You always could read me," he said, hoping to distract her to keep from answering.

"So, what's wrong?"

Right. She was as tenacious as he was.

"I'm worried this change in Avery is because of you and your family, not because she's accepting me. So when you go..." He shrugged because he didn't want to voice his concern, as he didn't really want to think it could happen.

"I think you're worrying for nothing." She swiveled to face him directly. "I saw Avery's face when she gave you the bracelet. She's smitten with the idea of you as her dad. And the nice part is you aren't replacing her mother because you're a guy. Avery's always wanted a dad, and now she has one."

"True." He looked at the bracelet.

"But?"

He shrugged again. "I guess since I've never been a parent before, I'm uncertain about everything when it comes to Avery. Like what does this bracelet mean? Is it as important to her as it is to me or is it just some craft project?"

"I think it's very important to her," Ryleigh said. "I've never been a parent either, so take my words for what they're worth. I suspect the way you feel is the way every new parent feels, whether their child is a day old or seven years old, like Avery."

"You think so?"

"I do. And I know if I became a mom right now, I would feel that way."

Oh, wow. That gave him so many visions of a future with her. But they'd never discussed kids. "How do you feel about becoming a mom? Do you want kids?"

She narrowed her eyes. "Yeah, sure. I'm just not sure how many. Or when."

Like maybe not now with a seven-year-old.

He'd been thinking so much about getting back together with her, and thinking the only obstacle to overcome was her wariness after the lame way he broke up with her, and that they lived in different towns. But the real obstacle was much bigger. Huge, in fact. How had he missed it?

He was a dad now and anyone he dated would have to become an instant stepmother.

He couldn't ask that of Ryleigh. Could he actually ask it of any woman?

The single moms at school came to mind. They'd been interested in him. Almost acting desperate for a suitable match. They were already mothers and didn't seem to mind that he had a child. So maybe that was his future. Taking on a wife who came with her own child or children.

Another wrinkle to get over. To live *with*, not in. No point in really thinking about any of it. He wasn't in the market for a wife. At least not one other than Ryleigh Steele, and she sure wasn't shopping for him.

"You're lost in thought," she said.

He waved a hand. "Nothing important."

She opened her mouth to say something, but her phone rang, and she grabbed it. "It's Kelsey."

Ryleigh tapped her phone. "Finn is with me, so I'm putting you on speaker, Kelsey."

Ryleigh set the phone on her knee nearest to Finn.

"We have the victim's DNA results back," Kelsey said. "And got a hit in CODIS."

"That's odd." Ryleigh looked at Finn. "CODIS is the FBI's DNA database, but Gates doesn't have a record."

"At least not that we uncovered," Finn said, his mind racing with how this could be true.

"Nick and Russ were thorough and would've turned up a criminal record for Gates if he had one." Ryleigh peered at her phone. "Wait. The database isn't just criminals, so why was his DNA in it?"

"I don't know if it is," Kelsey said.

Ryleigh's head popped up, and she blinked her long lashes. "But you said Gates's DNA matched a record in CODIS."

"No," Kelsey replied. "I said the *victim's* DNA matched the database, but Uri Gates isn't the victim."

～

Not Gates? How can that be?

Ryleigh's heart pounded as she watched Finn's mouth drop open. She let her gaze wander the room as she tried to process the shocking news.

Finn leaned closer to her phone. "Say that again, Kelsey."

Yeah, he didn't believe it either.

"The victim isn't Uri Gates," Kelsey said. "The DNA matches to a Dean Keenan."

"Keenan?" Ryleigh whipped her gaze to Finn, her heart thundering now. "It's Keenan. He died in the bomb."

Finn nodded. "No wonder he's not returning Eckles's phone call. But why was he wearing Gates's boots?"

Yeah, why? "Maybe he didn't want to get his other boots dirty. Or if Keenan set the bomb, he wanted to put Gates's boot prints at the scene to cast the blame on him."

"Maybe Gates knows the answer to that question," Finn said. "We have to find him. Find out if Keenan is our bomber, and he didn't get out in time."

Ryleigh planted her shaking hands on her knees to stem her eagerness to figure this puzzle out. "He could only be responsible for planting the first bomb, but since a photo-electric cell was found at both locations, maybe the same person made both of them."

"Could be. And if Keenan set bomb one, we must have a second bomber. He could be getting ready to strike again, and we have no clue as to his ID."

"So who is he?" Ryleigh asked.

"That's the million-dollar question," Kelsey said.

"Along with what happened to Gates." Ryleigh let everything they'd learned so far run through her brain but didn't come up with an answer as to where the guy might be.

"Maybe he *was* involved in setting the bomb," Kelsey said. "Maybe even set them both, and no one was supposed to die, but when Gates heard about the body, he went underground."

Finn nodded. "Sounds possible, but why leave his vehicle behind?"

"It's a very distinct model," Ryleigh said. "Maybe he ditched it to fly under law enforcement's radar." She looked at her phone. "Kelsey, have you called Russ with this information?"

"I tried," she said. "But got his voicemail and had to leave a message to call me. Oh wait, he's calling me back now. Got to go." Kelsey ended the call.

Finn jumped up and started pacing. "Okay, so Keenan is dead. How do we start looking for Gates or an unknown bomber?"

Finn's fidgeting made Ryleigh nervous, and she got up too. She strode around the room pondering the leads. A few minutes of pacing and she stopped next to Finn. "My first thought is the video footage."

"But Russ reviewed all of it, and there wasn't anyone who didn't have a legit reason for coming to the office."

"True."

"Then do we need to start looking at people who had a legit reason for being there or just focus on Gates?" Finn asked.

Ryleigh's phone rang. "It's Russ."

She answered. "I assume you talked to Kelsey."

"I did," he said. "With Keenan dead, there's no point in hanging out at the motel, so I'll send Carla to lockup until we can figure this all out and head back to my office."

"Shocking news, right?" Ryleigh asked.

"Yeah. If Gates isn't our victim, he could be our bomber. I put out an alert on him, but without his current vehicle, it'll be like finding the proverbial needle in a haystack."

"We should've done a better job," Ryleigh said. "We thought we knew where he was so we haven't been looking for him. That stops now. We can have Nick and Colin try to find credit card activity for him. Maybe for a hotel or rental car. Or maybe he owns another vehicle."

"I just ran his particulars through DMV," Russ said, his radio squawking in the background. "Only vehicle registered to him is the Jeep Gladiator, but I'll text Colin and Nick to start looking for other details."

"Let's hope they find something soon." She looked at the clock and the time was nearing eight p.m. "We only have about twelve hours before you have to call in the feds."

"Don't count us out yet." His intensity and determination flowed through the phone. "We still have time to find a last-minute lead, so let's get after it."

23

Finn couldn't take any more of sitting and looking at a computer. He and Ryleigh had dug into the Sovereign Earth members provided by Colin. For a solid hour they'd reviewed internet articles, trying to find out who could be behind the bombs. Ryleigh was in her element, but he was an action guy, not a sit and ponder guy. He'd been spoiled by analysts who'd done this work for his team— presenting him with the problem and the details behind it. Then his team formed a plan and executed it. The exact opposite of this drawn-out investigation without many leads.

"I can't sit here anymore." He got up to pace, instantly releasing tension with each step.

Ryleigh peered at him over the top of her laptop. "There's got to be a lead in here somewhere."

He spun to face her. "But where? We've looked at each ecoterrorist on Colin's list and none of them give us any reason to believe they would suddenly become bombers."

"Doesn't mean they didn't do it." She crossed her arms as if for emphasis on her statement's validity. "I think it's time to have Nick and Colin switch their focus to a nationwide search of Sovereign Earth members who embrace any type of violence."

More research, but at least Finn didn't need to do it. "Agreed, but it feels like we're starting over."

"Not totally." She shook out her arms. "We've eliminated a lot of things, but I get your point."

He went back to the table and rested his hands on a chair back. "More research will take time. Time we don't have. I know Russ hoped to resolve this by morning, but doesn't look like that'll happen."

"You're probably right," she said. "But as much as I want to help Russ avoid the feds, it's more important that this bomber is caught before he strikes again."

"Of course." Finn pulled out the chair and sat. "So let's get back at it."

"Thank you." She smiled at him. "I know sitting around is hard for you."

"With my job change, I need to get better at it."

"You will." She gave him an encouraging smile. "If my family of former law enforcement officers has managed it, I think you can too."

He took a good look at her, applying evaluative skills he'd learned as a SEAL to read people and digging deep into her eyes. "Do you miss being an agent?"

"Yeah, sure, but I chose to make the change. It wasn't forced on me like your change. It's not as big of a deal for me." She tilted her head and watched him. "Anything that's forced on us is harder to deal with than things we choose for ourselves."

Wow, so simple but so perceptive. She really had a good head on her shoulders. Lived her faith. Was a role model for him. He wasn't looking for more reasons to fall in love with her, but she just kept revealing them, and he was now finding her to be nearly irresistible.

"But if we remember that God only allows things in our lives for our own good," she continued, "then the unexpected can be easier to deal with too."

"Easy to say." He tried not to sound negative and to embrace her positive comment, but he wasn't quite there yet. "Hard to live."

"Oh, I know." She waved a hand. "I can preach it with the best of them, but living it? I'm not so successful a lot of the time. You know me. Impulsive. Act quick. At first, I don't always think to pray before I act. That usually makes it harder."

Oh, yeah, he knew her. And remembered some of the crazy predicaments she'd gotten herself into when they'd been together. The memories brought a smile. He could get used to a lifetime of rescuing her from similar comical situations.

A knock sounded on the front door.

Finn shot a look in that direction. "Who could that be at this time of night?"

Ryleigh cast a tight-eyed look in that direction. "Only one way to find out."

He went to the door and looked through the peephole. "It's Tobias."

Finn pulled open the door.

Tobias stepped in, slapping a newspaper against his hand. "This! I didn't think about this!"

He pushed past Finn into the family room and tossed the paper down on the table. "I forgot about this guy's grudge."

Finn picked up the nightly edition of the local paper and read the main story.

Ryleigh looked between them both. "What's this about?"

"Title reads *Local Hero Celebrated,*" Finn said. "It's about a guy named Barney Vick who rescued an autistic child who slipped unnoticed into the Oregon Caves and got lost."

She looked at Tobias. "And what does that have to do with the bombing?"

"Barney blames me for his father's death." Tobias plopped onto a chair. "His dad died nearly eight years ago, and I'd put it out of my mind. Barney's a real conspiracy theory nut, and I figured this was just one of his rants because I had nothing to do with the death. But now that I think about it, he might want revenge."

Finn's interest was piqued now. "How did the man die?"

"Prostate cancer, which Barney claims his dad got on the job." Tobias shook his head.

"That's absurd, right?" Ryleigh asked.

"To you and me and most reasonable people—but not to Barney." Tobias rubbed a hand over his tired face and then down his long beard. "Since I never heard from him again, I assumed he'd learned to deal with the loss, let it go."

"And now?" Ryleigh asked.

"I dunno." Tobias shrugged one shoulder. "I'm wondering if maybe I was wrong."

"But why wait eight years to exact revenge?" Finn asked.

"Yeah, that doesn't make sense." Tobias sat back and planted his hands on his thin knees. "I don't know. When you called earlier to say Keenan died in the bombing, I wondered if we'd gotten it wrong. That maybe we shouldn't be looking at ecoterrorists. Just a thought."

"And one worth looking into," Ryleigh said. "Thanks for bringing this to our attention."

"I'll see you to the door," Finn said, eager for Tobias to leave so they could get over to this Vick guy's place.

Tobias turned back on the porch. "Promise you'll let me know what happens with this."

"Will do." Finn closed the door and went back to Ryleigh, who was still reading the paper.

"Did you notice that Vick's a ranger? He works at the Oregon Caves." She looked up. "Could explain the marble dust found at the bomb site."

"We need to pay him a visit," Finn said, finally glad to have something to act on but with Avery asleep, he couldn't go until the morning.

"Let's give Russ a call." Ryleigh picked up her phone and put Russ on speaker. She succinctly updated him on the newspaper and visit from Tobias.

"We need to raid Vick's place," Finn said.

"Agreed, but it'll be law enforcement only, and you won't be in on the action," Russ said.

Not in on the action.

His gut cramped. Not good. He thought he'd dealt with that kind of response. Guess not.

But not in on the action was his life motto from now on, and he had to learn to fully deal with it. At least if he wanted to live a quality life that God wanted for all of His children.

An hour later, Ryleigh exited Russ's patrol car out front of Barney Vick's ranch home. The sixties house had a red brick exterior, black shutters, and older wooden windows and sat on an oversized lot at the edge of town. The windows looked like they needed replacing but otherwise the home seemed to be in good repair.

She marched straight to the door. Russ joined her, warrant in hand. The place was dark and buttoned up, but Vick could be sleeping. She knocked and stood back to wait. She rested a hand on her sidearm as did Russ. Vick didn't have a record of any sort—not even a traffic ticket—but if he was their bomber, he didn't care if people got hurt. That could include law enforcement officers who came to question him.

Her pulse tripping, she tapped her foot, but Vick didn't answer her knock.

Russ pressed him thumb on the doorbell a few times and pounded harder. No answer.

"He's not home," the neighbor lady yelled from her front porch. Ryleigh spun to look at her. "He went camping for the weekend and is going straight from there to work tomorrow."

"Hey, Lucy," Russ called out. "Thanks. You wouldn't happen to have a key, would you?"

"I do, but what for?" The older woman wore a flowery housecoat, and she eyed them from under pin curls held in place with bobby pins in an X shape.

"We just need to take a look around."

Russ's vague reply got a raise of the woman's eyebrows, moving the pin curls. "I know you're the law and all, but I'm not sure Barney would appreciate me giving you a key."

"He'd like it a whole lot better than me busting down his door." Ah, yes. Appeal to her practicality.

"I suppose."

Russ held up the warrant. "The judge approved this visit if that helps."

"Does indeed. Be right back." She spun, her housecoat flapping in the breeze.

"I didn't want to mention the warrant," Russ said. "Now it'll be all over town within an hour and people will be speculating."

Not good. "Let's hope Vick is really camping and doesn't get wind of it."

Lucy's screen door came open again, but didn't snap

closed behind her as a guy, likely her husband, peeked his balding head out.

"Evening, George," Russ called out. "Nice night."

Ah, yes, small-town policing, Ryleigh had never really understood what it involved until now. They were here to search the home of a potential bomber, and Russ was making small talk with the neighbor. He had to. As sheriff for a small county, Russ had personal relationships with many of the county residents. The FBI never had this dichotomy to deal with. If they had a warrant to serve and the occupant wasn't home, they would simply bust down the door and enter.

Lucy marched across the lawn, her backless slippers snapping under her feet. "What's he done?"

"I'm not at liberty to share anything at this time," Russ said. "But it could be nothing."

She raised a painted-on eyebrow. "He finally go off half-cocked on one of his conspiracy theories and hurt someone?"

"Conspiracy theories?" Russ asked.

"Seems like every week it's something new. Last time we talked he said he thought the war in Ukraine was fake. That Democrats were using it to make them seem like heroes as they saved us from Russia." She rolled her eyes.

"Do you know where Barney went camping?" Ryleigh asked to change the subject.

"He said, but I don't remember." Lucy faced her porch. "George, you know where Barney went camping?"

"You're the one who gets all the neighborhood gossip details, so I didn't bother to ask." His booming laugh traveled on the breeze.

"Thanks for the key." Russ smiled at Lucy. "But you best go on home now, just in case we encounter any danger."

"From Barney? Hah! I've always compared him to the big

purple dinosaur who shares the same name. No danger there." She walked off laughing.

Russ inserted the key in the lock.

"She could be right," Ryleigh said. "Our evidence is sketchy at best at this point."

"Then let's find something that isn't sketchy." Russ pushed open the door and announced himself.

No reply, just as expected.

Hand on the butt of his weapon, Russ stepped inside. Ryleigh followed him into an entryway boasting a flowery floor tile in orange and yellow sixties colors. That led to a step-down family room with a brick fireplace and older furnishings.

"Police," Russ yelled again. "If you're here, Barney, come out."

Russ waited a moment and then headed down a hallway toward the bedrooms. Stained carpet emitted a musty odor with each step. Ryleigh refrained from holding her nose as she followed.

Vick had set up the first room as an office. A newer-model computer sat on a vintage wooden desk painted an olive green. One wall covered with brown wood paneling held photos and internet articles about various conspiracies with red yarn lines anchored to colored pushpins and connecting items together.

She stepped to the board and paused by a top article written in Canada about a link to loggers and prostate cancer. She put on gloves and tapped it. "Check this out."

Russ came to stand beside her and study the page. "Loggers have a higher incidence of prostate cancer."

"Never expected to see that," she said. "They think the vibrations from chain saws may be the cause or emissions from the engines."

"See this?" He tapped the last part of the title that said

loggers and *cops* were among higher-risk occupations for prostate cancer. Twice as likely to get it. "They see it in truck and bus drivers too. Not liking my job at this moment."

"That's an interesting side fact." She looked at him.

"Vick might have some justification for blaming the job."

"But blaming Tobias is pretty far-fetched. Vick's dad chose to be a logger. Tobias didn't force him to do the job." She tapped the date noted at the top of the paper. "This article was recently printed. Vick might've just located this info, and it could be what set him off after all these years."

"Makes sense." Russ pursed his lips and stared ahead. "We need more information."

She turned to the desk and sifted through papers on the corner. Her mouth dropped open. "No way. Look at this. Bomb schematics using a photoelectric cell. Right out in plain sight. He must not have thought we'd ever connect the bomb to him."

"Guess we have the evidence we came for." Russ frowned when she expected him to smile. "I knew about his conspiracy theory garbage but never thought the guy was more than odd. At least not odd enough to blow something up."

Ryleigh stared at the wall. This was the work of someone not in their right mind. Totally not in their right mind. And someone willing to risk the lives of others to make his point.

That made him dangerous and unpredictable. And he was out in the Oregon wilderness doing who knows what.

What was he capable of doing? Had he set another bomb? If so, where?

A chill rolled over her body. "Looks like he went off the deep end."

Russ grimaced. "Yeah, but what does all of this tell us?

Carla's statement and her emails prove Sovereign Earth sent the threats."

"Or at least Keenan did, whether he was representing the group or not," she said, trying to ignore the danger this man presented and focus.

"The threats were big gossip in town, so what if Vick heard it and decided to piggyback off them? Set a bomb and place the blame on the group?"

She let that thought settle in. "Sounds like a good possibility."

"And that could also help explain why he decided to do it now. He thought he had a way to exact his revenge and not get caught." Russ got out his phone and snapped pictures of the wall. "Go through the desk. I'll check out the rest of the bedrooms. Maybe we'll find out where he's camping."

Russ strode off, and she sat in the old wooden chair on wheels.

She couldn't bear the thought of a half-crazed bomber being out there somewhere, not knowing where, and they couldn't stop him. She had to find something. Anything. Just a hint. That was all they needed to propel them forward.

She ripped through the drawers. Snatching up papers. Reading. Discarding.

Nothing. Nothing at all. Including no mention of his campground location.

Okay fine. She needed help. The campground could be on Vick's computer which she couldn't touch until they had an image made of the hard drive.

She texted Nick, who was a night owl and was sure to still be up.

Urgent. Top suspect identified. Can you come get his computer to image it?

Despite the time of night, his answer came right away. *Send me the address and I'll be there ASAP.*

She fired off a thank you along with Vick's address.

Russ came back and stood in the doorway. "Only things I found were several pairs of boots. They all have lug soles."

"We can try to match them to the prints lifted at the bomb scene," she said, though that wouldn't help them find Vick. Just prove he'd been at the scene.

"If you're done, we can do the living room, garage, and kitchen."

"I'm done, but I texted Nick to pick up this computer." She stood, took one last look at the creepy board, and followed Russ down the hall.

He took the living room and garage, and she searched through the kitchen with white flat front cabinets and orange tile countertops. A typical kitchen. Neat and tidy with a stack of mail on the corner of the counter. She flipped through the pile. Bills. Ads. Nothing of interest to move the investigation forward.

"Living room's a bust. Garage too. Only gym equipment." Russ pointed through the patio door. "I want to get a look at that shed."

He slid the door open, the vinyl sticking on the track, emitting an awful noise that the neighbors had to hear. Under the stars and a swift wind, they crossed a cracked concrete patio holding a rusty kettle grill to the solid-looking shed with a heavy-duty padlock.

"We need to get inside here, but not without it being checked out first."

She nodded. No way she would discover the bomber's ID only to fall victim to one of his bombs.

Thankfully, Grady was more than glad to come out with the robobugs and search the shed for booby traps. The roach did his job in minutes, and Grady declared the shed safe. And as a bonus he'd brought bolt cutters to remove the lock. He applied it to the lock and it dropped open.

Flashlight in hand, Russ stepped inside and pulled the string on a lightbulb hanging from the ceiling. The space flooded with dim light, revealing yard tools hanging in a row on one wall and a workbench on the opposite wall.

"Bingo!" He shot up a hand and flashed her a grin over his shoulder.

She stepped into the space that reeked of motor oil and spotted the reason for his enthusiasm. Several tubes of explosives matching the ones in Shadow Lake Logging's explosives' depot and various parts for constructing a bomb were laid out neatly on a worn workbench. Her gaze landed on a photoelectric cell.

Adrenaline cut a straight path through her body.

She moved closer, easing past Grady, her heart racing now. "Dates are written on the tubes just like the ones Tobias's company uses."

"Yeah," he said, sounding way too calm for this important discovery. "But how did Vick get into the shed? Or get past the cameras for that matter?"

"So maybe these aren't the missing explosives," she said.

"Explain," Grady said.

She glanced between the men. "If Vick knows the brand of explosives Shadow Lake Logging uses and how they handle inventory, he could've put a date on the tubes to make it look like these came from there."

"Then where are the missing ones?" Russ asked.

"Keenan took them and stashed them somewhere but never got to use them."

Russ nodded. "You could be right."

"Either way." She took several breaths and looked at Russ. "We could really have our bomber."

"Looks like it, but we need concrete proof." How he kept his tone so controlled, she would never know when her heart threatened to leap out of her chest.

Grady stepped closer. "These are the same materials used in our bombs. Or at least the same brand and the dates are similar."

"Then he could really be our bomber." Russ dug out his phone. "And we need this place secured as a crime scene then torn apart for leads."

"I'll get Sierra out here." Grady went to the door.

The men made their phone calls. Adrenaline flowing, Ryleigh couldn't stand around. She had to move. To do. But what? Maybe there were other buildings in the large yard. Other discoveries that could provide even more proof that Vick was their bomber.

"I'll take a look around outside." She fairly bolted from the shed and turned on her phone's flashlight. She shone the beam into the tall grass, weeds, and shrubs as she walked the perimeter filled with shadows. She took her time, making sure she didn't succumb to a trap set by Vick. With the plans out in plain sight and the shed clear, she didn't really expect one, but better to be safe than sorry.

The neighbor's dog barked on the other side of the fence, the little yips breaking the quiet night.

She took a long breath and continued down the fence line, found nothing. But what did she expect to see? They'd already hit the motherlode of evidence. Not only bomb schematics, but the materials to make them.

She reached her starting point. Flicked the light over the back of the shed. A shovel perched against the fence behind the small building caught her attention. Vick had neatly hung his other tools. Why would this one be outside?

She eased between the fence and the shed and came up short.

Oh no. No. No. He didn't.

"Russ!" she screamed. "You'll want to see this."

She held her flashlight in place, her hands growing clammy. Her breath shallow. The beam of her light still focused ahead. Illuminating the mounded soil. A rectangle about six feet long by three feet wide.

Russ came up behind her. "A grave? You found a grave?"

"Yeah," she said, her mind filled with implications. "Could be I just found Uri Gates."

∼

Nearing two a.m., Ryleigh watched Dr. Pierre Meadows, the medical examiner, clear away the soil behind Vick's shed. Russ had connections in the state ME's office and was able to get someone onsite right away due to a bomber on the loose.

Her adrenaline had fled long ago, swamping her with fatigue. The grave and lack of leads as to Vick's whereabouts had doused it. Nick imaged the computer, but Vick hadn't searched for campgrounds or made an online reservation with that device. He could've used his phone, but he would have that with him.

And it was too late to get anyone in the state's IT department to look up a reservation under his name. She ought to know. She and Russ had both tried to find someone to help them, but were told to wait until morning. Fine. They would have to do that and would have to arrest Vick at his work.

"We have a body," Dr. Meadows called out. "Hasn't been here long. Come take a look to see if he's your guy."

Russ marched toward the grave, no hesitation in his steps. Ryleigh got her feet heading in the right direction, but she wanted to run the other way. This part of the job had always been hard, and she was glad to have left it behind.

Thankfully, she'd only had to work two murder investigations in her career. No doubt Russ had seen a whole lot more victims.

They reached the open grave. The young ME with thick blond hair, dressed in the usual white Tyvek suit, stood back, his lips pursed in a narrow face with a pointed chin. He'd erected bright lights giving them a clear view of the dirt he'd mounded alongside the body. He'd also uncovered and brushed off the victim's face. It was bloated and discolored, but no question in her mind. The deceased was Uri Gates.

"It's him," Russ said. "No doubt."

"Yeah," Ryleigh added. "That's Uri Gates."

"Okay, then." Dr. Meadows clapped his gloved hands. "We'll finish the recovery and get him back to the morgue for the autopsy. I'll let you know when I have any information to share."

Russ eyed the man whose dark circles and bags under his eyes left him looking tired. "I know you don't usually work overnight, but any way we could get results by eight?"

Dr. Meadows frowned. "You're right. I don't work overnight."

Russ stepped closer as if he hoped his intimidating presence helped sway the ME. "It's just that I'd like to get the autopsy in before the feds take over and claim jurisdiction."

"Feds are coming?" Dr. Meadows perked up. "Well, why didn't you say so? Yeah. You'll have my findings by then."

Not wanting to linger on the death, Ryleigh stepped away and took a few deep breaths of the cool evening air to think.

"Looks like we beat my self-imposed time clock on the investigation," Russ said. "Should help with the feds taking me to task for not calling earlier. And since we aren't dealing with terrorism, I hope they'll just walk away."

"That would be good," she said absently, as it all seemed so irrelevant when another man had lost his life.

"If we don't find Vick's camping location soon, you'll have to make the arrest in the morning," he said. "I'll need to be here to deal with the feds. As much as I always wish I could be, I can't be in two places at one time."

"No worries. I can handle it." She filled her tone with a bravado she didn't feel.

"Can I get your contact info, Sheriff?" Dr. Meadows asked.

"Let me take care of this, and then we'll plan the morning takedown." Russ strode back to the ME, his steps filled with energy. Learning the truth brought him relief. She got that, but a sense of sadness clung to her and wouldn't let go.

Her phone rang. *Finn.* She didn't feel like talking to anyone. Not even him. She'd been keeping him updated, but he'd been his usual antsy self and chomping at the bit to be allowed onsite. So she answered.

"We just identified the body as Gates," she said. "So Vick is now wanted for murder."

Silence was the response. Not expected.

"Did you hear me?" she asked.

"I did, and you're still planning to go to the caves in the morning with Russ?"

"Not with Russ. I'll go alone. He has to be here for when the ATF arrives."

"No!" Finn's voice erupted over the phone.

Russ turned to stare at her. He'd heard Finn's outburst all the way across the yard.

"Sorry, but no." He'd lowered his voice. "I can't allow that. Put me on speaker so I can talk to Russ too."

She didn't want to comply, but Finn would just hang up and call Russ, and she wanted to be part of the conversation.

She motioned for Russ to join her. "It's Finn. He wants to talk to you, so I'll put him on speaker."

"Let's move further away for more privacy." He led the way to the back fence.

They were not only far enough away for the sound not to travel, but deep shadows of the night clung to them. She didn't like it. Not one bit. Felt eerie and uncomfortable as if Vick were watching them. He could be, she supposed, but doubted it as he didn't seem to think anyone would come for him and hadn't hidden his tracks at all.

"Go ahead, Finn," Russ said.

"You can't let Ryleigh go to the caves alone," he stated.

Russ cocked his head. "I'll be needed elsewhere."

"I won't let Ryleigh go alone." His adamant tone would give even the strongest of men a pause. "And before you suggest some green-behind-the-ears deputy accompany her, that doesn't work for me. If you don't go with her, then I will."

Russ frowned. "I can't have a civilian in on the arrest for when Vick goes to trial."

Finn didn't speak right away, and Ryleigh could easily imagine he was looking for the words that would get him his way.

"I'm going no matter what," he finally said. "So deputize me too if you want things to be by the book."

Shadows darkened Russ's face, but Ryleigh could imagine his frustrated expression.

"You don't have any law enforcement experience," he stated plainly.

"I'll let Ryleigh take the lead," Finn said. "And I'll just be backup in case she needs me."

"I don't know." Russ sounded like he was wavering.

Ryleigh would love to have Finn as backup, and she could help get Russ to side his way. "Finn does have experience where it counts. Apprehending very bad guys. If Vick gets violent, Finn would be great backup. Better than a young deputy for sure."

"Fine," Russ snapped. "The visitor center opens at eight-thirty tomorrow. Meet me at my office at six so I can swear you in and still give enough time for the two of you to get there before opening."

"Will do, and just so you know." Finn paused for a long moment. "There's no way I'll face a murder suspect without a weapon. I'll be carrying whether you like it or not."

24

With the arrest warrant for Vick in her pocket, Ryleigh looked around the chilly Oregon Caves National Monument and Preserve visitor's center. She and Finn were waiting for the ranger in charge to join them. And because she was outside Russ's county, they also waited for a deputy of the jurisdictional county to join as well. He'd been delayed by an accident on the way. She could still talk to Vick, but she had no authority to arrest him in this county. Hopefully, the deputy would arrive in time for that.

A female ranger in uniform with a Smokey Bear type hat passed them as she gave two families a tour of the center. It didn't surprise Ryleigh that so many people were already there. With such rainy winters, Oregonians flocked to state and national parks in the summer to get their fill of sunshine.

A male who appeared to be in his fifties came out from a door in the back and strolled their way. He wore gray-green pants and a lighter gray short-sleeved shirt with a nametag and badge pinned to his chest. He had on a similar hat to the other ranger and greeted them with a smile. "Ranger Otis. How can I help?"

"I'm Deputy Steele." She smiled to relax any concerns he might have about law enforcement asking questions and held out the temporary shield provided by Russ. "And this is my associate, Finn Durham. We're looking for one of your rangers, Barney Vick."

"Barney?" His eyebrows shot up. "He do something wrong?"

"We just have some urgent questions for him."

"He's guiding a tour right now." Otis looked at his watch. "He would've left about ten minutes ago and won't be back for nearly ninety minutes."

"Already?" she asked. "You just opened."

"The demand has been great this year, so we're scheduling a tour before opening each day. You'll have to wait until he gets back."

Russ couldn't wait for his answers. Not with the feds arriving on his doorstep any minute. "Any way we can catch up to Mr. Vick, and you can take over the tour so we can talk to him?"

Otis tilted his head. "We might be able to catch him. But we'll have to hurry."

"Then let's go."

He ran his gaze over them. "The cave is a constant forty-four degrees. I hope you brought jackets."

"They're in the truck," Finn said.

"Go ahead and get them quickly while I grab mine and tell my ranger that I'm going into the cave."

"Be right back." Finn fled the room and down the outside stairs toward the parking lot.

Otis strode over to the other ranger.

She and Finn had reviewed an online video giving them an introduction to the caves and had prepared accordingly, including wearing boots. What they hadn't prepared for was the deputy to be late. Still, Russ was waiting for news of

Vick's arrest, and she had to proceed, a deputy with them or not.

She stepped over to a placard and read more about the history of the caves until Finn and Otis both joined her again. Finn wore his jacket and helped her into hers.

"Let's move," Otis said. "We'll have to go at a fast pace, but you both look in good shape and should be able to keep up."

He led them down to the entrance, over metal grates, and into the cave's yawning mouth. They had to duck just to get inside the space lined with large rock walls, and they made their way down narrow pathways and up a set of stone stairs.

Otis looked back but kept moving. "There are more than five hundred steps on our tour. Be prepared to duck too as some ceilings are only forty-five inches high."

Ryleigh wished she were taking this tour as a visitor instead of a law enforcement officer looking for a suspect. What was she saying? She wished she wasn't going into a cave at all. In such a confined space, if Vick knew they were looking at him for the bombings and was prepared to do battle, things could turn ugly fast.

Otis paused and looked over his shoulder. "This is where people often find out they're claustrophobic. You both good with the small space?"

"I'm fine," Ryleigh said, though she felt the walls closing in on her, she wouldn't give in to her irrational fear.

Finn gave a sharp nod. Not a surprise. She couldn't begin to imagine all the tight spots he'd found himself in as a SEAL.

"Then we'll pick up the speed," Otis said. "We're headed uphill all the way through the mountain, so let me know if you get out of breath and need to rest."

Even if she were breathing hard, Ryleigh would never let

a man who was twice her age know it. She doubted Finn would either, but then she doubted this little hike would faze him at all.

They marched on and worked their way through narrow spaces. Under overhanging rocks and up steep wooden stairs before she heard a male voice leading the tour.

"They're just ahead," Otis called over his shoulder. "Go ahead and wait at the back of the group when we reach them. I'll take over and move the group on. Can you please wait to question Barney until we're out of earshot? Don't want to upset our tour members."

"We can do that," Finn said.

Ryleigh stuck close to Otis but stopped behind the last of the visitors, who were looking at Otis with open suspicion. He whispered something to Vick, whose eyes widened. Otis turned to the group and told them of his tour takeover. She vaguely listened as he described some of the rock formations, but she used the time to study Vick.

He was about six feet tall, and his uniform stretched tight against a muscular physique. He had on a hat matching the other rangers, but it sat high atop his head that was shaped like a Mr. Potato Head toy. Long black bangs stuck out under his hat and above his large nose. A narrow chin made his face even longer. He might be buff as if he worked out, which the gym equipment in his garage would confirm, but he had an oddball appearance, as if his features weren't put together in the right places.

Otis gave them a nod and led the group up a flight of stairs while Vick remained standing to the side of the narrow passage.

When the last guest reached the top stair and disappeared around a corner, she approached Vick and introduced herself and Finn.

He blinked rapidly at them. "What in the world could you want with me?"

"It's about the bombs at Shadow Lake Logging," she said, not beating around the bush when time was of the essence.

"What about them?" He started to put his hands into his pockets.

"Hands where I can see them," Ryleigh said, and he stopped. "We would like to talk to you about your part in building them."

"Me?" His squeaky voice rose up and echoed. "You have the wrong person."

"Then explain the bomb schematics we found in your house and the materials in your shed." Finn stepped closer, Vick shrinking away from his threatening look.

Ryleigh wished Finn hadn't moved, but he'd let his impatience get to him.

Vick clenched and unclenched his jaw. "I don't know what you're talking about."

Finn moved even closer, his hands raised.

Ryleigh stepped in front of him before his threatening behavior gave the guy a heart attack. "It's just a matter of time for our forensics experts to match your prints to the ones recovered at the bomb sites. And in Uri Gates's vehicle."

"Uri who?" His surprise seemed legit, but he couldn't be surprised when the man was six feet under behind his shed.

"You're testing our patience," Finn said. "The man you killed and buried behind your shed."

She fired a snarky smile at Vick. "Oh, yeah, I should've mentioned we found his body."

Vick's face paled in the dim light, as white as the marble rock behind him. He cast his gaze around, as if wondering if he could run and get away from them. He shoved a hand in his pocket and pulled it out before they could react.

His fingers cupped a grenade. He jerked out the pin with his left hand.

What in the world?

He sneered at them and waved the grenade like a man who'd lost his mind. "You don't want me to let go of the handle in a cave holding that lovely group of visitors."

No. This couldn't be happening.

She swallowed and let the grenade register in her brain. She glanced at Finn.

He was assessing their options, and his tight jaw said he didn't like them.

She looked at Vick again. "You can use the grenade to force your way out of here, but we have a deputy waiting for you outside." Ryleigh could only hope the local deputy had arrived by now.

"I'm not going to prison," Vick said, his voice high and tight. "I didn't mean to kill Gates, and I won't go to prison for something that's all that stupid Tobias Hogan's fault."

He confessed. He really confessed. Unbelievable.

And he was talking. That was good. They were in a hostage situation now, and one of the first skills in hostage negotiations was to get the hostage taker talking and keep them talking. If he incriminated himself even more along the way, all the better.

"I've had some problems with Tobias too." She fibbed to gain his trust. "What did he do that has you so upset?"

"Upset?" Vick's voice rose. "He killed my dad. You don't just get upset with that. You get mad." He waved the grenade. "You get even."

"Well, of course you do," she said, trying to keep her voice stable, which was nearly impossible with a crazed man waving a grenade in her face when the walls of the cave seemed to be closing in all around them. She worked hard to look empathetic too. "How did he kill your dad?"

"Prostate cancer."

Finn stared at the guy. "You know that Tobias didn't give your dad prostate cancer."

"He did too." Vick raised his chin. "Recent studies prove it."

"I'm afraid you'll have to explain that to me." Ryleigh understood, but she wanted to get his confession. "Because I really want to understand your situation so we can work out a solution."

He gave a firm nod.

Good. He was buying into her concern. "It's no secret that men who work as loggers have a higher rate of prostate cancer."

It'd been a secret to her until she'd read that article in his office, but she wouldn't interrupt him to tell him that.

"Even if that's true," Finn said, taking on the role of bad cop in this questioning, which allowed her to keep working on gaining the grenade-wielder's trust. "Your dad chose to work for Tobias."

"True. Yeah. Sure. But the old guy could've upgraded his equipment sooner so Dad wouldn't have had to manually fell trees so often." He relaxed his arms, a good sign that talking might be helping. "If he'd bought a motorized logger to fell a lot of the trees, Dad would've only had to do the difficult ones that the machine couldn't reach."

"I heard Tobias say a good quality machine, even a used one, could cost more than a hundred grand," Finn said. "He would've had to lay off a lot of the loggers to afford that. Plus, the machine would put men out of work, and then your dad might not have had a job at all."

"But he would still be alive." Vick glared at Finn.

"Maybe," Ryleigh said. "You can't know that for sure."

"What about your dad?" Finn asked. "Did he blame Tobias?"

"Nah. He said Tobias was a great guy and boss, and Dad's cancer was just the luck of the draw." Vick shook his head. "He was brainwashed by the old guy, but I didn't fall for it. The old dude could've acknowledged it was a possibility when I went to see him, but he didn't care."

Similar to Tobias's account, but she suspected the mill owner had been far more sympathetic than Vick was letting on. "Why wait until now to do something?"

"It was those eco-nuts." He smirked. "Their threats gave me the chance to act and put the blame on them."

"How did you know about the threats?" she asked.

"Please." He rolled his eyes. "Shadow Lake is such a small town you pretty much know what everyone had for lunch before the day is out. Once I heard that Sovereign Earth was suspected, I did some research and learned one of the members had plans for a photoelectric cell bomb. Figured it was so unique it would point right to them."

And it had. For a few days.

One thing was for sure. This guy was good at research if he discovered that fact. But then he probably spent a lot of time digging into conspiracy theories and had mad search skills.

"I can see you have what you think is justification for the bomb, but why did you kill Uri Gates?" she asked, as they had only been able to speculate on what had happened.

"Didn't want to." His lips dipped in a frown. "After I planted the bomb, I was taking off down the logging road and he showed up right before it went off. He was going to try to stop it. I couldn't let him do that. And I didn't want him to get blown up either. He could've died, like that eco-guy. I didn't even know he was there until after you all found him."

297

Interesting. Ryleigh assumed he hit Gates outside of the crime scene perimeter or the Veritas team would've found blood.

"You set the bomb," Finn said. "Gates showed up, and at some time the victim had also arrived to disarm it without you knowing about it."

"That's right. I was heading down the logging road and Gates pulls up in his flashy green Jeep. He starts to question me, and I learn he's a supervisor at the mill. Then he wants to know who I am." Vick let out a heavy sigh. "I didn't want him to stop the bomb, so I clocked him with a thick branch that was on the ground nearby. Only meant to knock him out. You know, so I could get away. Guess I hit him too hard, and he died. Loaded him in his Jeep and took off to think."

"Where did you get the explosives?"

"Stole them from a guy employed by a construction company that I worked at in college. They had the worst security and he took his share of the explosives to use in projects on his farm. I knew where he kept the stash."

"And you wrote dates on them to make them look like they were stolen from Shadow Lake Logging," Finn said.

"Yep. Figured I'd send you on a wild goose chase trying to figure that one out."

"Well, we did," Ryleigh said. "I need you to put the pin back in the grenade, and I'll have to arrest you."

He lurched back. "Not happening. I have nothing to lose, and I'm not going to prison." His gaze frantically searched the area.

"Don't do anything dumb," Finn said.

Vick jerked his hand in the direction of a small opening in the cave wall. "Over there. Both of you. Inside. Now."

She studied the tiny entrance, and her skin crawled with her fear of tight spaces. "But where does it go?"

"Just crawl in until you get to the opening at the end and

wait for me." He waved the grenade. "Try anything funny, and I'll let this go. The visitors might have a head start on us, but this will still take them out."

"You don't want to die," she said, panic settling deeper as she eyed the tiny opening.

"You're wrong there." He flashed a sickly grin at her. "I'd rather die than spend a lifetime in prison. And if I die, you go with me."

The area smelled earthy and yet held a chemical odor as Finn clawed his way through the narrow opening on the heels of Ryleigh's boots. Finn's shoulders scraped the rock, and he seriously questioned if he would fit, but Vick claimed he would. Before Ryleigh had climbed in, he'd wanted to hug and assure her that he would find a way out of this mess. But he'd kept his hands to himself. No way Finn would let Vick know he had a personal connection with Ryleigh. That would just give the killer further ammunition to use against them.

Ryleigh's feet disappeared down an incline, and he followed to spill out into a small room with low ceilings. Ryleigh huddled over near the far wall. Fear darkened her eyes already dusky in the shadows of her phone's light.

"Focus your light on the opening," Finn said to Ryleigh and scrambled to his feet to crouch near the space they'd just exited.

She changed the light's direction, illuminating the thick cave walls and leaving herself in the dark. Even if he wanted to comfort her now, he had no time. Vick was crawling right after them. If he came out arms overhead, Finn could clamp his hand over the jerk's grenade hand to stop it from detonating, then Ryleigh could extract the grenade from his grasp.

Vick's head poked from the opening, his grenade hand tucked tight against his body.

"Back up, He-Man," Vick said, eyeing Finn. "To the far wall."

Finn let out a frustrated breath and moved away. No way he could take over now. This guy's buff build said he was strong, and Finn had to take that into account for when he struck. And strike he would as there was no way this man was going to get away with terrifying Ryleigh. Or killing two men. Finn would just have to bide his time and be sure of his move before he took action.

"Okay, now what?" Ryleigh asked, keeping her flashlight beaming at Vick.

He wiggled out and got to his feet. "We go deeper into the cave."

"Then what?" Finn asked.

"Then I leave you here and take off."

"We'll just come after you," Finn said, not caring if that upset this creep.

"If you do, I let go of the grenade and blow up those lovely people you just met. Maybe bring the whole side of the mountain down and kill the other visitors too." He fixed his gaze on Ryleigh. "Do you want that to happen?"

She glared at him. "You know I don't."

"Then let's move. Go ahead to your left. Over the boulder."

Ryleigh went first, the light fading with her as she scrambled over a large rock and into a narrow crevice. Finn followed, his body brushing against the stone worn smooth by others who'd taken this route before him.

He exited the tight path to find Ryleigh bent over in a

smaller space where they couldn't fully stand. She searched the area with her phone's light.

"Is this the off-trail route?" Finn asked the moment Vick emerged to join them.

"At one time, but this section's closed now due to the potential for collapse. Just think of it as my own private little tour for you." He cackled, and the sound bounced off the low ceilings. "Keep going, veering to the right. The walls on the right side are the most unstable. Try not to touch them."

Finn took out his cell and flashed the light down the narrow path he would have to traverse upright this time, catching a glimpse of Ryleigh ahead. No way his shoulders would fit through there without scraping against the wall. He would have to sidestep through it. At least the ceiling was high enough to stand upright.

He turned to enter, but two feet in, he shone his light back at Vick, wondering if he could take him before going deeper into the caves.

The guy gave him a nod of approval. "Dumb-looking jock like you. I didn't think you'd figure out how to safely move through there."

"Not a jock at all." Finn fired back at Vick. "But still no sweat. As a Navy SEAL, I was in situations far more dangerous than this."

Shock and awe, coupled with unease and uncertainty claimed Vick's face. Good. Just the reaction Finn was going for.

The creep held out his fist again, waving the grenade. "Keep going."

Finn probably should've kept his mouth shut—don't poke the bear and all of that. But he figured if the guy was a little less certain, he might be easier to overpower.

Finn put away his phone and sidestepped his way down the narrow path and into another small room. Bats fluttered to the ceiling. Ryleigh cringed as her light revealed guano caking the room.

Vick eased out of the opening, and Ryleigh pinned him with her light.

He had that same grin, the one that said he wasn't mentally all there. Delusional in his conspiracy theories. "Take the last opening you see ahead, and you'll be done."

"Then what?" Finn asked. "Is that when you leave us?"

Vick nodded, the smile turning snide and uglier. "And you shouldn't try to follow me. If not for the visitors' sake, then for yours. Too many side shoots and false paths. You'll never find your way out of here."

"Then what do you expect us to do?" Ryleigh asked, her tone higher than normal, her fear cutting into Finn's heart.

"Wait an hour, then backtrack to get out." He cocked his head. "But you should know if you're dumb enough to think you can track me, there's no cell service, and no one will come looking for you on this route. No one at all."

25

Time had run out. Finn had to act fast. But what should he do?

He couldn't let the guy leave. Finn couldn't be left behind to die in this rocky hole either. Avery needed him. And he sure didn't want Ryleigh to suffer any more than she already had.

Vick eased toward an opening in the rock that he could back through and keep an eye on them at the same time. His shadow in Ryleigh's light was long, narrow and fluid, looking other-worldly.

"Wait," Finn called out, his mind racing to figure out how to get close to this guy. "Don't leave yet."

Vick spun and snorted. "Begging isn't an attractive quality for a big bad SEAL."

Finn swallowed down his anger at the taunt. He wanted to rush the guy. Punish him. Take him out. But he shoved his hands into his pockets instead. All rushing him would do was give him time to release the grenade.

No one wanted that to happen.

But if Finn got close enough, he could simultaneously clamp his hand over the grenade and throw two swift disabling punches. He knew the moves—had used them often enough. One to the back of Vick's head and one to his liver. Finn would strike with lightning-fast precision. Vick wouldn't know what hit him, and he would take a nosedive into the stone.

Problem was, Finn had to get close, and so far, Vick had been too smart to allow it.

Then outsmart him. It's now or never!

Finn had to try some subterfuge or Vick would get away. Maybe kill someone else.

Finn pulled his right hand from his pocket, fist closed around a quarter. "You'll want to take this with you."

Vick's eyebrow rose. "Take what?"

Great. He'd taken the bait.

"It's better if I show you." Finn held out his closed fist and started forward. If Vick were as smart as he thought, he would tell Finn to stay put, but he focused on Finn's hand just as Finn wanted.

Perfect.

Finn quickly closed the distance.

Vick's focus remained on Finn's fist.

Finn flashed his free hand out to clamp the grenade. Vick startled but Finn smacked him behind the head with his closed fist. His head and upper body jerked to the side.

Vick's hand loosened on the grenade.

Finn clamped tighter. Threw another punch to the area just below Vick's ribcage—to his unprotected liver.

Vick cried out and plummeted to the ground. The pin went flying. His fingers released the grenade.

Finn took firm control, holding tight to the grenade so it wouldn't detonate. Protecting him. Protecting Ryleigh. The others.

All over in five seconds or less.

Ryleigh rushed forward, dropped her phone, and

flipped Vick over. The light shone up at the ceiling and reflected down. Just enough for Finn to see her put a knee to the back of the man who was writhing and moaning and trying to clutch his gut. She got out her cuffs and slapped them on his wrists behind his back.

"Got him." She grabbed her phone, shone the light up, and grinned at Finn.

Wow. Amazing. The most joyful grin he'd seen to warm his heart. Well, maybe it equaled the one from Avery before she'd kissed his cheek. His heart was full. Complete. More love than he could ever imagine he would experience.

Another rush of adrenaline flooded his body. Right. Forget the love for now. He still had a job to do. Secure the grenade so they could get out of there. "I need to find the pin."

"Yeah." She let out a shuddering breath and picked up her phone. She focused the light in the direction the pin had gone flying.

Finn got down on his knees. Swept his free hand over the rough floor. His finger felt the cold metal butted up to a boulder. He picked it up and slid it into place. Safe. They were safe.

He let out a long breath.

Thank You!

He pocketed the grenade and went back to Ryleigh. Tears flowed from her eyes and down her cheeks.

Vick continued to writhe in pain and didn't seem as if he even noticed they were in the room.

Finn touched her cheek. "It's okay, honey. You're safe now and so is everyone else."

"I've seen guys disabled like this in the movies but never in person." She gave him a wobbly smile. "You were impressive."

"All in a day's work." His face heated with a blush. He

305

didn't take compliments well. "Or it was for me. Once anyway."

He waited for the pain of loss to take hold and it didn't. At least not that gut-wrenching, sick-to-your-stomach feeling. Sure, he had a niggling of unease, but more than that, he was thankful he possessed the skills needed today and in the end, he was still alive to care for Avery. And just as important, Ryleigh was alive and well too.

Because he wanted her in his life. He didn't know how he would make that happen, but she would be by his side for life if he had anything to say about it.

~

A grenade. The guy had actually pulled a live grenade on them. Unbelievable.

Ryleigh fought against her weak knees to exit the last tunnel with Finn, her rescuer and rock. What a takedown! She'd experienced some hairy situations as an agent, but this one would go down as the scariest day of her life.

They'd had to remove Vick's cuffs to let him crawl out but she slapped them on him again.

"Not so tight," he complained.

She had no sympathy for him.

"Move." Finn took a solid hold on Vick's arm and prodded him ahead until they stepped into the sunshine that was beaming down on the cave.

She took in a deep breath and let it out, the air tasting and smelling sweeter.

She was alive. *Alive*!

Thanks to Finn. The man who saved her. Saved so many people as he'd done for years as a SEAL, but she'd never been witness to his prowess before. Some might say his move was foolhardy, but not with his skills. No, it'd been a calculated attack he knew he would win. Or he wouldn't have risked their lives.

There was nothing she could face that would be harder to overcome than this. At least nothing with Finn at her side. She wanted that. Him with her for the future. For sure. Facing death at the hand of a killer had made it crystal clear. Her other problems were small. Minor. Tiny. And conquerable.

And she planned to tell Finn that—after she got Vick solidly locked behind bars.

She scanned the area ahead until she spotted the deputy and his patrol vehicle. She took out her phone and called Russ. She gave him a brief version of what had happened. "I could bring Vick in, but is that what you want or do you want the local deputy to book him?"

"As much as I'd like him under my control," Russ said, his voice tight. "Let's not call attention to being out of jurisdiction and let the locals book him. You go along and bring back a copy of the booking report for the feds."

"Will do."

"And, Steele, I'm surrounded by feds, and you speak their language, so double-time it back here." He laughed and ended the call.

She chuckled too, releasing some of her adrenaline, and then shared the information with Finn. She pointed at the deputy. "Let's get Vick transported."

Finn shoved Vick ahead, visitors staring. If they only knew the danger they'd been exposed to, but the grenade remained in Finn's pocket. It was freaky to her, but probably something he'd carried many times in the past.

The deputy frowned at them and took control of Vick. He pressed him up against the car for a thorough search, read him his rights, and put him in the backseat. He secured the door and turned. "Not gonna lie and sugarcoat this. You should've waited for me. Won't help our agency goodwill."

"Couldn't be helped," she said, trying to diffuse the situation. "Besides, we're giving you the collar. Bringing in a bomber and murderer will give you bragging rights. That should count for something."

"Yeah, yeah, it will." He cracked a half smile. "I'll meet you at booking to take your statements."

He slid behind the wheel, and she didn't wait for the door to close but started for Finn's truck before her wobbly knees gave out on her. He strode by her side, their fingers close but not touching. Man, she wanted to reach out. Feel his solid presence. She wouldn't. Not with the deputy still in the area.

They reached his truck well out of view. She waited for him to open the passenger door as he always did. He came close. Stopped. Pinned her against the door and kissed her —hard.

Wow! Oh wow! Her senses swam. Her head dizzy. Her knees now threatening a total rebellion.

He came up for air, his forehead furrowed as he gazed into her eyes. "I could've lost you."

She felt his worry deeply inside. Echoed it. "But you didn't, and I could say the same for you."

"It's just, I never should've broken up with you. I hope you've truly forgiven me, and we can make a go of it now. I can't lose you again. Not to a grenade and not out of my life at all."

"I have, and we can."

He swept her into his arms and kissed her again. More gently this time, but his lips were insistent. Urgent. Needy.

She let herself enjoy it. Feel all the feelings. Deepen the kiss even more.

But he soon lifted his head. "You know I'd move to Portland in a heartbeat, right? But I can't ask Avery to move right now."

"It's okay." She ran a finger down the side of his face, enjoying her exploration of the plains and valleys up close. "We'll have to figure out logistics, but if we have to date long-distance for a while, I'm okay with that. As long as we don't give up on each other again."

"Never," he said emphatically. "Never."

Labor Day.

On the long dock on the Maddox property, with Avery on one side and Ryleigh's grandad and father on the other, Finn cranked in his fishing line. The bait skimmed across the glistening lake, cutting a path toward him. Summer was coming to a close and rain would soon set in again for the winter and spring, but the sun shone bright over Shadow Lake today. A glorious day for fishing.

A glorious day to be alive.

Finn turned to look across the beach at Ryleigh, who reclined on a lounger next to her sister Teagan. Ryleigh's shorts revealed her creamy long legs and a tank top displayed her toned arms. He couldn't see her eyes behind her dark glasses, but she still looked beautiful. And peaceful.

He knew the feeling. He hadn't felt such peace, such calm, since he'd broken up with her. And today was the last day he would be in her company. Or her family's company for that matter. As much as he enjoyed the afternoon on the Maddox property with all the Steeles who had comman-deered Shadow Lake Survival's property for a family reunion of sorts, he would rather grab her hand and find a secluded spot for just the two of them.

Then what? He'd tell her that he loved her and demand she move here to be with him?

Yeah, right. That wouldn't work. The opposite. She'd hightail it out of there faster than the deer he'd seen bounding across the meadow on the drive in today.

She did still have Tobias's account to manage. For now, but once he felt sure that the threats were over, and he'd rebuilt, Tobias would likely cancel the contract. He'd been upfront with her about that, so she knew what to expect. But for now, she would occasionally come to Shadow Lake.

Artie nudged him. "You gonna keep staring at her all day, son, or go talk to her?"

Finn flashed a surprised look at the older man. "Who says I want to talk to her?"

"Come on, now. Even little Avery can see you're in love with my granddaughter."

"He's right. It's gross." Avery wrinkled her nose.

"It's not the right time." Finn pointed his attention to his fishing.

"But at the end of the picnic, Ryleigh's gonna leave," Avery said, her big eyes looking up at him. "And she'll take everyone with her."

"Yes." The thought closed Finn's throat and the word stuck like damp sawdust.

Avery frowned. "No fair. I want them to be our family."

Artie rested his free hand on Avery's shoulder. "I'm pretty sure I'm right when I speak for the family to say we'd like the same thing."

Avery pouted. "So why can't you do something about it?"

Finn pulled his line out of the water and knelt next to Avery. "Our lives are here in Shadow Lake, and Ryleigh's is in Portland with her family and work. We've talked about it, and we can't figure things out just now. Maybe in the future."

"It's easy. We can move there." Avery challenged him with a sharp look.

Finn had to fight to keep his mouth from falling open. He'd never expected this from her, and he didn't know if it was just a passing thought, if she'd get over it, or if she really wanted to move. "But you love your house here."

"I know, but isn't loving people more important?"

"Wise child, this one." Artie grinned.

"I don't know, Peanut," he said, ignoring Artie. "You feel this way now, but what about when it's time to go to school, and you have to go to a new one? Make new friends? Will you think moving is such a good idea then?"

"I can do it for a family." She turned and hugged Artie's waist. "He wants to be my grandad, so can't you let him? Please?"

Finn didn't know how to answer. He had to make the right decision for Avery, not for himself, and he didn't know if he could separate those feelings to do the right thing.

"I'll think about it, Peanut," he said.

She frowned but held out her little finger. "Pinkie promise?"

He bent down and crooked his finger in hers as she'd taught him to do. "Promise."

She threw her arms around his neck. "I love you, Finn. Bunches. Will you adopt me and marry Ryleigh?"

His heart melted into a liquid puddle in his chest, but panic followed. They'd talked about adoption. He'd offered. He didn't know if his heart really had been in it then. He'd offered more out of wanting to make her feel secure, but right after Felicia had died, he'd thought about having a child for the rest of his life and the thought had strangled him. Now?

Now, he'd truly taken her into his life, and she was his forever. He had to finalize the adoption as she'd said, but that was just a formality. He was Avery's father now, and proud and thankful he could fill the role. It beat the joy of being a SEAL a thousand times over, and he would never regret his decision to parent this little girl.

He didn't feel the least little twinge of fear for their future together. Anxiety over doing a good job as a parent, yeah, but that was what parenting was all about.

And that meant making the right decision now. He couldn't fail her.

Please, God, please. This child has been through so much. Help me do the right thing for her. For my daughter.

Ryleigh feigned reading her book, but she covertly watched the dock where Finn was fitting right in with her family and the Maddox family too. He'd been deep in conversation with the brothers and Colin several times today, but she had no idea what they'd been discussing. Seemed serious, though. Maybe he was just thanking them for their help as she'd done earlier.

Maybe. But if that was true, she might've expected some backslapping or fist bumping. Neither of which had occurred.

Teagan poked Ryleigh in the arm, then pointed at the dock. "Wonder what's going on over there."

Ryleigh pretended to just then notice Finn, Avery, and Ryleigh's grandad engaged in what looked like a very serious conversation as her father looked on from nearby. And Ryleigh didn't miss seeing Avery toss her arms around Finn's neck and hold him tight. How far they'd come in a few weeks.

No, that wasn't right. The change had really taken months, with much rejection from Avery. It was just the last few weeks that he seemed to finally break through to her somehow.

Ryleigh's heart soared for him, but fell in a flash. Ryleigh wanted to be around to see how they fared together. More than that, she wanted to be part of their story. In what form, she didn't yet know because once her emotions all calmed down from the grenade incident and she could think, she knew becoming a mother was a big step that she needed to consider. To pray about. So she wouldn't hurt this little girl more.

"You know God wouldn't have put him in your life again unless He wanted you to follow your feelings this time," Teagan said.

Ryleigh flashed her gaze to Teagan. "What?"

"You didn't think I knew about him, did you?" Teagan laughed. "Well, surprise, sis, we all know—have known for ages that he hurt you."

"Even Mom and Dad? Gran and Grandad?"

"Yep, everyone. The cousins, Uncle Gene and Aunt Iris too."

Ryleigh couldn't believe this. "But no one said anything."

"Because we respected your privacy and figured if you wanted to talk about it you would."

Ryleigh gaped at her sister. "Since when does privacy mean anything in our family?"

"Since you were so very devastated and couldn't even talk about it. We thought you would at some point, but then time passed and you were all right, so no one brought it up."

"That's as shocking as running into Finn again." She shook her head. "I'm surprised Grandad didn't deck him."

"Me too." Teagan laughed. "Dad probably would've if

he'd been the first to see him, but Grandad has convinced everyone that Finn's a great guy."

"He really is." That was not in question. Not in the least.

"I know he hurt you, but looks like you've forgiven him." Teagan swung her legs over the edge of her chair and nodded at Reid's small fishing boat puttering toward the dock. "Looks like Drew is back, so I'm going to go meet him."

She'd recently gotten engaged to Drew Collier, and she wanted everyone in the world to be as happy as they were. So maybe her advice was a bit prejudiced.

She stood and squeezed Ryleigh's shoulder. "Finn's a keeper. Don't toss him back in."

Ryleigh got up too and grabbed a cane pole plus a bucket of worms and went to the dock. Not knowing what she was going to do or say, she stopped short of Finn and Avery, hoping Finn would come to her so she didn't seem like she was stalking him.

She sat on the wooden dock, dangling her legs over the shimmering water, and dug into the bucket for a big fat juicy worm that she slid onto her hook just like her grandad taught her.

"Ew," Avery said, coming up to her. "You do your own worms?"

Ryleigh wiped her slimy fingers on a towel and tossed her line into the water. Her red and white bobber popped up and floated on the surface. "Grandad wouldn't take us fishing if we didn't handle our own bait."

"He did mine for me." Avery set down her small pink camo pole that Ryleigh's grandad had gotten just for her and plopped down next to Ryleigh.

"Yeah, he does that the first time to get you hooked on fishing." Ryleigh winked at Avery. "Then the next time he makes you bait your own hook."

She looked uncertainly up at Ryleigh's grandad. "I don't know if I can do it."

Ryleigh leaned closer to Avery. "I'll tell you a secret. I didn't think I could either, but he joked with me the whole time I was hooking the worm, and we laughed so hard that I was distracted and had my hook baited before I knew it."

"Maybe I can do it." She scrunched up her eyes like she might cry. "If I ever get to go fishing with him again."

Ryleigh tried to smile away the child's sadness. "I'm sure if you ask, he'll be glad to come down here to take you fishing."

"You think so? Even if he might not be my grandad?"

Ryleigh had no idea what she meant by that and didn't know how to answer.

"I want a grandad just like him." Avery looked longingly down the dock.

"He's a good one for sure," Ryleigh said, wishing the same thing for this child.

"Finn said maybe we can move to Portland so that can happen."

"He what?" Ryleigh's voice shot up.

Avery startled.

"Sorry, sweetie. That just surprised me. Tell me exactly what he said."

"I asked him if we could move to where you live. He said he would think about it."

"When was this?" Ryleigh glanced at Finn, who caught her gaze and put down his pole to join them.

"Just now." Avery looked up at Finn. "I know I'll miss my friends, but I want a real family. One who can't go away at any time, and you have the best family ever. They stick together. I want to be part of it."

"We know you do, Peanut," Finn said. "But there are a lot of things to consider."

"Papa and Nana." Avery cast a wary glance at Ryleigh. "Your mom and dad said I could call them that."

"That's nice."

"They said they were so happy to have me in the family. That I would be the perfect grandchild." Avery frowned. "I don't think I can be perfect, but I'll try."

"Oh, sweetie." Ryleigh took the child's hand. "They don't expect you to be perfect. They just meant they've wanted a grandchild for a long time and it would be perfectly wonderful to have one."

"Oh, okay." A long breath slipped out. "I'll still do my best to be good and not make them wish I wasn't there."

"You just need to be you," Ryleigh said emphatically. "Nothing else. And they will always love you no matter what."

"How do you know that?"

Ryleigh searched for the right way to explain. "You know how your mom loved you even when you got into trouble?"

Avery's head bobbed in a forceful nod. "Yeah, she was the best."

"Well, grandparents are like that too."

"And so are Ryleigh and me," Finn added. "We will always love you no matter what."

Avery launched herself at Finn. "I love you too, even when I don't like you."

Finn grinned at Ryleigh over Avery's head.

Avery looked up at him. "So we can move to Portland?"

"Yes."

"Yay!" Avery released Finn and danced around.

"Shh," Ryleigh's grandad warned. "You're going to scare the fish away."

"Oops." A sweet grin lit Avery's face. "Guess I was already naughty."

Finn ruffled her hair. "I think Grandad will be okay with it when he hears why you were so excited."

She frowned.

"What's wrong, Peanut?" Finn asked.

"Nana said if you wanted, I could come live with them for a little while so you and Ryleigh can be alone. You know to get all mushy and stuff."

Finn looked like he was trying hard to stifle a laugh. "But you don't like that idea?"

She shook her head so hard her braids done expertly by Finn slapped her face. "But I'll do it if you want me to. If that means we'll be a family, I'd stay two months."

"No need." Finn hugged the child. "I might let you do some sleepovers with them, but otherwise you're stuck with me, kiddo. Forever."

She blinked her big blue eyes up at him. "Promise?"

Ryleigh had no idea how he could possibly refuse that adorable face. "Promise."

"I'm going to tell Grandad that he's my grandad now too." Avery pushed away and bolted down the dock, her sandals clapping on the wood.

"I'm glad Avery wants to move," Ryleigh said. "But what about your job?"

"I've been talking to the Maddox brothers about setting up my own business to teach survival skills." His eyes narrowed. "We figure if I could buy some land on the outskirts of the metro area that I could have a thriving business. Would you be okay with not living in the city?"

"Okay?" She smiled, glad he knew how much she wanted a future with him, and he was thinking of her. "Remember I'm a farm girl, and I'd love it. Maybe Grandad would even sell you some of their land since they're getting older."

"That could work."

"Of course, you'd have to be good with living near my parents and grandparents." She looked at her grandad as he helped Avery bait her hook. "But honestly, no matter where we would live, my grandparents would be around all the time anyway."

"And speaking of them. It's time for some privacy." Finn took the pole out of Ryleigh's hand, put it in a holder, and looked at her grandad. "We're going to take a walk. Mind watching our poles?"

Grandad put an arm around Avery. "We've got it, don't we, sweetheart?"

She gave a serious nod. "And I'll even put on a yucky worm if I have to."

Ryleigh chuckled and trailed Finn down the dock and to the woods ringed by tall trees and holding an old stone firepit in the middle.

She looked at Finn. "My sisters, cousins, and I used to hang out here with the Maddox brothers and plan our future takeover of the world."

"Guess that means I have to watch for your plots of world dominion." He laughed.

"No worries. I have everything I want, and the world will just have to do without me taking it over." She snuggled her arms around his solid body and rested her head on his chest to listen to the solid thumps of his heartbeat.

"If that changes let me know, and I'll be your able assistant."

"Good to know." She leaned back and looked up at him.

"As I told Avery, you're stuck with me. Forever."

She blinked up at him as Avery had done and held out her little finger. "Pinkie promise?"

He cupped the side of her face. "Promise. Forever and ever."

He kissed her and her heart soared.

"This wasn't how I planned to propose, so I want a do-over on that once I have a ring. And I have to ask your dad's permission too."

"Just a formality."

He nodded. "Still, your dad can be intimidating. Your grandad too."

"Take a look in the mirror if you want to see intimidating." She caressed his cheek. "But not at the moment. Right now, you seem very approachable."

"That's good because since we're alone and can't gross Avery out, I intend to get all mushy and stuff."

He lowered his head and before his lips even touched hers, she knew that forever with this man might involve having to find private time for the mushy stuff, but the challenge was worth the reward and then some.

Thank you so much for reading *Edge of Steele*. If you've enjoyed the book, I would be grateful if you would post a review on the bookseller's site. Just a few words is all it takes or even leave a rating. Click or tap HERE, and you will jump to the right place to post your review.

Though this is the end of this series, you'll be happy to hear that there is a new series coming soon!

SHADOW LAKE SURVVAL SERIES
Coming SOON - When survival takes a dangerous turn and lives are on the line.

SHADOW LAKE **SURVIVAL**

WWW.SUSANSLEEMAN.COM | SUSAN SLEEMAN

The men of Shadow Lake Survival impart survival skills and keep those in danger safe from harm. Even if it means risking their lives.

Book 1 – <u>Shadow of Deceit</u> - August 2, 2023

Book 2 – <u>Shadow of Night</u> - October 2, 2023

Book 3 – <u>Shadow of Truth</u> - December 2, 2023

Book 4 – Shadow of Hope March 2, 2024

Book 5 – Shadow of Doubt – June 2, 2024

Book 6 – Shadow of Fear – October 2, 2024

For More Details Visit -

https://www.susansleeman.com/shadow-lake-survival-series/

Susan Sleeman

~

Shadow of Deceit - BOOK 1

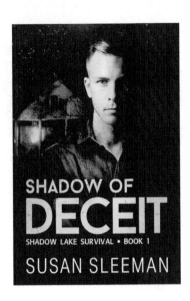

SHADOW OF DECEIT
SHADOW LAKE SURVIVAL • BOOK 1
SUSAN SLEEMAN

When returning to her past threatens her life and a murder occurs…

When Mia Blackburn returns to Shadow Lake to inherit her uncle's property, she doesn't expect a threatening warning before she even reaches the rustic resort. And when a fire traps her in the burning barn that very day, she fears she won't get out alive. Just in time, Ryan Maddox, her ex-boyfriend and Shadow Lake Survival owner, rescues her from the deadly blaze. She's thankful for his rescue, but after their tumultuous breakup, he's the last person she wants to see.

Will she be the next victim?

Despite the threatening warning and her residual feelings for Ryan, Mia won't let anyone scare her from the rustic resort before she fulfills the terms of her uncle's will and inherits the property. Ryan insists on keeping a close eye on her, and soon Mia feels safer and closer to Ryan than ever before. Yet the threats haven't stopped, and soon Mia's inheritance includes a murder, and she could be the next victim.

For More Details Visit -
https://www.susansleeman.com/shadow-lake-survival-series/

ABOUT SUSAN

SUSAN SLEEMAN is a bestselling and award-winning author of more than 50 inspirational/Christian and clean read romantic suspense books. In addition to writing, Susan also hosts the website, TheSuspenseZone.com.

Susan currently lives in Oregon, but has had the pleasure of living in nine states. Her husband is a retired church music director and they have two beautiful daughters, two very special sons-in-law, and two amazing grandsons.

For more information visit:
www.susansleeman.com

Printed in Great Britain
by Amazon

24272508R00189